"TEHAN IS OLDER THAN I AM. HE CAN HAVE THIS ONE."

Tehan picked up the white man's knife and withdrew it from its scabbard. He walked to the captive, thumbing the blade's edge. Dropping to his knees, he laid the edge against the man's chest and drew downward to the stomach. Bright red blood welled up in the cut and a low moan escaped the white man.

Lone Wolf stepped closer. "Tehan, you are now locked into a battle with this man. If he dies without crying out, he will take your medicine with him. You cannot allow that to happen. It will mean bad luck for all of us, but it might mean your death!"

Tehan blinked rapidly, lower lip clenched in his teeth. He slashed across the man's thigh, cutting him to the bone. The captive only grunted and gasped for breath. Then suddenly Tehan grabbed the man's right hand, and with a quick swing, severed his index finger at the second joint. The captive screamed, but it was short, almost a shout—an explosion of sound cut off as easily as the finger.

Lone Wolf pulled the captive's other hand free of the stake and thrust it into the fire. The man shrieked as his flesh caught flame. He flopped on the ground like a landed fish.

"The screams are the medicine leaving," Lone Wolf said. "Feel the medicine!" he bellowed, still wrestling with the white man. "Feel it course through your body!"

Tehan felt it. His whole being hummed like a plucked bowstring, the vibrations making his teeth ache. He was light-headed, giddy, almost delirious with the power passing into him. "Yes!" he shouted, wrapped in ecstasy.

WARRIOR'S BLOOD

Walter Lucas

PINNACLE BOOKS
Kensington Publishing Corp.
http://www.kensingtonbooks.com

PINNACLE BOOKS are published by

Kensington Publishing Corp.
850 Third Avenue
New York, NY 10022

All Kensington Titles, Imprints, and Distributed Lines are
available at special quantity discounts for bulk purchases for
sales promotions, premiums, fund-raising, educational or in-
stitutional use. Special book excerpts or customized print-
ings can also be created to fit specific needs. For details,
write or phone the office of the Kensington special sales
manager: Kensington Publishing Corp., 850 Third Avenue,
New York, NY 10022, attn: Special Sales Department,
Phone: 1-800-221-2647.

Pinnacle and the P logo Reg. U.S. Pat. & TM Off.

First Printing: August, 2001
10 9 8 7 6 5 4 3 2 1

Printed in the United States of America

One

July 12, 1874

As the last stone rolled back, the sightless skull of Ord-lee faced the sun for the first time in three summers. Kiowa warrior Boytale gazed at the skeleton. He wondered what the dead Comanche warrior's life was like in the Happy Hunting Ground.

Boytale was of Mexican birth, adopted by the Kiowa as a small boy when a raiding party passed through his village.

Tall and thin but well-muscled, he bore almost no resemblance to those he considered family, other than skin darkened by years of exposure to the plains sun and winds. His hair was the right color, black with blue highlights, tightly plaited and tied with scarlet strips of cotton. His black-brown eyes, too, reflected his people, but there it ended.

Boytale had a long, thin nose, straight, without the aquiline hump of the Plains Indians. His head was ovoid, with flat cheeks that narrowed to a chisel-point chin. His face betrayed his Spanish heritage, left to him by some unknown Conquistador from a time even his great-grandfather never knew.

At seventeen, he was one of the youngest members of the revenge party.

The other men gathered around him had been recruited by the famed Kiowa war chief Lone Wolf. He meant to avenge the deaths of his son and nephew by taking at least one white scalp. But Boytale knew that Lone Wolf needed to renew his medicine after the disastrous fight with the white buffalo hunters on the Canadian River.

Boytale had been forbidden to go, but he'd heard the combined Kiowa, Comanche, and Cheyenne forces had numbered over three hundred. A Comanche medicine man had said the attack was the will of the Great Spirit. He'd said they would be invincible, protected by a magic yellow paint from the Great Spirit himself.

Instead, they'd lost, beaten by a few men hidden in dirt lodges.

Blame was placed on the shaman, but Lone Wolf argued otherwise. He said the spirits abandoned the Kiowa for using the Comanche medicine.

Boytale didn't know, but he wondered what kind of gods would leave people helpless against an enemy.

Wind blew over the hilltop and moaned through the mesquite trees and scrub brush. Boytale felt a shiver run down his spine. Was Ord-lee telling him to watch his thoughts? Was the Great Spirit warning him not to lose faith?

"Lone Wolf."

Boytale looked up. Feather Head pointed down the hill.

Below them four white men rode, slowly and relaxed. They had no idea fifty Kiowa warriors were less than a quarter mile away.

"Quickly," Lone Wolf ordered. "Everyone get on his horse."

Boytale mounted. As he did so, another horse kicked a loose stone that tumbled down the hillside.

He saw a white face turn in his direction. The cowboy yelled and took off at a gallop. His companions glanced back, then joined him.

With a shout, Lone Wolf charged down the hill. His men followed closely, the thunder of hooves all but drowned out by war cries. The chase was on.

The cowboys turned west, a move that caught the Kiowa off guard. Then the cowboys turned south before starting a long sweeping circle to the east.

Lone Wolf immediately swung southeast. "They are trying to get home!" he shouted over his shoulder.

Grassland gave way to rocky flats. Almost at once, Boytale's horse slowed and whinnied in pain. Looking down, he saw jagged stone covered the land.

He grunted. These white men weren't stupid. The unshod feet of the Kiowa horses were cut to pieces on the rocks. He dismounted and led the animal back to grass, stopping close to his leader. A dozen other warriors behind him did the same.

Bear Mountain, Lone Wolf's lieutenant and possibly the largest Kiowa in the tribe, rode up. "How is your pony?"

The chief shrugged. "He will be better once his feet are wrapped." He strung his bow and pulled an arrow from the quiver. "I see your horse is not hurt."

"I stopped when I saw what was happening to you." A slow smile spread across Bear Mountain's face. "Sometimes it's a good thing not to be first."

Lone Wolf returned the smile with a rueful grin. "Sometimes." He pointed to a small stand of cattle nearby. "String your bow. Since the white man led us here, his meat can fill our bellies."

Lone Wolf's brother, Red Otter, and the Owl Prophet, Mamanti, led their horses next to Lone Wolf's. The war chief regarded Mamanti.

"You said we would get a scalp today," Lone Wolf said.

Mamanti scowled. "The day is not over yet. When the sun sets, if you are still empty-handed, come to me then."

Several calves were shot. The warriors cut long strips of hide from the animals and tied the still-bloody skin to their horses' feet, a makeshift moccasin.

Movement to the north caught Boytale's eye. As he stared, he saw strange forms moving rapidly along Salt Creek, obviously following the war party's path. When they got close enough to separate into individuals, he realized the group of riders were all wearing white hats.

At Lone Wolf's command, the Kiowa climbed on their horses and rode up a long draw into the hills, each breaking off until their trail narrowed to one horse. The warriors circled back around on either side of the draw, dismounted, and waited.

The last thing Major John B. Jones wanted was to tangle with a large party of Indians. He'd arrived the previous day after a sixty-mile forced march based on a rumor of Indian trouble. Earlier that morning, he sent a patrol of Rangers under a very young Lieutenant Wilson to find the trail.

Now Jones and two dozen members of the newly formed Frontier Battalion of the Texas Rangers followed that trail. It was wide and well-worn. He estimated as many as fifty hostiles in the party—twice his number.

Still, he wasn't worried. This mission was to locate and calculate the strength of the enemy. When the time came for attack, he had seventy-five more men waiting at the base camp.

Moving at a gallop, Jones and his men followed Salt Creek, passing the marker erected to the members of the Warren Wagontrain Massacre, a grim reminder of what determined Indians could do. They had passed the fifteen-mile mark, and the trail became fresher.

They came to the Western Crosstimbers and slowed. Here the land changed from grass to breaks. Arroyos and dry streambeds cut between hills whose sides were covered in scrub brush and post oak. As the Rangers entered a ravine known as the Lost Valley, they slowed more, then stopped.

Another trail of unshod ponies clearly intersected with the one they had followed. Jones waved his cousin, Walter Robertson, forward.

"What do you think, Walt?" he said, pointing at the tracks. "Look like they met up with another war party to you?"

"Cain't say, John. If they did, we'd be outnumbered four to one."

Jones nodded. "I reckon." He turned to his men. "Listen, we're going to continue the chase. Keep an eye out for hostiles. I don't want to get ambushed."

Jones rode into the valley watching the surrounding hillsides. He noticed the trail with thin, individual sets of horse tracks leading into the breaks. Soon all sign of the Indians disappeared. He reined to a halt again.

"Damn!" he muttered, then louder: "Captain Stevens, if you please."

Captain G.W. Stevens, company commander of the Rangers now under Jones, rode to his leader's side.

"Yes, sir, Major Jones."

"Divide the men into small patrols and have them

scour the countryside until we can find the trail again.
You and Lieutenant Wilson will accompany me."

"Very good, sir."

Stevens wheeled his mount and began to shout orders. The Rangers split into small groups, quickly fanning out. Within a few minutes, Jones was alone with his five remaining men.

"We'll keep to the creek," he said, and started at a walk, the others following closely.

Jones removed his hat and ran his fingers through his hair. The white Stetson was covered with trail dust and looked beige. A darker reddish-brown line ran around the crown where sweat had mingled with dirt and stained the felt. He faced his second in command. "Tell me, Stevens, you ever fight Indians before?"

Stevens shook his head. "No, sir, never fought anybody. Too young for the war."

"I fought with Terry, but that was against Bluecoats," Jones said, replacing the hat. "I've not met the red men on the field of battle."

"What will we do if we're attacked by a hundred or more?"

Jones regarded Stevens closely, but saw no fear in the man's eyes. That was good. Caution made a man careful, but fear paralyzed. He'd seen it in the War Between the States, and had heard of it happening to soldiers now, especially when facing Indians.

"I don't know, Stevens. I've heard tell that they don't like to take casualties. If we spank them good, they should run. But if that is not so, we will simply ride back to the camp."

Stevens grinned. "At a good clip."

"That goes without saying, Captain."

"Yes, sir, Major."

Lieutenant Wilson brought his horse in line with

the others. "But what if the hostiles follow us?" he asked in a shrill voice.

"All the better," Jones replied.

Wilson's voice squeaked, "Better?"

"What the major means," Stevens began calmly, "is that if we can get them to chase us, they'll be facing fresh men and horses. Indians don't care much for even odds." He looked at Jones. "I heard that from a buffalo hunter."

Jones nodded, but said nothing. He scanned his surroundings, wondering where he'd hide if he was a Kiowa or Comanche running from the Texas Rangers. He wanted to catch this war party and punish them. Word of the loss would spread from tribe to tribe. Maybe next time, these bucks would think twice before raiding into Texas again.

He pulled a handkerchief from his vest pocket and mopped at the sweat on his face. He couldn't remember the last rain he'd seen on the plains. Some buffalo hunters who'd come south after the Comanche raid on Adobe Walls said they'd had rain the day before the attack. That'd be June 25, he thought. No rain since, and precious little before.

From the distance came the familiar pop of a pistol shot. The sound echoed off the hills surrounding Jones and his men.

"Which way?" Jones barked.

Stevens pivoted in his saddle and anxiously looked around. "Who the hell knows? Goddamn hills bounced it every which-a-way."

Scouting parties appeared along the hillsides and galloped toward Jones. From the south came a lone rider, flat against his horse and in full flight.

Before Jones could utter a word, he heard the war cries of Indians. Almost immediately, the war party rode into view. Jones issued orders and placed his men in a skirmish line. The rider passed the front line and slid to a stop.

"Jesus, Joseph, and Mary!" he yelled. "There's gotta be three hunnert of them red bastards!"

Jones's reply was terse. "Quickly, man, take your place on the line! You others, don't shoot until they're within pistol range. Forget your rifles. In the time it will take to reload, you'll be dead."

Stevens took a moment to assess their situation. Twenty-five Texas Rangers trapped on open ground by many times their number.

He shouted to Jones. "Major, we will all have to get to cover or be killed."

Jones stared at the captain. Was Stevens mad? No, he'd just stated the obvious, something Jones had overlooked. He cursed himself. They'd been led by the nose by these Indians, and he'd allowed himself to be caught without protection. He looked around.

"We seem to be surrounded, but I do remember a ravine to the south," said Jones.

Stevens nodded. "Yes, sir, I recall. We'll have to fight our way through."

"Rangers, we shall ride to the south, to a gully or wash there. Keep together and focus your firing on anyone who impedes us."

On Jones's order, they charged straight at the Indians. The warriors scattered and made for the hills. Encouraged, Jones continued the chase past the ravine to the southwest side of the valley. During the chase, a Ranger named Moore managed to kill one of the Indian's horses, unseating its rider. In the next second, a bullet shattered the bone in his leg just below the knee. The last Jones saw of Moore, he was afoot, limping into the bushes.

The Rangers crested a ridge just in time to see the war party wheel their horses and counterattack. Jones screamed for retreat, and his men reversed direction back toward the arroyo.

Jones saw a man named Lee Corn slump forward in his saddle. Blood ran freely down his arm and back. Even on the run, Jones could see the wound was bad. Corn veered off to the north, and was caught by another Ranger Jones didn't know. The last the major saw of his two men, they were nearing Cameron Creek.

Jones slid to a stop and leapt from his horse into the ravine. It was about five feet deep and close to a hundred yards long. He shouted encouragement to his men, urging them to come on. Lagging behind was a Ranger Jones knew as Glass. Closing on the others, he suddenly fell back and out of the saddle. Landing face-first in the dirt, he remained motionless.

"Christ!" Jones swore, pulling his pistol. He emptied the weapon at the oncoming Indians though he knew they were still out of range.

When the remaining Rangers had made the shelter of the ravine, Jones took a head count. "I saw Moore, Lee Corn, and Bill Glass go down. Are we missing any others?"

The men exchanged glances, mentally picking out those they knew.

"I think everyone else is here, sir," Stevens said.

Lieutenant Wilson stared at Glass's body. He felt ill. Other than relatives, Glass was the first man he'd seen dead, and the only man he'd ever seen killed. "What about Bill?" he asked quietly.

"Glass is dead!" Jones said harshly, brown eyes flashing. "As will we all be should the Indians have their way."

Lone Wolf and his men quickly spread themselves among the trees. In the open area separating them from the white men lay the man Tsen-au-sain had shot.

The Kiowa waited patiently, and as fire from them stopped, the shooting diminished from the other side. Soon the scene was quiet except for insects and the occasional snort of a horse.

Lone Young Man and Little Mountain crept through the brush trying to get close to the body. One would count coup and take the scalp; the other would touch the body for a coup as well.

The trapped white men saw the young warriors and immediately opened fire. Bullets kicked dust high into the air and whined through the vegetation. Lone Young Man jumped to his feet and ran for cover, zigzagging. When the gunfire concentrated on him, Little Mountain also leapt up and ran, diving into the first dense brush he saw.

Boytale slid behind a tree to avoid stray rounds. He gazed at Lone Wolf. The Kiowa chief didn't appear upset in the least. He smiled at Boytale.

"Time is on our side," he said. He gazed at the sun. "Can you feel the way the dry heat sucks the moisture from the air? White men have a bad habit of not carrying enough water and drinking what little they carry too fast. The only water to be found is half a mile away."

He sat up straighter and signaled to Bear Mountain. As the massive Kiowa drew close, he said, "I want you to take some warriors and hide near the water hole. Before long, at least one of these whites will try for water. We'll let him go; you stop him."

Bear Mountain nodded and crawled away, calling men's names.

"Can I go?" Boytale asked.

Lone Wolf slowly shook his head. "When you are

older. I should send you back among the rocks to keep you safe."

"But—"

Lone Wolf lifted his hand. "Don't worry. This war was forced on us by the whites. The young must learn to fight quickly, some before they're ready. You will stay, but close to me."

Red Otter made his way over. "What are we going to do now?" he asked.

Lone Wolf shrugged. "Wait."

"But what of the dead white man? I need his scalp for my son."

"There he is," Lone Wolf answered, pointing at the body. "Take his hair. Satisfy your need for vengeance."

Red Otter frowned. "You don't want it?"

"Not as much as you." A small smile played at his lips. "And certainly not as much as *they* do."

Red Otter turned and shouted to the unseen warriors. "I am going to count coup on the dead white man. Who will go with me?"

Hunting Horse glanced at the form on the ground. Mamanti had prophesied that he would honor himself. This had to be his chance. Still, he remembered what happened to Lone Young Man and Little Mountain. The task would be twice as hard now that the whites knew what to expect. He rose. "I will go, Red Otter."

Red Otter grimaced, but said nothing. He broke cover and ran to a nearby tree. Once in position, he signaled for Hunting Horse to join him. The young warrior took his elder's lead and ran to the same tree.

Using this alternating pattern, the two continued moving from tree to tree until they were a hundred yards from their comrades and close to their goal.

The whites had refrained from shooting during the

advance. Perhaps they hoped for an easy target. Red Otter withdrew his knife.

"From here we must crawl. I'll take his scalp for my son, but I want you to have first coup."

Hunting Horse grinned. First coup was a high honor among the Kiowa. The only higher was killing an enemy in hand-to-hand combat. Mamanti's prediction would come true, and Hunting Horse would have a grand story.

The young warrior had just gotten to his knees when he saw the body move.

"Red Otter, he's still alive!"

The older warrior looked up sharply. "What?"

"I saw him move. He's not dead."

Red Otter and Hunting Horse watched the fallen man closely. A low groan came across the clearing, and the head raised a bit before dropping back down into the dirt.

Red Otter was excited. "You must move quickly. Kill him, and take the scalp." He handed Hunting Horse his knife. "Do this and all the honors are yours. I will not even take second coup."

Hunting Horse's heart pounded. Mamanti had said no one in the war party would die, but that still left being shot. Hunting Horse clenched Red Otter's knife between his teeth and dropped to all fours.

He had no sooner begun to move when the white man's head raised, eyes blinking rapidly. The two locked stares. Hunting Horse had never before looked a man in the eye that he intended to kill. For that matter, he'd never killed anyone. This was his first war party. As the youngest member, he knew he'd be kept near the back, protected by the old warriors. He'd expected excitement, perhaps shooting with little danger, but not this. Not to be looking into the eyes of a helpless man.

"Go, Hunting Horse!" Red Otter hissed. "Hurry before the others see he's not dead."

The young man moved slowly into the open. The white man screamed and flailed at the ground managing to turn himself around. Still shouting words Hunting Horse didn't understand, he pulled himself toward the arroyo.

Hunting Horse crawled faster, fearing his quarry would escape. He had closed to within feet of the white man when a thunderous roar filled his ears. The ground erupted as bullets crashed into the soil less than six inches from his hands. He was showered in dirt, grass, and small rocks.

He dropped to his belly as more rounds passed overhead. They sounded like hornets buzzing through the air. His heart had stopped beating altogether. In response to the white men's shooting, Kiowa fired back, and above all this, the wounded rider screamed and inched his way toward safety.

Fear paralyzed Hunting Horse. What had been a chance for war honors now turned into a very real possibility of death. He pivoted quickly and slithered back to the trees.

From his hiding place, he saw three white men run from the ditch. They grabbed the wounded man under the arms and dragged him into the arroyo. Hunting Horse understood their actions. No warrior left his dead or wounded behind.

As though angered by the warriors' attempt, the men in the ravine directed all their fire to the tree behind which they hid. Bullets smacked into the bole; bark peeled away and flew into the warriors' faces. Hunting Horse and Red Otter ran for their lives using the trees around them for any shelter possible. Reaching Lone Wolf, the pair fell to the ground exhausted.

Staring at the clearing they'd just left, Hunting

Horse saw where blood had discolored the sand. That could have been his blood. A tremble started in his hands and crept its way down his body until he shook uncontrollably. He felt a little sick to his stomach, but exhilarated. What a story!

Major Jones looked at the man they'd rescued. Glass's eyes were wide and vacant, his face a mask of horror. His breath came in hard, agonized gasps. Jones shook his head. Glass was already dead; he just didn't know to quit breathing.

Looking at his command, Jones easily read the fear in their faces. These men weren't combat veterans. They were farm boys and city boys looking for the high excitement of being a Texas Ranger.

Jones climbed to the top of the ravine. "Listen to me, men. We are faced with a determined enemy, but they're not Texas Rangers, by God. We can outshoot 'em, outcuss 'em, and if need be, outrun 'em."

He paced the bank, hands behind his back as though on a leisurely stroll. At five-feet eight and some 140 pounds, he knew he was hardly an imposing figure, but he still believed he'd attract the Indians' attention. Within seconds, bullets whined through the air. The men ducked for cover, but Jones continued his walk.

"Now, I'm not going to say that this will be easy, far from it. But we can do it. I know you won't fail me." He paused as a round kicked dirt over his boots. "See? I am a prominent figure, yet they can't hit me! Don't worry, boys, I'll get you through."

Jones stopped near a scrub oak tree and looked through his field glasses. Dissatisfied with the image his shaking arms gave him, he leaned against the tree for support. Bullets crashed into the trunk; cut leaves showered the ground.

"I want half of you boys to switch to rifles." He lowered the glasses and stepped back into the ravine. "Watch for the smoke, then shoot at it. Don't waste ammunition. They shoot, you shoot back. Even if we can't kill them, we'll keep their heads down."

Sudden shots from the rear sent all the Rangers scrambling.

"Where the hell's that coming from?" Jones shouted. He scanned the tree line and saw telltale smoke on a ridge to his rear. "Dammit, they're behind us now!"

He had to find relief or the Indians would surround them and kill them one by one. Desperately looking for additional cover, he saw a bald ridge about 150 yards away. The only sign of visible vegetation was an old large oak tree. He signaled to his cousin.

"You see what's happening, Walt?"

Robertson nodded.

"Good." Jones pointed at the ridge. "See that lone oak? I want you and one other man up there."

Robertson studied the position and its relation to the Rangers. "Sure, John," he said. "I reckon I'll take Bill Lewis with me. He's just about the best shot we got."

The three men took off at a dead run under covering fire from the remaining Rangers, and reached the oak without mishap. Winded, Jones sat heavily.

"Damn, I'm gettin' too old for this kind of foolishness." He grinned at Robertson. "Helluva fight, eh, cuz?"

Robertson pulled his tobacco plug from his shirt pocket and cut a chaw. "You know it's gonna get mighty hot up here soon's those Injuns know what we're up to."

Jones nodded. "Yes, sir, I do. Still, from here you can watch my back and still have a clear line of fire at the main party. I don't intend to run, but I'd like to keep my options open."

"Amen, brother," Robertson replied, putting the tobacco in his mouth.

Jones turned to Lewis. "Well, son, you ready?"

"Yes, sir, Major! We'll keep them redskins off'n your back."

"Never doubted it," the major replied, rising to his feet. He dusted off his pants and gazed down the hill. "Time to get back." He looked at his rear guard. "Boys, stay here until they get you or until the fight is over."

Boytale glanced at the sun. His mouth felt dry, but he was used to it. Kiowa learned to live without food or water for days if necessary. Life on the plains demanded it.

Lone Wolf stood and walked to Mamanti's hiding place. Boytale trailed close behind.

"I am going with some men to the water hole," Lone Wolf told Mamanti. "I want you to keep the rest here."

"There will not be many of us. What if they charge?"

"They won't. Whites cannot go long without water. Soon the thirst will madden them, and they will try for the water hole. Bear Mountain is waiting north of the creek. If they evade him, I'll be in the bushes."

As the shooting slackened, Jones saw hope in some men's faces. "Lieutenant Wilson," he called.

"Yes, sir."

"Talk a walk. See how Robertson and Lewis are faring."

Wilson's voice was small. "Yes, sir."

Jones looked at the young officer. "Buck up, son. I made it up there and back. So shall you. If either of them is hurt or dead, shout or fire your weapon three times. We'll come runnin'."

Wilson left at a ground-eating lope. He crouched as low as he could without having to slow. When no one shot at him, he straightened a bit and pressed on faster. Feeling as though he had flown up the ridge, he burst upon Lewis and Robertson in a rush. Clearly startled, the two raised their weapons.

"Hold up, boys!" Wilson screamed, hands out thrust. "I'm with you!"

Robertson swore. "Good God, Lieutenant! You oughta holler or something. You scared us plumb to death."

Wilson took a huge breath. "Sorry, men. Major Jones sent me up to see how you're doing."

Lewis grinned. "We're doin' right good, sir."

"You're both all right? No wounds?"

"No, sir," Robertson replied. "Not 'less you count a splinter in Bill's little finger."

Wilson stared at the two Rangers, then looked at the bullet-scarred tree. Huge chunks of bark were missing, stripped away by the Indians' shooting. He plopped on his butt.

"Goddammit! No-good, bushwackin', murderin', red-nigger son-of-a-whores!"

"Lieutenant, you ought not swear like that," Lewis said seriously. "Don't you know that you might be killed at any moment?"

Wilson removed his hat and used it to fan his face. "Forgive me, Lewis. I'm not really myself today. You're right. I should not like to meet my Maker with a sin on my lips."

Robertson deposited a healthy spray of tobacco

juice on the ground close enough to Wilson that the lieutenant jumped. "If that's the case, sir, I reckon most of the men below us are hell-bound for sure."

The Indians suddenly fired at the trio. Bullets zipped past the men as they lay in the dirt as close to the oak as possible. One round cut through the foliage overhead, clipping a dead limb. The severed branch fell, striking Wilson on the head.

The lieutenant screamed and grabbed his head. "By God, boys," he exclaimed, "I'm shot, sure as hell!"

Robertson nearly choked on his plug.

Jones licked his dry and cracked lips. The sun seemed to drain the life out of each man. He'd seen several digging in the bottom of the ravine, hoping for a drop of moisture. The best they'd found was damp sand.

"Major, shootin's eased a mite."

Stevens's voice sounded like a croak. Jones was sure his was no better. "I'm well aware of that, Captain."

"The men need water bad."

"I know that as well. For that matter, so do the Indians."

"You don't think they lit out? Lotsa times Indians will just quit for no reason."

Jones had heard the same stories, but couldn't see why any commander would quit the field of battle when he was winning. Red or white. He'd already allowed himself to be led into an ambush, surrounded, and cut off from any source of water. Not again. He did not plan to leave the ravine until he was positive the Indians had deserted the area.

"Captain, the order stands. No one leaves the group to get water." It was a good eight hundred yards to the water hole. Too far, too dangerous.

As word of Jones's decision was passed around, voices rose in complaint and anger. A sudden commotion at the far side of the unit brought Ed Carnal on the run.

"Major! Major Jones! You gotta stop 'em!"

"Stop who, Carnal?"

"Porter and Bailey, sir. Them fools is making a water run."

"Goddammit!" Jones pushed his way through the group. "Stop those men!" he bellowed.

Carnal trailed behind Jones and Stevens. "I tried to tell 'em they's three hunnert redskins out there. But they was plumb loco for water. Said no one could stop 'em short of killin' 'em."

Jones reached the far end of the ravine in time to see Porter and Bailey ride away. The others crowded around him.

"I right sorry, Major," Carnal continued. "Really I am. I told 'em, but they wouldn't listen. No, sir. I said—"

Jones held up his hand, silencing the Ranger. "I'm sure you did your best. All right, men, get your carbines."

"But Major," Stevens exclaimed, "them carbines ain't got that kind of range!"

Jones regarded his second in command coolly. "Pray tell me, Captain Stevens, what else can I do? Would you have me send more after them? Weaken my force anew? If, by the grace of God, they do make it there alive, the least we can do is offer what protection we have for the ride back."

Stevens sagged, the wind driven from him as surely as if he'd been punched. "Yes, sir." He watched the quickly receding riders. "Godspeed, boys," he whispered.

* * *

Boytale watched the approaching riders with keen interest. The first led the other by fifty yards. As the first white man slid his horse to a stop, he jumped from the animal and dropped canteens into the water hole. Lone Wolf waited until the second was within range.

As the Kiowa burst from the brush, Boytale heard shots from the arroyo. The white man saw the Kiowa at the same instant and wheeled his horse back to the south. Had he turned east, away from the war party, he might have outrun the Kiowa ponies, but the warriors attacked at an angle and quickly surrounded the rider.

Do-hauson drove a lance deep into the white man's side. As he fell, Mamay-day-te touched him, getting first coup. The others let him fall to the ground.

Boytale was excited. They had their kill, maybe two. He heard a splash, several seconds of quiet, then a rapid burst of gunfire. Looking in the direction of the shooting, he saw Tahbone-mah riding toward them leading a bay stallion.

"Did you get a kill?" Lone Wolf asked.

Tahbone-mah shook his head. "He's hidden somewhere on the creek. We will never find him." He grinned. "But I do have this fine animal."

Lone Wolf smiled, dismounted, and made his way to the dead white man. He drew his knife, bent, and quickly scalped the corpse. Then he pulled out his brass hatchet-pipe and methodically pounded the man's head into mush. Again he took the knife, cutting and hacking at the body, until finally stretching out the man's intestines between bloodstained hands.

At his signal, the remaining members of the party either shot arrows into the body or stabbed it with their lances, until what was a man more resembled a mutilated porcupine.

When all had finished, Lone Wolf waved his men together.

"My mourning is now at an end. My heart flies free of the pain of the loss of my son and nephew. I want to thank each of you for helping me, for helping my brother, Red Otter."

Pointing at a young warrior, he continued. "Mamay-day-te has on this day shown his worth. He has been a good friend to my family. For his loyalty and bravery, I am giving him my name. Now he will be known as Lone Wolf. Let us go home."

"What of the other whites?" Feather Head asked.

"Leave them. Mamanti said we would kill one man today. We have. As he predicted, we have lost no warriors. It is ended."

Jones stared bleakly at Bailey's mutilated corpse. He'd seen almost as bad in the war, but to the others in his unit, the sight must have been horrendous.

"What do we do with him, sir?" Stevens asked quietly.

"Do?" Jones said brusquely. "We bury him, Captain. That is what we do."

Stevens glanced about. "Here, sir? Shouldn't we take him home?"

Jones regarded his second in command closely. "Listen to me, Stevens. The only reason we know that this is Bailey is because Porter's standing over there. It's bad enough I got to tell his folks he's dead, but there is no way in hell I'll let them see his body!" He stepped away from the distraught Stevens. "Lieutenant Wilson!" he shouted. "You will form a burial detail, and put this poor bastard into the ground."

"Yes, sir," Wilson replied. "Then we go after the Indians?"

Jones shook his head. "No, sir. Those redskins are heading to Indian Territory. We will ride home and take the matter up with the U.S. Army."

HEADQUARTERS
ARMY OF THE UNITED STATES

Washington, D.C., July 15, 1874

Lieutenand General P. H. Sheridan
Commanding Division
Chicago, Illinois

Dispatch of today received.
Don't you think it would be well to order the 6th and 10th Cavalry to converge on Fort Sill and settle this matter at once. . . .
Unless something is done now, the rascals will merely rest awhile and start afresh.

W. T. SHERMAN
General

HEADQUARTERS
ARMY OF THE UNITED STATES

Washington, D.C., July 20, 1874

Lieutenant General P.H. Sheridan
Chicago, Illinois

The following communication has been just received from the Secretary of War and is sent to you for your information and guidance:—

War Department
Washington City
July 20, 1874

In accordance with the suggestions and recommendations received today from the Acting Secretary of the Interior and the Commissioner of Indian Affairs, the guilty Indians will be pursued and punished wherever found and the Reservation lines should be no barrier to such operations. . . .

W.W. BELKNAP
Secretary of War

By command of General Sherman:

Wm. D. WHIPPLE
Asst. Adjt. General

Chicago, Ills.
July 21, 1874

Genl. W.T. Sherman,
The telegram of the Secretary of War which you transmitted to me yesterday came duly to hand. . . .

P.H. SHERIDAN
Lt. Gen.

Two

Private James Augustus Rambling slowly slid the cleaning rod down the bore of his Springfield rifle. He extracted the patch, then examined the barrel.

A careless lock of light brown hair fell to his forehead, and he impatiently brushed it away, his face set in a frown, pale blue eyes narrowed in irritation.

As the curl drooped again, he laid the Springfield across his knees and swept both hands through his hair. It was then he noticed Bob Larsen.

Larsen was a private in Rambling's outfit, Company I, Fifth Infantry. He was tall and thin, with a long neck and bobbing Adam's apple. His ears stuck out, his face narrow and pinched, all topped with a shock of short, greasy black hair.

But it was his eyes that people remembered. They were brown, so dark they looked black. They glowed with some fire that burned deep within Larsen. At the moment, they seemed to bore through Rambling.

"Jim, gotta moment?" Larsen said in an unremarkable tenor voice.

Rambling smiled. "Sure, Bob." He'd known Larsen over two years since training camp in 1872. The fiery gaze didn't bother him anymore.

Larsen glanced around the barracks, then sat on the bed next to Rambling. He leaned in close.

"You are a Christian, right?" he said in a low voice.

"Yes. I was raised a Methodist."

Larsen frowned a moment, then nodded. "I was worried there, but then I remembered that Jesus was a Jew."

Rambling raised his eyebrows. "Really?"

Larsen nodded. "Not that I got nothin' against Jews. I just mean you never can tell where a savior might come from, y'know?" Larsen looked around the room again. "I have something very important to talk to you about. Grant is a Mason."

"The President?"

"U.S. Grant himself," Larsen said with a slow nod. "Doesn't that mean anything to you?"

Baffled, Rambling shook his head. "Should it?"

Larsen's eyes widened in disbelief. "You don't know, do you?" He leaned closer. "Grant is not only a Mason, he is the Grand Potentate of the Great Masonic Lodge in Washington. During the war, he and other Mason officers designed a way to rule the world while they orchestrated the slaughter of thousands of Christian men on the battlefield."

Larsen sat back, a small smile on his thin lips. "You know how to tell he's a Mason?" He glanced at the barrack's door, then looked back at Rambling. "His watch. Ever notice how in every picture, Grant's always wearing that watch? Well, on that same chain is a key to a secret room hidden in the basement of the White House. Lincoln found the room, and Grant had Booth, another Mason, kill him."

Rambling's father carried a watch, but he wasn't a Mason. "Many men have pocket watches."

"They're all Masons." Larsen snorted. "Course some of them deny it, even claim they've never been one, but then why . . . why carry the watch?"

"Even if what you say is true, what has that to do with us?"

A pained look crossed Larsen's face. Rambling felt like an idiot who'd missed some obvious fact.

"Jim, it has everything to do with us. It is Grant's intention to send us into the wilderness just like Pharaoh sent out the Jews. There the Indians, who're just pawns of the Masons and don't even know it, will kill us all. Afterwards, Grant will fill the ranks with more Masons until he has an army of his own kind."

"Do you think Captain Lyman will stand for that?"

Larsen laughed. "He's one too. If he dies, he becomes a martyr, but that won't happen."

"Why?"

Larsen stood and paced the floor. "The Masons worship their own savior. A man named Hiram Abiff that they claim died and was brought back to life." He stopped and gazed at Rambling. "Actually, he was killed by Romans. See? Lyman believes that even if the Indians do kill him, he'll just get back up again."

Rambling sat back. "I don't know, Bob. It's really rather hard to believe."

"But you must!" Larsen shouted, and sat back on the bed. "You must," he repeated, his voice pleading. "Because you are the key! You, Jim, hold all of our destinies."

"What?"

"It's true, it's true. Oh, can't you see? Pharaoh sent the Jews to die in the desert, but Moses saved them. And who was he? A shepherd. Just like David who slew the Philistine Mason, Goliath."

"But I'm no shepherd," Rambling protested. "My family's in the shipping business."

Larsen groaned. "No, no, no! You don't understand! The shepherds are the lowest members of their society. And who are we if not the lowest of the low in the Army."

He stood and raised his arms in supplication, his voice climbing in volume. "You will overcome the evil of the Mason Lyman and lead us out of the wilderness. Then the Christians will march on Washington and storm the White House. We'll wrest the key from Grant and open his secret room." He lowered his arms. "Know what we'll find? The Book. The grand plan for Masonic world domination."

Larsen gazed into the distance, rapt in his vision. "Between its pages," he said quietly, "are the names of all the Masons in the world. We will be able to eradicate this threat to the Christian world at last." He looked at Rambling. "But it lies with you, Jim. As the evil is thrust upon us, you must fight for Man, for God, for the very salvation of everyone. I will be there in the ranks, but I am merely the prophet. I need you to fulfil my destiny as you do your own."

Rambling rubbed his face, unsure what to say. That Larsen was unbalanced was obvious, but if he thought he was being mocked or disbelieved, would he be violent?

"Bob, have you told anyone else about this?"

Larsen frowned and looked away, chewing his lip. He turned back, eyes wide in sorrow.

"I—I talked to Lieutenant Lewis about it." He fell to his knees and gripped Rambling's arm. "Forgive me! I thought he was the one, but as I told him I watched his eyes. I saw the change, and I knew." He squeezed harder. "But I know it's you! You have a savior's eyes. You will save us. You will lead us out of the wilderness!"

Rambling gently pried Larsen's hands from his arm. It had gone numb in his viselike grip. Larsen was much stronger than he appeared. Maybe it was the madness. Rambling stood and pulled Larsen to his feet.

"Listen," Rambling said, "don't tell anyone else about this. I'm sure the Masons have spies everywhere—and they won't be wearing the watch."

Larsen nodded eagerly.

"We'll have to be careful," Rambling continued. "We have to bide our time. Strike too early and we'll fail. Understand?"

"Yes. Yes."

"Good." He slapped Larsen on the back. "I'm glad you came to me, Bob. We'll keep prepared just in case we ever get sent into the wilderness. Fair enough?"

"Don't you worry, Jim, I'll keep quiet and wait."

"No matter how long it takes?"

Larsen frowned, then nodded. "However long. You are our deliverer, and I'll abide by your wishes."

"That's good, Bob. We can't rush destiny, can we?"

Larsen stared at the floor and shrugged. "I suppose not."

Private Joshua Smith burst through the barracks door. "Guess what, fellows. We're off to fight the Indians!"

Shocked, Rambling sat on his bed. "What? Are you sure?"

Smith smirked. "Heard from a clerk I know what works for the general himself. He's says we're to go into Texas, out on the plains. He says there ain't nothin' but miles and miles of nothin' out there. Leastwise nothing but redskins."

"Into the wilderness," Rambling mumbled. He glanced at Larsen.

The private smiled at his savior and slowly nodded his head, tapping himself on the side of the nose three times.

Three

Muttering to himself, Rambling dug through his steamer trunk, finally pulling out a pair of gray woolen socks. He quickly shoved a hand into the first sock, groaning when his finger poked through a hole in the toe.

He returned to the box and took out a small sewing kit known as a "housewife." After threading the needle, he sat on his bunk and started to darn the sock.

"Rambling!" a voice boomed from the other end of the empty barracks.

He looked up from his darning and saw the square frame of De Armond just inside the open doorway. "Yo, Sergeant."

"Get your butt up to the commandant's office."

Surprised, Rambling blurted out, "On Sunday?"

De Armond strolled down the center aisle. "The issue here is not the day of the week. The issue is just how fast can you respond to an order."

Rambling jumped to his feet, threw the sock and sewing kit into his locker, and reached for his hat. "Sorry, Sergeant. I wasn't questioning the order. I was just surprised to be called to the commandant's on a Sunday. I'd have thought General Miles had more important things to do."

"You're not to see the general. You got visitors."

Rambling paused and looked over his shoulder. "Who?"

"I don't know, son," De Armond said, with a sigh. "Lieutenant Lewis tells Mitchell, who tells me. I tell you, you go. That's the way it works."

Rambling pulled the kepi on, the bill just above his eyebrows. He sidestepped De Armond and ran down the length of the barracks. Outside, he quickly crossed the parade ground and made his way to the office of Nelson Miles, commander of the Fifth U.S. Infantry Regiment at Fort Leavenworth, Kansas.

Inside, a blond-headed lieutenant he recognized as Miles's adjutant, Baird, sat at a desk. Rambling came to attention and saluted.

"Private James Rambling, sir, reporting as ordered."

Baird stood and returned the salute. "Follow me, Private."

Rambling was ushered to Miles's office. Baird closed the door behind him.

The office was spartan, which surprised the private. A low bookshelf stood against one wall beneath a photograph of President Grant. On another wall was a large oak desk. One leather-bound chair was behind the desk, two in front.

In one of the chairs sat a woman in her fifties, her sandy hair neatly brushed and combed in place beneath a small hat adorned with lilac tea roses. She looked up as he entered the room, blue eyes widening in recognition. A small smile played at the corners of her well-formed mouth.

"Mother," Rambling said.

A tall figure standing by the window turned at the sound of his voice. James Daniel Rambling was sixty, thin, with large hazel eyes flecked in gold, set above a hooked nose. His thin-lipped mouth, turned down at the corners, added to his foreboding, hawkish image. With his gray-streaked black hair swept back, he looked every inch the dour Puritan from whose stock he came. His gaze swept Rambling from head to toe.

"You look thinner," he said in a strong tenor voice.

"I'm well, Father. The food here isn't wonderful, but it is plentiful."

Elizabeth Rambling stood and hugged her son. "You look wonderful," she said. "I've missed you so very much."

Rambling smiled. His mother had always radiated as much warmth as a Franklin stove. "It's good to see you again, Mother. I'd hoped to come home earlier, but we've been very busy. And now . . ."

The elder Rambling cleared his throat. "That's precisely why we've come."

"Hush, Papa," Elizabeth said, waving him off. "That can wait." She bent and picked up a basket next to her chair. "Look, James, we've brought gifts." She raised the lid. "There's smoked oysters and Underwood Devil Ham. And some of those smoked sausages you like so much." She lifted a jar. "Here's some Dijon mustard."

Rambling stared into the basket, all but drooling. "This is fantastic, Mother! I don't know what to say."

"Shush, dear. That's a mother's job." She looked back into the basket. "Now, Cook made molasses cookies, and Mrs. Johannson's cook sent boysenberry preserves, and Mrs. Reilly's cook a small but very nice Virginia ham."

"Thank you. Thank you so much. You can't imagine how much we'll enjoy this."

"We?" Elizabeth asked.

"The rest of the men in my company. I can't keep this bounty to myself. We're a unit, Mother. We share and share alike." He lowered the lid. "But I don't think you've traveled all the way from Baltimore to bring me a picnic basket."

"Indeed," Rambling Senior intoned from the window. He stepped closer to the soldier. "We are well aware of what is happening."

Rambling wasn't surprised. His father owned one of the largest shipping companies in Baltimore. During the Insurrection, he'd gained favor with the government by cutting his cargo rates in half for Federal shipments. The gambit paid off after the war when he was placed at the top of the list of contracted companies. He had many friends in Washington.

"I think it's time you came home," the elder Rambling continued. "You've gotten to play soldier for two years now, but I need you to learn the family business."

"I can't leave, Father."

"Nonsense! I know I can buy off your enlistment. You could leave with us today."

"No, Father, I won't quit."

"This is ridiculous," his father said, his face turning red. "You spent but a year at Oxford, another at Yale. You had no compunction about quitting then."

Rambling flushed. "The Army isn't a factory job or school where I can walk away as I choose. I must serve the rest of my enlistment. If I decide not to reenlist, I still have time to learn the shipping business."

"What can you hope to gain from this? Do you know where you're going? Do you know what it is that you'll face?" His father turned back toward the window. "I've lost one son to a meaningless war. I refuse to lose another."

"Daniel is not dead!" Rambling shouted.

The elder Rambling turned. "He may as well be. He sits and mutters to himself. Sometimes he drools. Lately, he's been given to wandering the neighborhood. I've had to hire a man to watch over him. Do you call that living?" He sighed. "This precious Army of yours took my eldest son, whole and healthy, and returned a white-haired shell of a man with his mind and one hand buried in some Pennsylvania field!"

Rambling remained silent. He was ten years old when his older brother returned from the war. The shuffling, hoary-headed human wreck that shambled into his house little resembled the vibrant twenty-one-year-old who'd left three years earlier.Over the next eight years, Rambling tried to understand what had happened to Daniel. What had he witnessed or done? He talked to him, but the answers were always a jumbled mix of phrases, curses, and shouts. At times he held his brother as Daniel cried and screamed in terror at the visions in his head.

Rambling snapped from his reverie as his father addressed him again. "Excuse me?" Rambling said.

"I said I can force the issue."

"How, Father? I am of majority. You cannot compel me to leave."

"I can cut off your allowance." The elder Rambling leaned closer. "Think you can live on thirteen dollars a month?"

Rambling stood his ground. "Actually, Father, most of the money is in a bank. I've only taken enough to have new boots made. The rest is yours if you want it."

"Dammit, son, money is not an issue!"

"James, please," Elizabeth chided. "Your language."

Taken aback, Rambling Senior gaped at his wife a moment, then closed his mouth. "I am trying to save your son from himself," he said.

Elizabeth rose and brushed at the folds in her traveling dress. "Well, you can't. He's a Rambling and

Ramblings have always been men of action. We've fought the English twice, and in the War Between the States. Now, we have a new soldier to brave the frontier." She reached and placed her hand on her son's cheek. "Do be careful, James. And when you feel you've satisfied whatever need brought you here, come home."

Later, back in his barracks, Rambling thought over the visit from his parents as he divided the basket among his comrades. At first he thought his father had been trying to run his life like he did his business. Then he realized that the old man was frightened, scared that another son would come home broken—or not at all.

As he opened tins and jars of preserves, he heard a distinctly nasal voice.

"Well, well, what have we here?"

Rambling glanced up at Seth Hitchcock. He stood with arms crossed over his chest, a look of disdain painted on his thin, pockmarked face. His light brown hair was unkempt and draped his ears like a scraggly tablecloth.

Though his stance seemed casual, Rambling read the challenge in his brown eyes. Hitchcock had two other privates standing just behind him, Bailey and Ketzel. The three comprised a group of toughs who enjoyed bullying other soldiers. Until now, they'd ignored Rambling.

"This is a gift from my mother," Rambling said evenly. "You're welcome to share with the rest of us."

Hitchcock laughed. "Oh, I intend to. In fact, I think I'll start with those oysters. They're my favorites."

Rambling rose and faced Hitchcock. "You can have some, not all. My mother didn't bring this basket from Baltimore just so you could pick it clean."

"Really?" Hitchcock lowered his arms to his sides. He glared at Rambling, ready to take what he wanted. Then his eyebrows rose. "Baltimore?" A leer twisted his mouth. "Baltimore," he repeated. "My, oh, my. You boys know what we got here? A Baltimore Rambling."

"What's that mean?" Bailey asked.

"You wouldn't know, but I do. I'm a wharf rat. My daddy used to unload ships in the harbor when he was sober. Me, too, until I joined up. Now Daddy was always talkin' about the rich men he worked for, but he said the richest was named Rambling. He owned the biggest and fastest ships afloat. Ain't that right, Jimmy-boy?"

Rambling clenched his jaw. He'd never hidden his background until he was in training camp. When the other soldiers found out who he was, he became an outcast. The poor men hated him for his wealth, though he never lorded it over anyone. The snobs appealed to him to join their clique as American aristocrats. When he refused, he had to fight the men they hired to beat him. He won most of the battles, as well as the respect of his opponents, but no one offered him friendship of any kind. Now he was in danger of having the same thing happen with I Company.

"What if it is?" he asked through clenched teeth.

"Nothin'." Hitchcock smirked. "Course, I seem to recall another Rambling come home from the war a little different." He laughed. "Yessir, that doughboy come home all crazy and pissin' his—"

The punch started at Rambling's hip and caught Hitchcock on the jaw, snapping his head to the left. Before the startled soldier could react, a second punch came from Rambling's right and caught him flush in the face. His nose broke instantly, blood spattering bystanders. Hitchcock's eyes rolled white and he fell straight back, landing heavily on the wooden floor.

Rambling faced Bailey. "You got something to say?"

Bailey looked down at his unconscious leader, then back into Rambling's cold, hard eyes. He slowly shook his head.

Rambling looked at Ketzel. The soldier lifted his hands in surrender.

"What in the hell is goin' on here?" De Armond's voice echoed through the silent building.

"Nothing, Sarge," Larsen said. "Seems Private Hitchcock tripped over his own big feet and fell."

De Armond walked down the center aisle, the crowd parting as he neared. He stopped and knelt next to the prostrate Hitchcock.

"Clumsy son of a bitch must have fallen flat on his face judging by that nose." He stood and motioned Bailey and Ketzel. "You two drag that piece of shit to the infirmary." While the men picked up their comrade, he turned and nodded at the basket. "What's that?"

Rambling drew a deep breath and released it slowly, willing himself to calm. "It's a gift from my folks. Help yourself, Sergeant."

De Armond glanced over the goods arranged on one of the company dining tables and chose a smoked sausage, which he liberally smeared with Dijon mustard. He bit in, chewed, then smiled.

"I just love these things. One day, we're gonna make us a company smokehouse." He raised the sausage. "Thanks, Rambling."

De Armond turned and started back down the aisle to check on Hitchcock. Then he stopped and looked back.

"A word to the wise, son. If you hit with the flat of your fist, you're not as likely to bust a knuckle."

Rambling stared at the departing sergeant until he felt a hand on his shoulder. He turned and gazed at Larsen.

"Are we gonna eat this," Larsen asked, his face solemn, "or wait for the Masons to take it?"

Rambling started to chuckle, then he laughed. "Dig in, boys!"

Four

The five sat around the campfire in Lone Wolf's lodge, the war chief in the center, facing the door. To his left were Lone Young Man and Little Mountain. Boytale and Hunting Horse sat on the right.

The pipe had been passed around many times, each man thankful for the successful raid. Others, like Hunting Horse, had much more to be thankful for. Lone Wolf's wife served a simple dinner of corn mush and roasted beef.

"I feel good," he said at length. "I have avenged my son, and his spirit now rides among the buffalo in heaven. My wife smiles again. That is as it should be."

As Lone Wolf paused, Boytale glanced up at the fresh Tejano scalp stretched on a hoop and hanging from a pole.

"But," Lone Wolf continued, "we must talk of the future. I am speaking to you young men because soon all the old warriors will be gone. It is you who will carry the fight."

Hunting Horse shifted uncomfortably. "But who are we to follow? You tell us one thing, Striking Eagle tells us another."

Lone Wolf stared into the fire. "That is what's wrong with the People today. We used to sit in council and make up our minds together, but now the peace chiefs meet and make decisions for us all. The young are left with no real leader because the Kiowa have no real leader."

He glanced at Hunting Horse. "Striking Eagle was once a great fighter, his heart hardened against his enemies. But now, his bow is unstrung, and he talks only of the white man's road. Even White Bear has given up his lance and war shield. They are *onde*, warrior aristocrats." He pointed at the men around him. "You young men cannot become *onde* without war. So who will lead the People? Who will protect them from our enemies?"

Lone Wolf picked up a twig and tossed it into the flames. "Soon, though, matters will change. Big Tree still hates the soldiers. With him, the balance of power shifts again to the fighters. Then the issue of war will be raised anew."

Stretching, Lone Wolf gained his feet. The others stood quickly and followed him through the tipi doorway. Blinking against the sunlight, he gazed toward the fort, about a mile to the west. "We will stay here until our friends arrive from Texas. In the meantime, let the Indian agent Haworth feed us."

Boytale saw a rider approach.

Lone Wolf waved and called. "Red Otter, welcome to my lodge."

The warrior reined to a halt. "My brother, you look well."

"I am. My medicine feels powerful, and soon Big Tree will be here again. I smell change, Red Otter. The very air reeks with it."

Red Otter's smile faded. "There is a stink, but perhaps not what you wish."

"What do you mean?"

"Striking Eagle wanted to come into the fort for

blankets and bullets, but Haworth said he was not allowed in without the interpreter. When asked why, the agent said the Great White Chief in Washington told him that all the Kiowa must move here."

"Here?" Lone Wolf said, looking around him. "They cannot. I am here, and so is Mamanti's band. There is barely grass for our ponies. If everyone moves here, the horses will starve."

Red Otter nodded. "That was what Sun Boy said, but there is more. It is not just the Kiowa. The Comanche, Cheyenne, Wichita, Caddo, and even the Arapaho must all move here or to another agency. Striking Eagle said he thought the Comanche would go to Anadarko."

"What is happening?" Lone Wolf asked.

Red Otter shrugged. "I don't know, but I did hear Haworth say that after all the tribes have gathered, our names will be written in a book, and we will be counted every day."

"I see," Lone Wolf said, nodding vigorously. "Yes, I see all too well. The white man gathers his cows all in one place. Then he counts them and writes in his book. Remember? Remember when we get the beef?"

Red Otter thought a moment. His mouth fell open. "They herd the cattle into a pen, then slaughter them!"

"That is what they will do to us!" Lone Wolf shouted. He turned toward his lodge. "And I do not intend to be here when it starts."

Boytale watched the rabbit sizzle and sputter over the fire. In the days since Lone Wolf had led them from the fort, they'd spent the time roaming the plains, camping where and when the mood took them. They hunted freely and feasted at night on buffalo and antelope.

He listened when the chiefs and old men gathered around the campfire. They told stories of days long gone and past battles, warriors, and great chiefs. Sometimes, Mamanti inflated his owl, and the bird would tell him of events to come. Boytale never questioned whether the Owl really said anything. He just knew that Mamanti was right more times than he was wrong.

Boytale liked his life as a Kiowa. He had been captured as a boy when the tribe raided his village in Mexico. His birth parents were a faint memory. If he had siblings, he couldn't remember them. The family that took him in was kind and raised him as a brother to their other children. Still, he knew there were those in the tribe who looked down on him because of his Mexican birth. And it was those old men who could stop him from becoming *onde*.

A rider approached the camp. Every night someone came from the fort with the day's news. They returned the next day only to be replaced by another rider at dusk. This rider rode straight to Lone Wolf's tipi.

Boytale rose and walked to the war chief's lodge, as did others in the band, eager for news. The door flap was pulled aside, and Lone Wolf emerged, followed closely by Mamanti.

"Goose!" Lone Wolf hailed the rider. "It is good to see you. It's been a long time since we rode together."

"Too long, Lone Wolf," Goose replied, smiling. "Since before the fight with the buffalo hunters."

"Soon, maybe, we'll ride again. What news? Has Big Tree arrived yet?"

Goose shook his head. "Word came today that he

is close, but there is other news. The interpreter from the fort told Striking Eagle that the soldiers will come in three days to count them."

"What did Striking Eagle say?"

"Nothing. He just nodded and went into his lodge."

Lone Wolf rubbed his face wearily. "Does he not understand what the soldiers will do?" He glanced up. "You there, Boytale. Find Bear Mountain and bring him here."

The four riders approached the camp quietly. As they crested a nearby hill, the fort spread out before them into the distance. The soldiers' lodges were nothing more than black shapes with bright yellow squares on their sides. Occasionally a door opened, spilling more light into the roadways.

Directly below them lay the tipis of Striking Eagle and the other peace chiefs and their bands. Each home glowed warmly from the cooking fire within, tendrils of smoke coming through the top. They clearly saw the massive horse herd as well as individual ponies staked by the lodges.

Lone Wolf pointed and Boytale started down the hill. He tied his horse to a bush on the outer edge of the village and walked in. He wore no paint nor did he carry a weapon except his knife. To any who might watch and tell the soldiers, he was just a boy visiting his chief.

Boytale quickly located Striking Eagle's tipi and announced himself.

"You are part of Mamanti's band," Striking Eagle said as he emerged from the lodge. "I thought all of you had moved away."

"We have, but Lone Wolf has learned that the count will start soon, and wishes to meet."

Striking Eagle frowned. "He knows he is always welcome to my lodge. Tell him to come down, and we'll talk."

"Actually, he wants you to come with me."

The peace chief gazed evenly at Boytale, who felt uncomfortable with the scrutiny. *Maybe he thinks I'm leading him into a trap.*

"There are only four of us," Boytale said, "Lone Wolf, Mamanti, Bear Mountain, and myself."

Striking Eagle nodded slowly and turned back to his tipi. "Very well," he said over his shoulder, "let me saddle my horse, and we'll go."

"Thank you, Striking Eagle. I will meet you at the southern edge of the camp."

The pair rode the short distance to where the others waited. On the back side of the hill, an almost flameless buffalo-chip fire had been started, and blankets lay on the grass nearby. Lone Wolf sat in one corner, holding a pipe. Mamanti sat to the war chief's right. Bear Mountain had withdrawn to attend the fire.

The riders drew to a halt, and Boytale leapt from his pony. He quickly grabbed the halter on Striking Eagle's mount, and held the animal still as the peace chief dismounted.

Striking Eagle drew himself erect and walked to the blankets. His bearing wasn't haughty, but dignified, as though to remind Lone Wolf and Mamanti who they were dealing with. The formality of his approach belied the informal surroundings. He sat across the blanket and between the others finishing the triangle.

As Striking Eagle sat, Bear Mountain rose and carried an ember to Lone Wolf. The war chief lit the pipe, offered it to the cardinal directions, and passed it Mamanti. The Owl Prophet also offered smoke to the gods and handed the pipe to Striking Eagle, who did the same.

The pipe was returned to Lone Wolf, who cradled the instrument in his left arm. "Striking Eagle," he began, "I welcome you to our camp, such as it is."

"Thank you. But we could have met at my tipi. I would never turn you away. Our differences are only in the path we choose. I know you only want what is best for our people."

"I would have enjoyed your hospitality, Striking Eagle, but there are those, even among our own people, who would have told the soldiers I was there. They would do this for whiskey or even tobacco."

Striking Eagle stared at the blanket, its patterns faintly visible in the dark. "It's true. There has been a great change in the Kiowa. Many have been poisoned by the peddler's cheap firewater. Even some of our women have been corrupted and leave their homes to lay with the soldiers for money. I fear there may be no Kiowa one day."

"Your fear is no greater than ours," Mamanti said. "I have consulted the Owl, and he tells me of danger ahead for the People."

"What kind of danger?" Striking Eagle asked. "Disease? Soldiers? What can befall us now?"

Mamanti shrugged. "Much of what is to happen depends on what happens next."

"Spoken like a true medicine man," Striking Eagle said with a wry smile. "Enough threat to worry, but not enough information to act."

"I feel the danger lies with the count," Lone Wolf said. "I believe they mean to count us, then slaughter us like their cattle."

"Nonsense," Striking Eagle countered. "The agent, Haworth, would not allow this to happen."

Lone Wolf persisted. "How can you be so certain?"

"Haworth is what the whites call a Quaker. He is like a peace chief. He protects us from the soldiers."

"Ha!" Lone Wolf barked. "One man against the all the soldiers? How can this be? Does he wield some great magic that stops them?"

"No," Striking Eagle returned evenly. "The Great White Chief in Washington has given him the power over the soldiers. This is true because I've heard them complain to Haworth. Some of our people speak their language better than they think, so they don't hide their thoughts from us." He leaned forward. "There will be no slaughter unless you fight the soldiers."

Lone Wolf sat silently for a few moments, marshaling his thoughts. Finally, he said, "There are some things worse than death in battle. The whites will put us in cages and let us starve while pretending to feed us. They will turn our warriors in to dirt-scratchers like the Caddo, or worse, into drunken old women. We will have to beg for anything we need. This is better than death? This is preferable to living on the plains, hunting the buffalo, and watching our sons grow into men?"

"They will soil our blood with theirs," Mamanti intoned. "We will be defiled until there is no pure Kiowa left."

Boytale felt the heat rise to his face. He wasn't sure if Mamanti's comment was directed at him, but at the moment, he was ashamed of his Mexican heritage. He had never wanted anything more than to be accepted by those he considered his people.

Striking Eagle laughed. "We have been taking wives and children from among the Mexicans since before my father's father's time. Who here can say he has no blood other than Kiowa? Since the whites came, we have adopted their children as well. We marry Comanche and Cheyenne. All are now some part Kiowa as we are a part of them."

"That is true, Striking Eagle," Mamanti agreed. "But it has always been of our choosing. The white man will take our children, our women. They will forget their language, their gods, their families here."

Striking Eagle rose. "Perhaps. Yet if we seek the war road, these same women and children will die. If the worst comes to pass, as you suggest, and the whites take my children or grandchildren, at least they will be alive. And as long as they live, deep in their hearts, they will always be Kiowa. That no man can take."

Five

The heat, the swaying car, and the rhythmical clack-ety-clack of the wheels conspired to lull Rambling to sleep. He sat, arms crossed, eyes closed, chin to chest, on the hard, horsehair-stuffed seat and allowed his mind to wander.

He recalled his parents' visit—how his father had stormed from the office when he refused to leave the Army. His mother had paused in the doorway and looked back.

"Do you really believe you can help Daniel by doing this?" she'd asked.

He'd paused a moment. "I don't know," he replied truthfully, "but I'll *never* know if I don't try, will I?"

She'd said nothing, just offered him a small smile, turned, and left.

"How can you sleep in this heat?" Larsen demanded.

Reverie broken, Rambling lifted his head and wiped a hand across his face. "Wasn't asleep," he said with a yawn. "Train's making me lazy."

"I can't see how." Larsen's worn fatigue coat was unbuttoned, revealing the neck and chest areas of his red long-handled underwear shirt darkened with sweat. He mopped his brow with a sodden handkerchief. "Lord above, I feel like I'm gonna bust into flames!"

Rambling shrugged. He'd grown up on the docks of Baltimore's Inner Harbor. Summers there were not only hot, but oppressively humid. The heat in the car, growing dryer as they moved westward, didn't bother him that much.

"If I didn't know better," the other persisted, "I'd think the Masons'd done something to the sun."

A small smile played on Rambling's lips. "Maybe they did."

"What?" Larsen stared at Rambling, mouth slightly open. Then he laughed. "You're just joshin' me. Had me a-goin' there, too." He slowly shook his head. "Heat's addled me, only excuse I got."

Rambling chuckled and looked out the window. The featureless prairie slid by in waves of yellow and sun-scorched green. "I was told that not two years ago trains had to stop on the way to Dodge and wait while millions of buffalo crossed the tracks. Now there's nothing but empty land."

" 'And let them have dominion over the fish of the sea, and over the fowl of the air, and over the cattle. . . . ' " Larsen grinned. "Genesis. We are meant to be the masters of this world. I reckon that includes buffalo and such."

"I suppose."

The door at the front end of the car swung open and Sergeant De Armond strolled through. He was wearing his dress uniform, buttons gleaming. Rambling wondered how the man kept himself looking as though he just stepped off the parade ground.

"All right, you lazy bastards," De Armond growled, "time to start earning that thirteen dollars you get. We will be pulling into Dodge City within the next fifteen minutes. Before then, I expect you to grab your gear. When the train stops, you will immediately move to the rear of the car to disembark."

As soon as De Armond left, Larsen rose and pulled his equipment from the shelf above his head. He moved to one side.

Rambling gained his feet and retrieved his gear, grunting under the weight of the seventy-pound brace. He slipped the brace on like a coat, shrugged it into place, and buckled the belt's plate.

The brace system consisted of a yoke worn over the shoulders like suspenders. The waist belt attached to the yoke in the front and rear. Everything else hung from the belt or shoulder straps.

Rambling's gray woolen blanket rode across his shoulders. Inside were his groundsheet and shelter half. Beneath the roll hung the valise-knapsack with his clothing and personal items. A canvas haversack rode in the small of his back containing his meat can—in which he could carry up to four days' ration of pork, other food items, eating utensils, tin cup, and condiments.

Hagner pouches hung on both sides of the haversack, each holding twenty-four rounds of .50–70 ammunition. Two more pouches were attached to the front of his waist belt. He wore a twenty-one–inch triangular bayonet on his left hip. His wool-covered canteen hung from a back strap and rested on his right hip.

The last piece of equipment he gathered was his forage cap. It was blue broadcloth with a short patent–leather visor patterned on the bummer caps worn by Yankees and Rebels alike during the War Between the States. This new version had been issued the previous year. The smaller infantry bugle was made of stamped brass and was pinned in the middle of the three-inch crown. Inside the bugle's loop, a brass "I" denoted Rambling's company.

Dodge City's reputation as a wide-open town was well-known, and as the train slowed, the men crowded to the left side, trying for a glimpse of the dance halls and saloons legendary for their wickedness.

"When I get in," Rambling heard a soldier say, "I'm gonna git me a new whore every night." The man laughed. "Hell, mebbe two!"

"Bullshit!" another said. "By the time you get done drinkin' that bust-head whiskey of theirs, the only thing's gonna be stiff is your neck from sleeping on the table."

The first soldier snorted. "The hell you say. There ain't enough whiskey in all of Kansas to keep Ol' Throbber down. You just wait and see, sonny."

"My God!" Rambling recognized Hitchcock's nasal voice. "The thought of seein' you and 'Ol' Throbber' is enough to keep me limp for a week!"

Laughter rang through the railcar. Even Rambling smiled, though he still intensely disliked Hitchcock and his friends.

The train pulled into the station with grinding breaks and the squeal of metal on metal. It finally jerked to a halt, and the troops filed out the back door.

Rambling stood beside the pup tent he shared with Larsen. He sighed. The five-mile march from Dodge City to Fort Dodge had been boring and dusty, with no highlight but the sporadic cheering from townspeople gathered on the sidewalks.

The new arrivals were camped outside the fort proper, ranged along a river. The neat rows of tents were dominated by the company commander's conical Sibley tent. Rambling had heard some companies housed their troops in the tipilike structures, as many as twenty men per tent. He preferred the two-man shelter. At least a body could stick his head out for a breath of fresh air.

The company standard snapped in the breeze outside the commander's tent. The short flag served as a signpost, helping soldiers to tell their camp from the others. Without it, the camps looked identical.

Larsen crawled out of their tent, stood, and stretched.

"I wish they'd let us go to town," he grumbled. "Won't be long before all the good-lookin' girls get taken up by the pony soldiers."

"And Masons," Rambling murmured.

"That goes without saying." Larsen stared at the ground a moment, then looked at Rambling. "Say, Jim, you think they got a lodge here? Makes sense, don't it? They could start the weeding process right here by only sending Christians out on patrol. Hell, with the Indians just across the river, it'd be easy. In fact, I heard tell of a teamster got himself scalped just outside the fort."

"I suppose anything's possible, Bob." Rambling gave Larsen a sidelong glance. "Of course, we can't spread this around."

Larsen raised his right hand. "I swear, Jim, mum's the word." He looked around the camp. "Since we got a couple hours before chow, I'm gonna see if I can scare up a poker game. You in?"

"If you need an extra hand, let me know. If not, I think I'll pass."

Larsen nodded and started away. "Fair enough, buddy."

Rambling turned and made his way to the latrine. It sat in the middle of a pasture well away from the campsites. A crude structure, it was built like a series of outhouses connected together and placed over a slit trench. Still, it was better than what he'd use once they were in the field.

As he rounded the corner of the latrine, he came face-to-face with Hitchcock and his friends.

"Well, as I live and breathe," Hitchcock said with a smile, "if it ain't my old friend, Jim."

Rambling turned on his heel, only to feel hands grab him from behind.

"Wait a minute, hoss. What's your hurry?"

Rambling turned back around, Ketzel and Bailey gripping his upper arms, and faced Hitchcock. "I'm not looking for trouble."

Hitchcock smiled. "Me neither. I'm just lookin' to talk." He rubbed the bridge of his nose. "Course, last time we talked, you busted my nose. Still pains me."

Rambling said nothing. He felt the grip on his arms tighten.

"Yes, sir," Hitchcock continued, "still hurts from time to time. Know what they did to me, Jim? They stuck sticks up my nose and pulled 'em back out. Post surgeon said it was so's I could breathe right." He shook his head. "Can you imagine? Sticks! I just thought that lucky punch of yours hurt." He grinned. "I don't hold no hard feelings, but we got unsettled business."

A privy door swung open, and the hands on Rambling's arms let go. He gazed past Hitchcock and saw De Armond glaring at them.

"Goddammit!" the sergeant yelled. "Man can't even take a shit without you yahoos tangling." He stomped over to the quartet. "We're going to settle this once and for all. I do not intend to spend my time nursemaiding you assholes." He looked from Hitchcock to Rambling. "Tonight, one hour before Taps, behind the sutler's store. Be there, the both of you." He jabbed a finger at Hitchcock. "You got business here?"

"No, Sarge."

"Then get your ass gone." He hooked a thumb at Bailey and Ketzel. "Take your lackeys."

As the three men drifted off, De Armond spun back toward Rambling. "What's your sad tale?"

"Nothing, Sarge. I was just coming here to take a leak."

"Then get to it, soldier." As the private turned away, De Armond continued. "And Rambling . . ."

"Yeah, Sarge?"

"You better take him, son, or he's gonna make your life hell."

Rambling picked at his supper, acutely aware of the stares of the men around him. He and Hitchcock sat with I Company, and Rambling knew they were being compared. Once odds were determined, the bets would fly. Wagering, like the fight itself, was against regulations, but it offered a welcome relief from the boredom of camp life.

He rose and made his way back to his tent, Larsen on his heels.

"I bet money on you, Jim. After this fight, we're going to Dodge and live high on my winnings."

"What makes you think I'll win?" Rambling asked.

"It's a lead-pipe cinch. You have a mission to fulfil, something we both know about. Do you think that you-know-who is going to let it all ride on the outcome of a fight?"

Rambling stopped. "What are you talking about?"

"Look," Larsen said patiently as though addressing a very young, very stupid child, "it's like when David faced Goliath. Now God knew all along who was going to win, but it was important for the army to see the fight. It made them respect David as a leader and a warrior. The same thing was true of David. He needed to win to gain the confidence to rule Israel. See?"

Rambling pursed his lips and frowned. "Doesn't it spoil the effect for me? I mean, knowing the outcome and all?"

"Of course not. You already knew. I told you." He laughed and slapped Rambling on the back. "All you got to worry about is making it look like he might win. That way folks'll see that you can take a licking and come back."

They continued to the shelter and Rambling crawled inside.

"I guess I better rest before the momentous occasion," he said dourly.

"You do that, Jim." Larsen beamed at his tent mate. "You rest up. I'll make sure you're not late."

"Thank you," Rambling mumbled, knowing the sarcasm was wasted.

A hand on his shoulder brought him instantly awake. He glanced out of the tent and saw the sun riding low on the horizon like a flaming orange. Rising on one elbow, he yawned and scratched his head.

"Man alive!" Larsen said, awed. "You're a cool one."

Rambling turned his head toward his tent mate. "What should I do?" he snapped. "Bite my nails? Wring nervous hands?"

To be honest, he was worried. What little he'd eaten at supper lay in his stomach like lead shot being slowly ground to dust by his twisting guts. He'd never fought a cold, calculated fight. Most of the time, his fights resulted from oral arguments leading to blows, but this was an entirely different matter. He was expected to calmly beat the hell out of another man with no provocation, no malice. He felt like an assassin.

With a grunt, he crawled from the tent and gained his feet. "Let's get on with this," he said, brushing his hands on his pants.

Rambling and Larsen walked through Company I's campsite and headed for the sutler's store. Rambling felt the looks. Even passing through the areas of other companies, he saw the appraising stares of the soldiers. Officers stepped from their tents and stood, hands on hips, carefully regarding the privates. Word had spread quickly.

A sour taste filled Rambling's mouth as they neared the sutler's store. He felt a burning at the base of his throat and feared he might vomit. Could he be that afraid of fighting Hitchcock?

He climbed the three steps, crossed the gallery, and pushed into the store. Conversation stopped immediately, every eye in the house on him. Then the heads turned toward the bar. Rambling followed the gazes and saw Hitchcock standing at the far end of the bar. He looked up and caught Rambling's eye.

"Come on in, Jim!" he called, raising a whiskey glass in salute. "You're a mite early." He waved Rambling over. "C'mere."

Rambling crossed the store, his boots ringing on the wooden floor. When he stopped next to his opponent, Hitchcock threw an arm around his neck.

"How you feelin', pard?" Hitchcock was drunk. He was loose, smiling at nothing, feeling good, and glad to be alive. He tapped Rambling on the chest. "I know how you feel. You got that sour stomach like you been eatin' bad meat. Feels like you're fixin' to shit your drawers, right?"

Rambling said nothing. He just stared at the reeling

man attached to him, taking in the sloppy grin, the bleary eyes.

Hitchcock raised a finger. "You don' gotta say nothin'. I know." He thumped himself on the chest. "B'lieve me, I know. Been there myself." He released Rambling's neck and poured another shot from the bottle in front of him. "An' you know what? You wanna know what's really sad? Huh, pard?"

"What?" Rambling's voice was flat.

Hitchcock glanced around the room as though he were about to reveal a great secret. "S'too late. Ain't nothin' we can do now. Why, I could give you a big ole sloppy kiss, and tell the world I loved you"—he grinned—"but s'too late." The grin faded. "Damn, I hate this!"

He straightened and looked Rambling in the eye. "I should not be here. Nossir, I shouldn't. I'm a happy boy. I oughtta be out givin' what for to a sportin' lady. But, no, I gotta beat the shit outta another fool—another fool like me." He killed the shot and grimaced. "Ain't right, pard. Y'know?"

"If you feel that way," Rambling said quietly, "then why not call off the fight?"

Hitchcock laughed. "Don' you get it? I cain't call off what I didn't call. 'Sides, there's money done been bet. People want their show, an' we got to give it to 'em. We're like them gladiators back in old Rome."

The store's front door swung open and De Armond stepped inside. He glanced around the room until he spotted Rambling and Hitchcock.

"You girls ready?" he asked. Then he turned and left without waiting for an answer.

Hitchcock bowed low at the waist and waved Rambling forward. "Caesar awaits."

The men walked through the door and down the

steps. They rounded the building, Hitchcock occasionally hanging onto Rambling for support.

"Thank you," he'd say after each misstep. "You're a fine gen'leman."

Behind the store, De Armond waited. A small crowd had gathered, but only enlisted men. Since the fight was illegal, any officer caught there risked his career. When they reached the sergeant, De Armond sent Hitchcock to one side of a clearing, Rambling to the other.

"All right," he barked, "here's the rules. No knives, no brass knuckles. You can bite, but you can't bite anything off. No eye-gouging, no cat-scratching. Other than that, most things go. Questions?"

"Jim?" Hitchcock called. "I gotta favor to ask."

Surprised, Rambling stammered, "What—what can I do?"

"Don' hit the nose. It has suffered greatly as of late."

Chuckles rippled through the crowd, and Rambling grinned. "I'll bear that in mind."

"Thank you, sir." Hitchcock again bowed. "You are a fine, fine gen'leman."

"If you girls are through socializing . . ." De Armond growled. He glanced from one man to the other, then stepped back. "Fight!"

Rambling moved toward the center of the clearing. Hitchcock had removed his shirt, revealing a torso crisscrossed with scars. He approached slowly, catlike. The men circled each other cautiously, looking for an opening.

"Jim," Hitchcock said, "you start."

Rambling shook his head. "Don't think so."

Hitchcock sighed. "Well, hell, we ain't ever goin' to start at this rate."

He suddenly stepped in and hit Rambling low on

the right side of the body under the rib cage. Rambling grunted and shifted to punch, but was struck by a blow to the same location on the left side of his body. He placed both hands on Hitchcock's chest and pushed him away, taking a step back to widen the gap.

Again the men circled. Rambling noticed that Hitchcock dropped his left fist as he went for the punch, and hoped he'd do it again. Hitchcock stepped in and swung. Rambling turned away from the blow and hit Hitchcock high on the cheek, knocking him down. Rambling backed away.

Hitchcock got to his hands and knees, shaking his head. He looked at Rambling and grinned. Then he gained his feet and started forward, closing in rapidly. Two swift blows went to Rambling's mid-body, then a jab to the face, and a right uppercut.

Rambling countered with a left to Hitchcock's jaw. He then threw two fast, hard punches to the stomach. As Hitchcock staggered past, Rambling delivered a quick rabbit punch to the kidneys.

Hitchcock grabbed his back, then spun so quickly Rambling never saw him move. His right leg shot out and caught Rambling high on the left thigh. Pain exploded in the leg, staggering him. When he grabbed the limb, Hitchcock closed with sharp blows to his head and neck. Rambling straightened, only to receive several quick punches to his stomach. He reeled, bright stars dancing before him.

In sheer desperation, Rambling spun on his heel, fist held high. He connected with Hitchcock's jaw, the force from the spin driving the fist home. Hitchcock flew back into the crowd of soldiers, who tossed him back into the clearing.

Rambling wasted no time. He moved in, delivering blows to Hitchcock's face and body. At one point, Hitchcock raised straight up. Rambling drew back and swung, but realized his blow was aimed at the other's nose. At the last second, he pulled the punch to one side.

Hitchcock showed his appreciation by hitting Rambling in the stomach with a short, vicious blow. Rambling doubled over, more stars, much brighter this time. As he gasped for air, Hitchcock delivered a hard rabbit punch to the lower part of his back. Rambling yelled in pain as the scene before him dissolved into a swirl of colors. He landed flat on his stomach.

Chest heaving as he struggled to fill his lungs, Rambling slowly gained his feet. Hitchcock stepped in and kicked him in the stomach, emptying his lungs again. Then he landed a sharp blow on the right side of Rambling's face. Rambling went down.

He pushed himself to his hands and knees, then made it to one knee. Hitchcock caught him with a left-right combination to the head, and he went down again.

"Stay down, Jim," Hitchcock said, his speech muffled by swollen lips.

"Can't," he grunted.

Rambling forced himself up to his knees. He got one foot on the ground, then the other. He rose, knees shaking, one eye swollen shut, vision blurred in the other, his whole body on fire. He raised his hands, but his legs betrayed him. He fell to his knees.

The crowd started shouting.

"Kill him!"

"Finish him off, boy!"

"Do it! Do it now!"

Hitchcock stared at Rambling. He lowered his hands and spat blood into the dirt.

"Let it be," he said. He retrieved his shirt and limped away.

Larsen ran to Rambling's side. "Are you all right?"

Rambling looked up with his one good eye and grinned. "Never been better, Bob."

As he smiled, the stars fell from the sky and he plunged into darkness.

Six

The old Comanche chief, Nakoni, had ridden to the agent Haworth and told him to stop the soldiers from coming to the Kiowa camp—but they came anyway.

Lone Wolf turned to Boytale. "You see," he said. "It is as I foretold. The whites will not listen to the agent, so he cannot protect us. We must be prepared to fight."

During the night, the warriors from Lone Wolf's and Mamanti's bands had quietly entered the village. They'd stayed with friends. Late, under the light of an almost-full moon, all the men had met. It was then Lone Wolf had told them of his fears and predicted that the soldiers would come, no matter what. When word arrived of the soldiers' appearance, the men ranged themselves in two lines in front of their lodges, bows and rifles at the ready.

The white men were led by a soldier chief riding a black gelding. His light blue pants had a red stripe down each leg, and his dark blue coat bore shiny brass buttons. More brass gleamed on his shoulders. He wore a hat, but it had no brim like those worn by other whites, just a crown topped with tall white feathers. The strap went under his chin.

The walking soldiers all wore the same kind of

clothes as the soldier chief, but their hats had no feathers, only some kind of white ball like a rabbit's tail. Some men had red marks on the arms of their coats. Boytale thought these must be their medicine signs, and wondered what kind of medicine those with unmarked sleeves used.

One soldier had three red bands on his arm, forming peaks like the tops of mountains or arrowheads. Boytale nodded slowly. *I will make the sign of the arrow on my arms, one for each battle.* He was sure that they would soon be covered.

The soldiers carried rifles with long knives attached to the barrels. The soldier chief also had a long knife, but his stayed in its sheath at his side.

The soldier chief rode to Striking Eagle's lodge and stopped. The Kiowa peace chief emerged, face unreadable. Silence swept over the village. The soldier chief raised his right hand and spoke in even, measured tones, but his face bore a haughty expression that said he thought himself superior to the Kiowa. The post interpreter translated his words into a combination of bad Kiowa and signs.

"This white-eye is called Captain Sanderson. He is here to count your people."

Striking Eagle looked around. "So count them."

The soldier chief's eyes narrowed as he listened to the translation. Then he barked a reply.

"He says you need to bring them forward," the interpreter said.

Striking Eagle regarded his counterpart closely. He took a deep breath and shrugged. "You warriors, listen to me," he said, turning to face his people. "I want you to come forward and lay down your guns and be counted." When no one moved, Striking Eagle stepped toward them. "We have agreed to the white man's terms. We have agreed to be counted."

"And killed!" Lone Wolf shouted. He brandished the scalp he'd taken at Lost Valley. "This is what we should be doing. Take the life, take the hair. The whites lie. We all know that. What has happened to all the promises they made at Medicine Lodge?"

Murmurs ran through the gathered warriors, enhanced by catcalls and jeers from Lone Wolf's men. Striking Eagle raised his hands for silence.

"I don't expect any warriors but my own to come forward. I will not speak for Lone Wolf or Mamanti. I will not try to control their bands, but my warriors have gone along with my promise, so now, step forward and be counted."

A few men shuffled their feet and stared at the ground, but no one broke ranks.

Striking Eagle tried again. "Otter? Summer Grass? Will you not do as I ask?"

An argument started between the soldier chief and the interpreter. The soldier chief's face was red with anger, and he spoke in clipped tones. The interpreter raised his hands as though pleading, but the soldier chief cut him off. He pointed at Striking Eagle, talking quickly.

The interpreter looked worried, but he nodded and faced Striking Eagle. "My chief says that Striking Eagle has no more respect from his warriors than an old woman." He paused and licked his lips. "He says that if you can't control your men, he will."

"Are we to stand for this?" Lone Wolf shouted. "How dare this white-eye talk to a Kiowa warrior this way!"

Murmurs started again and the warriors' faces hardened.

"I say, maybe we'll teach this white man why the Kiowa should be feared," Lone Wolf continued. He smiled as voices grew louder, and lifted the scalp.

"Why should I be the only one with a new trophy? There are enough whites here for everyone to add to their scalp pole."

"I wouldn't mind adding to my collection!" a warrior shouted.

"Neither would I," said another.

Lone Wolf stepped toward the soldier chief, shaking the scalp. "You might be powerful among your own kind, but my knife will lift your scalp as easy as this Tejano's."

As the post interpreter frantically translated Lone Wolf's words, the warriors roared their agreement.

The soldier chief's face went ashen and his eyes widened. He looked around him at the warriors, shouting and holding their weapons high. He spoke rapidly and turned his horse to leave.

"My chief says that if you want to be called friends of the white man, you must bring all of your people to the fort tomorrow." The interpreter spun his horse and raced after his leader.

Shouts came from among the walking soldiers, and they started to march. As they passed back through the camp, women and children emerged from the lodges. They called the soldiers names and threw pebbles and buffalo chips at them, laughing whenever one struck home. Warriors started singing victory songs and dancing.

Boytale laughed. They had beaten all those soldiers without a single bullet or arrow.

Striking Eagle watched the retreating soldiers, then slowly turned and gazed at Lone Wolf. Though the peace chief's face was expressionless, Boytale thought he saw a glimmer of amusement in his eyes.

That night the Kiowa danced and feasted and told humorous stories at the soldiers' expense. Finally, late into the night, the men drifted home, exhausted.

* * *

As Boytale ate a breakfast of corn mush and berries, he heard another warrior say that Striking Eagle had called for a meeting with Lone Wolf and Mamanti. He dropped the bowl and followed the other men.

The two chiefs and the Owl Prophet sat in a small circle in front of Striking Eagle's tipi. They were passing the pipe just as Boytale arrived, grateful that he'd missed nothing yet. Other warriors and old men gathered around the trio.

Boytale smiled as he recalled being a child and running to council meetings. He'd squirm in as close as possible, hoping to hear a bit of news he could lord over his friends. But the information could not be kept secret, because as soon as the council dispersed, the village crier would ride from one end of the camp to the other shouting the results of the meeting.

Now, as a man, he stood among his peers. Standing next to him was Tehan, a red-headed white captive. Tehan was Mamanti's adopted son. He was tall and lanky, with freckles that showed through his sun-bronzed skin. He went to great pains to keep his hair clean, the coppery curls glinting in the sunlight. His buckskin leggings were edged in scarlet cloth and slashes of crimson paint crossed his chest and face. He grinned.

"You think Striking Eagle's going to war?"

Boytale shrugged.

Striking Eagle received the pipe from Mamanti and held it in the crook of his arm. "I have worked hard and long for peace for my people, yet I was angered at the way the soldier chief spoke. The whites are supposed to be our friends."

"Perhaps now you'll join with Mamanti and myself and fight," Lone Wolf said.

Striking Eagle gazed at the war chief, taking in the hard eyes, the close-cropped hair gently moving in the breeze. He shook his head. "No, the warpath still means the destruction of our people. We will go to the fort today and be counted." He smiled gently. "You are welcome to come with us."

"I won't be treated like a dog," Lone Wolf replied.

"Thanks to you, old friend, we may not be treated as such either. You saw the fear in the white man's eyes. You saw how the soldiers almost ran away." He laughed. "That was a good thing. It was wise of you to remind them just who we are."

"Yes," Mamanti said, "what Lone Wolf did was wise, but I believe he intended more to remind *us* of who we are. The white man fears us today. He respects our warriors, but what happens when you're in the fort? Who is weak then?"

"Mamanti's right," Lone Wolf said, nodding. "What happens when we're not around?"

After a brief hesitation, Striking Eagle replied, "I don't know. I do know that to fight means the end of us. I hope that by making peace, the People will have a chance to go on."

"And if you're wrong?"

Again Striking Eagle offered the gentle smile. "If I am wrong," he said, "I won't have long to regret it. I hope the spirits allow fools into the Happy Hunting Grounds."

Lone Wolf rose, Mamanti joining him.

"You're leaving?" Striking Eagle asked. The question was a formality. He knew Lone Wolf and Mamanti's horses had been packed since dawn.

The war chief nodded tersely. "There is no reason to stay. We need to rejoin our bands and decide where to go to escape the soldiers."

Boytale and Tehan ran to their horses and threw

on blankets and grass saddles. They gathered their belongings and mounted, hurrying to catch the older men.

As they waited to leave, Tehan faced Boytale. "Can you believe that? Striking Eagle is willing to give up being a warrior." He shook his head. "Not me. Not my father. We'll fight to the end."

Lone Wolf waved farewell and started out of camp. The people remaining behind lined the warriors' pathway waving and singing songs of encouragement and good luck. Before they passed over a ridge that would block their view of the village, Boytale turned to see his people one more time—perhaps the last. The thought saddened him.

"Don't look back," Tehan said, his voice harsh and flat. "There's nothing back there except old women."

Seven

Lone Wolf's mood was ugly as the small band of warriors made their way back to their families.

"Don't those fools understand that the white man plans to kill them?" he growled.

Mamanti shrugged. "It is the road they have chosen," he replied quietly.

"Bah!" Lone Wolf retorted. "If they choose for their bands, then so be it, but they have chosen for us as well! We cannot fight the soldiers and win without their help."

Mamanti did not respond.

Lone Wolf gazed at the Owl Prophet. "Nothing to say? What about the bird? Has it no vision to assure me of the future?"

Mamanti frowned. "I will consult the Owl later," he said.

Lone Wolf turned toward his lieutenant. "And you, Bear Mountain: What are your thoughts?"

The giant Kiowa pursed his lips and a crease formed between his eyes. To Boytale, the crease looked like a furrow cut by the white man's plow.

"I have heard," Bear Mountain said, "that the Cheyenne and Comanche suffer as we do. The Comanche have gone as far as to disavow the Penateka, saying they have already turned white. Some Cheyenne have also moved to the reservation, but there are others like us who will fight to stay free, to live as warriors."

Lone Wolf carefully considered what he'd heard. Then he nodded. "When we fought the buffalo hunters, Comanche and Cheyenne warriors fought as well as any of us. If it were not for the bad medicine, we would have won."

He swung back toward Mamanti. "When you talk to your feathered friend, ask him if the others will join us against the soldiers."

When the warriors arrived at their camp, they could smell the evening meal being cooked. Some warriors retired to their lodges to eat with families. Other joined friends for the meal. Mamanti disappeared immediately after reaching camp. Tehan joined his father, but Boytale ate with Lone Wolf and a group of unmarried men.

Talk during the meal centered on what would happen next and what fate awaited Striking Eagle and his followers. The consensus was that the peace chief had betrayed the People.

"Striking Eagle has led his people down the white man's path," Lone Wolf said. "He has chosen to turn his back on Kiowa ways, on tradition, on all those things that we were given by the spirits. One day, he will pay. The gods will have their vengeance."

Mamanti walked up to the men, and they fell silent one by one until the sounds of insects and the crackling fire could be heard clearly. The shaman looked exhausted, as though he had wrestled with a great being and won, but not without cost.

His gaze traveled from warrior to warrior. "I have consulted the Owl," he said, "and he warns of great danger ahead. Still, he says we can be victorious if we join with other Indians who think as we do."

Lone Wolf grinned. "Then why the long face? I hear nothing but good news."

"It is not so easy, Lone Wolf," Mamanti replied. "We will be victorious on the battlefield, but the Owl does not promise the Kiowa will remain free."

The smile slowly faded from Lone Wolf's face. He frowned, then shrugged. "It's good enough. I have no intention of dying an old man. I am *onde* by birth and deed. If I die tomorrow, at least I will be able to say I died a man, a warrior, worthy of the title of war chief!"

Lone Wolf's words broke the tension, and the others burst in to acclamation, shouting and laughing. They offered their own versions of Lone Wolf's speech. Then they rose as a mass and started dancing—not a war dance, but a victory dance, for in their hearts they had already beaten the whites.

Boytale noticed that Lone Wolf pulled Mamanti aside. Curious, he worked his way closer.

"Does the Owl know where we might find our friends?" Lone Wolf asked.

"In the canyon of the hard wood," Mamanti replied. "The one the Mexicans call Palo Duro, at the edge of the great plains."

Boytale rode his pony up a nearby mesa and stopped near its eastern edge. He watched the Kiowa below him move slowly across the land, a thick trail of dust marking their passage. Mamanti had chosen a path for them that avoided areas where whites were known to live. He took particular care to keep them away from the lodges of the hunters on the Canadian River. He said there was bad medicine there, evil and unnatural.

The People could only move as fast as the slowest

horse. All rode, but the intense heat and lack of water quickly wore the horses down. When some of the women complained, Mamanti told them they would get to water soon enough, but his path kept them away from the soldiers.

Boytale had lost count of the days they traveled. He had been given more water than most since his duties included scouting ahead of the others, but the constant riding and vigilance was tiring. As he gazed at the caravan, he was happy to be here atop the plateau away from the choking dirt.

He turned at a sound behind and below him. He saw Tehan scramble over the edge of the mesa, his paint pony working hard. He rode up next to Boytale and reined to a halt, staring over the edge.

"I'm glad I'm not down there," Tehan said.

Boytale nodded. "Me, too. I remember having to ride a travois when I was little."

"So did I." Tehan laughed. "Everything tasted like dirt for days."

"And it seemed like every day someone fell off, and we'd have to stop and get them strapped back on."

Tehan sighed. "My grandfather fell off once, but no one laughed."

"No, they wouldn't, would they? I mean, he was just old and too weak to hang on."

"True." Tehan gazed along the horizon, taking in the great expanse of land colored in yellows and greens.

The dirt and rocks were red, and the ground was covered with low, rolling hills with occasional outcroppings of stone and mesa like the one they were on.

Sage, chinaberry, mesquite, and cactus grew in abundance. Wild plum trees, heavy with fruit, and vines bearing blue-black grapes lined canyon walls.

All manner of animal, including buffalo, were plentiful and waited for the hunter's arrow. It was as if they rode through the Happy Hunting Ground.

"Boytale."

"Yes?"

"Look to the northeast. Do you see trail dust? Not heavy but thin—like only one rider."

Boytale looked where Tehan indicated. Soon he saw a white thread, like tendril of smoke.

"I see him," he said, feeling the tension build. "Do you think he's a white man?"

Tehan shrugged. "Who knows? But if you look down near the base of those hills, you'll see warriors gathering to meet him."

Suddenly the tension that had been building turned into fear, the fear that something momentous was about to happen and they were going to miss it. The young warriors faced each other, mouths agape.

"What are we waiting for?" Boytale cried. "Let's get over there!"

With a shout of joy, Tehan wheeled his mount and bolted for the mesa's edge. Boytale urged his mount after him, and they plunged over the rim to fly down the side, their horses barely keeping their footing on the crumbling surface.

They galloped across the plain, riding low on their horses. They skirted the caravan, and only slowed when they came into view of the others.

The rider had already been intercepted, but he was only a Comanche. No sport at all.

The Comanche was dressed in leggings trimmed with fringe and tufts of horse hair. His shirt was plain except for a line of fringe along the sleeves. He wore no paint and had no feathers in his scalp lock. Yet Boytale saw he was powerfully built and carried himself like a chief. He rode a magnificent sorrel with scalps plaited into its mane.

The warrior addressed the others in Kiowa, explaining that his mother had been Kiowa and had taught him her people's language. He was called Brook, and he declared he had a right to carry himself with pride, for he was a descendent of Do-hauson the elder, one of the truly great Kiowa chieftains.

Lone Wolf was unimpressed. "Where are you going in such a hurry? Are soldiers chasing you?"

"No," Brook answered. "The soldiers are handing out pieces of paper to all those who mark their book." He paused long enough to pull a folded sheet from a bag around his neck. "This is what they gave me," he said, handing the document to Lone Wolf.

Lone Wolf unfolded the paper and stared at it. "It means nothing to me," he said.

"Me either." Brook grinned wryly. "But to the whites it means I'm their friend."

"And are you?" Lone Wolf asked, returning the paper.

Brook shrugged. "Perhaps. At least this will keep them from shooting at me, and if I need a scalp or a pony or two . . ." He grinned.

Lone Wolf laughed. It was the first time in many moons Boytale had seen the chief in good spirits.

"I'm going to tell Quanah about it," Brook continued. "If you put your mark in the book, they will let you have food and blankets—even bullets for hunting."

Lone Wolf frowned. "Do you think Quanah will move onto the reservation?"

"Of course not! But we can get supplies for the winter. That's why Big Red Meat is sending me to Quanah's camp."

"We could do the same," Mamanti said.

"Yes, we could," Lone Wolf answered. He gazed at the medicine man. "Can the Owl get us there safely?"

"I can but ask."

"Good enough." He turned back to Brook. "When you see Quanah, tell him we are going to the Comanche agency. We will write in the book and get our food. Then we will come to him in the canyon for the winter."

Brook waved his farewell. "I'll tell Big Red Meat, too. He'll look forward to meeting with real warriors again."

"Lone Wolf," Bear Mountain said, "shouldn't we send the women and children to the canyon?"

"No, all will come. We will gather many blankets and as much food as we can carry. Then we'll take all the bullets they have to offer."

The warriors rejoined their families and the procession swung to the north. Later, they would turn east and head straight toward the Comanche agency. Boytale and other men were again sent to scout the trail ahead.

Several days later, as Boytale and Tehan walked their horses back to camp, they crossed paths with a small party led by Lone Wolf and Mamanti. Tehan asked his father where they were going.

"To meet with some Cheyenne," Mamanti replied.

Tehan looked at Boytale, raised his eyebrows, and nodded toward the men.

Boytale paused a moment, trying to decide between a meal and satisfying his curiosity. Curiosity won. He shrugged and looked at Tehan.

The pair fell in behind the departing warriors and quickly matched their pace.

Their destination became apparent as they rode

toward a bluff jutting from the plains. Boytale saw a thin, dark green line on either side of the bluff, and knew water was nearby. What better place to meet on a hot day than in the shade of a tree by a river?

They rounded the bluff. Boytale saw horses. Then the Cheyenne came into view. Seeing only men and boys, he suspected the main camp lay somewhere on the river.

Beneath an old cottonwood tree, blankets had been arranged to seat a large group. A semicircle of Cheyenne warriors occupied one side of the blankets. They were mostly older men, and Boytale decided they must be chiefs or shamans.

A large, powerfully built warrior seemed to lead the group, but it was a tiny, wizened man who commanded the most respect. Each time he opened his mouth or gestured, every Cheyenne present paid close attention.

The Kiowa reined to a stop and dismounted. Lone Wolf, Mamanti, and Bear Mountain approached the waiting Cheyenne. They sat without comment.

An ember was brought from a nearby fire, and the big Cheyenne lit the ceremonial pipe. He offered smoke to the cardinal directions, then drew slowly. Exhaling, he passed the pipe to the man next to him. The second warrior smoked and passed the instrument on. No one spoke during this ceremony. The smoking of the pipe was sacred, and all who partook swore to tell the truth.

As the pipe was finally passed back to the first warrior, he gently cradled it in the crook of his arm. He took a deep breath.

"It is good to see our friends, the Kiowa, again."

Lone Wolf nodded. "We, too, are pleased to see you, Stone Calf, and our Cheyenne brothers. It has been too many moons since we hunted together."

Stone Calf grunted. "If the whites have their way, we'll hunt no more. At least not in the old way."

"What you say is true. That is why we chose to ride here. Have you heard what the soldiers are doing?"

Stone Calf shook his head.

As Lone Wolf told the Cheyenne about the recent events at the Kiowa agency, Boytale wandered to the river's edge. He squatted on the bank, cupped his hand, and got a drink. The water was fresh and cool.

He watched as two warriors walked toward the meeting. They looked to be about his age. One strutted arrogantly as though everyone were there to see him. He was dressed in leggings and a breechclout, his bare chest painted with vermillion and yellow ochre.

The other seemed tentative, or perhaps cautious. He wore buckskin, and his face had two white stripes under each eye.

Boytale stood. The two warriors glanced at him, then continued on to the meeting. Boytale made his way back as well.

Lone Wolf was speaking. "Ride with me and my warriors. Together we'll take what we want—live free again!"

"It is a good idea," the big Cheyenne said. "Let them count us and give us the peace paper. Then we will take our food and come back to the canyon."

Boytale walked to his pony. By the time he had mounted, the meeting was over, and the remaining Kiowa were walking his way. They quickly climbed on their horses and left, with Lone Wolf in the lead. Mamanti followed the war chief, then Tehan. The others fell into place; Boytale joined at the end, but Bear Mountain moved behind him to take position as rear guard.

The warriors wasted no time returning to their

camp. They had a long trek ahead of them, and their families must be told to prepare for an early departure.

Boytale was excited. The Kiowa were one step closer to freedom.

Eight

The days after the fight passed quickly, filled with routine. Rambling spent most nights playing poker—trying to win back the money Larsen had lost betting on him.

One night, however, they went to Dodge City on Rambling's money. He didn't have much, but it was enough for a good meal and a few drinks.

He'd had no more trouble with Hitchcock. They were by no means friends, but each now held a grudging respect for the other. That suited Rambling.

On the morning of August 9, he'd heard shooting near the river. Asking around, he learned that General Miles was testing the marksmanship of his scouts. According to what came down the grapevine, Lieutenant Baldwin, Chief of Scouts, had been bragging about the men in his command and Miles had sought to bring him down a notch.

Then one of the scouts zeroed in on a log over half a mile away. The general called for the trunk; the scout hit it. Then the general said to take off a limb; the wood flew into the river. The general ordered the scout to pick his own target, and a small branch on the end of the log spun through the air. In the end, Miles was left with his jaw hanging as slack as an empty flour sack.

Two days later, Major Compton gathered his Second Battalion and left without fanfare. He took four cavalry troops, all the Indian trackers, and most of the white scouts. The column was trailed by a single wagon driven by an old black Army cook known as Nigger Clark. Rambling was sorry to see him go. Most of the other cooks were mediocre, at best.

Compton and his men had been gone but two days when word came down that there would be an inspection of the company by its commander, Captain Wyllys Lyman. Rambling knew nothing of this officer except that the man was from Vermont and spoke with a formality that made some of the men claim he was British.

The chain of command for Company I, Fifth Infantry, was Lyman to Lieutenant Lewis, who passed the word on to First Sergeant Mitchell, who, in turn, told the troops. Any complaints took the return path. Anyone who broke the chain of command faced quick and harsh punishment at the hands of Mitchell or one of the other sergeants.

Immediately after breakfast on the thirteenth, Mitchell mustered the company. He ordered the troops to circle around him so all could hear.

"All right, laddies," he called in a rich Irish brogue, "gather round."

Mitchell was everything Rambling had ever imagined an Irishman to be—red hair, bright, green eyes, a fiery temper, and a strong affinity for drink. His face and the back of his neck were permanently sunburned. He was powerfully built, with muscular arms ending in large, strong hands showered with freckles. As the soldiers drew near, he tucked a thumb under each gallus.

"Now, ya all know what's goin' on. We're to take a stroll on the prairie and have a go at some Indians.

I'm to take the lot of you and make three squads with one sergeant, one corporal, and ten privates. So, listen up!"

Mitchell walked toward the circle of men, which parted to let him pass.

"First squad forms here. Sergeant De Armond and Corporal Kelly, step forward. Sergeant Hay, you and Corporal Knox have the second squad. That means third squad goes to our Prussian friend, Sergeant Koelpin, and Corporal Johnny Jones. William, you will be short, but any replacements will come to you first."

Koelpin frowned, his steel-gray eyes narrowing, and the ends of his massive handlebar mustache drooping. "Giff dem to Fred Hay," he said, clipping the words. "New recruits is a pain in de ass!"

"And ya ken where ya can stuff that, yer Prussian bastard!" retorted Hay with a Scottish burr. He scowled at Koelpin. "I got enough to do nursemaidin' his lordship, the cap'n, and this Irish galoot. I can no be watching yer hatchlings."

Koelpin leaned closer. "If you were haff de soldier—"

"I'd still be twice—"

"Jaysus and Mary!" Mitchell roared. "The way you two spit and spat, you might as bloody well get married."

Hay regarded Koelpin a moment, then turned to Mitchell and grinned. "Make him shave the mustache, and I'll think about it."

Chuckles sprinkled through the crowd. Koelpin's eyebrows and handlebar rose at the same time. Then he grinned widely.

"Vy should *I* haff to shave? You vear de dress."

Hay felt his face redden. "It's no a bloody dress. It's a kilt."

"Ja, ja, ja," Koelpin said, brushing the comment

aside. He turned to Mitchell. "If *mein* choices is de recruits or a short, Scottish man in a dress, I'll keep de recruits."

The men cheered and laughed.

"I'm tellin' ya," Hay shouted, trying to be heard over the soldiers, "it's no kind of a bleeding dress!" Then he quieted, for the more he protested, the louder the laughter grew.

Mitchell lifted his eyes to the heavens. "Praise be, there's peace at last." He frowned at his squad leaders. "Now, if you girls is through, there's still a small matter of an inspection to be had."

The rank and file seemed content to continue the banter. They laughed and joked among themselves ignoring Mitchell. "Shut yer cakeholes!" he yelled. The soldiers fell silent. "You men fall in, single file on my nose. First ten men go with De Armond, the next ten with Hay, and the rest with Sergeant Koelpin."

As the troops moved to their assigned positions, Mitchell bellowed, "Me lads, there are only three things I expect you to remember. First, what squad you're in. Second, the position that your squad leader places you in.

"Finally, if you embarrass me, the cap'n, or Lieutenant Lewis, I will personally knock you arse over tit and piss on your battered body!"

Rambling stood at attention, rifle at the ready. He felt sweat run down his sides. Beads of moisture covered his forehead; a thin trickle started at his left sideburn and trailed down his cheek to disappear inside his coat collar.

The company had formed three ranks by squad.

To the left stood the sergeant, then the corporal, and finally the privates, arranged by height.

Rambling found himself in De Armond's squad, Hitchcock to his right. Larsen and Bailey were in the second squad, and Ketzel was stuck in Koelpin's squad.

First Sergeant Mitchell stood three paces from the center of the first rank. Lieutenant Lewis was three paces in front of the first sergeant. Lyman faced the company, three paces from Lewis.

Lewis saluted crisply. "Company I, Fifth Infantry, ready for inspection, sir!"

Lyman saluted. "Very well, Lieutenant. Shall we have a look?"

Lewis executed a textbook about-face. "First Sergeant Mitchell, prepare the men for inspection."

"Yes, sir," Mitchell replied with a salute. He about-faced. "First squad, one step forward. Third squad, one step back. March!"

The company spread as ordered, allowing Lyman enough room to navigate the ranks, accompanied by Lewis, and trailed at two paces by Mitchell.

Lyman's examination of his troops was cursory. He quickly passed down the lines, making small comments of approval or correction. Then he returned to the front of the formation.

"First Sergeant, I should like to address the men."

"Yes, sir." Mitchell faced the company. "Company I, order . . . arms! Stand easy." He pivoted again and saluted Lyman. "They're all yours, sir."

Lyman returned the gesture. "Thank you, First Sergeant." He stepped past Mitchell and stopped, feet placed at shoulders' width, hands clasped behind his back.

"Gentlemen," he said. "We are about to embark

on a mission. . . ." He paused and lifted a finger. "No, a *grand adventure*, on behalf of the United States Army.

"It seems some Comanches and Kiowas have been bothersome to various farmers and ranchers," he said as he paced before the command. "General Miles has graciously offered our services to round up the miscreants and escort them home to the reservation." Lyman stopped and placed his hands on his hips. "I have assured the general that Company I shall fulfil any needs he has, and I leave it up to you men to carry out the tasks assigned to you with great vigor."

He resumed pacing. "As to the Indians, we expect a few to object to going home, but this is expected and shall be dealt with. Believe me, gentlemen, there will be time, opportunity, and Indians enough for all to share.

"We leave tomorrow at first light. Our initial path takes us through Dodge City, so I want everyone clean and uniforms looking sharp. You can get further details from First Sergeant Mitchell."

He stopped again and looked his troops over. "Thank you, men, and good luck."

As Lyman walked off the field, Mitchell yelled, "Company I, attention! Before you hit the racks tonight, I expect you to write letters home, pack your gear, and settle your affairs."

He gave the men a wicked grin. "Come the morrow, boyos, the fun begins."

Nine

Barked orders broke the early morning stillness of August 14, 1874, and Miles's column began its long-awaited campaign. At well over a mile long, the column was divided into four distinct sections—infantry, cavalry, artillery, and the supply train.

Nelson Miles rode at the head, followed closely by his adjutant, First Lieutenant George Baird. The regimental surgeon, named Waters, rode left of Baird and directly behind Miles. To the doctor's left was a scout named J.T. Marshall, a Kansas newspaperman who would chronicle the campaign.

Next came the regimental color bearer, a corporal and, to his left, the regimental trumpeter.

Captain H.B. Bristol, Fifth Infantry, led his four infantry companies from horseback. The companies, nearly 150 men strong, were lined up by unit designation with Company I in the last position.

Captain Lyman headed the company, three feet in front of and to the right of the guidon bearer. Lieutenant Lewis marched in Lyman's tracks fifteen feet further back. Sergeants De Armond, Hays, and Koelpin led their squads on Lewis' heels. Finally, First Sergeant Mitchell marched three feet behind the last rank and centered on the formation.

Thirty feet to Mitchell's rear, Major James Biddle,

Sixth Cavalry, rode at the head of his four companies. They were arranged in much the same fashion as the infantry units, the main difference being they rode in two columns.

Second Lieutenant James Pope, Fifth Infantry, was in charge of the third section—the artillery detachment Miles had requested. The first weapon in line was a ten pound Parrot, a small cannon mounted on a two-wheel carriage. The Parrot was designated a light field artillery piece because it was mobile and, at less than a thousand pounds, considerably lighter than its larger brothers. It boasted a three-inch bore in a rifled barrel, and could hit targets two thousand yards away.

The gun required nine men and fifteen horses for transport. Four horses were hitched to a limber, a two-wheeled cart mounted with a box containing powder, shells, and primers. The ring on the cannon's carriage, called a lunette, was slipped over a hook behind the limber's axle, turning the two vehicles into a four-wheeled cart that pivoted in the center. One man rode the left-hand horse of each team and carried the reins for the second.

Two more teams, with their riders, pulled a second limber, to which was attached a third type of two-wheeled cart called a caisson. Carrying two boxes of ammunition, plus a spare wheel for any of the other vehicles, it hung on the limber's pintle hook.

A fourth cart, called a battery wagon, carried the supplies to maintain and repair the cannon. Hanging off the back of a third limber, it was pulled by the final two teams of horses. Normally, the battery wagon was part of an entire artillery battery and serviced several cannons, but since the Parrot was to be used in remote areas, it was deemed necessary to send it along.

The remaining three men of the gun crew, including the corporal in charge of the weapon, rode on horseback, helping to guide the teams over rough terrain as needed.

The last two pieces of artillery for the campaign were Gatling guns. Chambered for the .45-70 round, these hand-cranked weapons had six barrels and could fire six hundred bullets a minute at up to a thousand yards. They had a crew of five men, including a corporal who served as gunner. The guns were dragged behind a limber like the Parrot, with a second unit pulling a limber-caisson combination. Tools for repair and maintenance of the Gatlings were carried in the battery wagon.

The ambulance followed the last Gatling gun and led the fourth section of the column, the supply train.

Seventy-two wagons rolling single file down the road stirred up thick clouds of dust. The sounds of curses, clinking gear, and creaking wheels filled the surrounding air and mingled with the flying dirt.

Bringing up the column's rear was the horse herd, several hundred strong, loosely bunched by cavalry soldiers assigned to care for them.

The scouts rode to either side of the column. Their primary mission was to locate Indians, but for the ride from Fort Dodge to Dodge City, they were content to pace the column and avoid the trail dust.

Rambling felt good. He didn't have to eat dirt, and only had to step over the occasional horse apple. He wore one of the old uniforms he'd brought and carried another in his valise. He had on new boots that fit well. All the soreness from the fight two weeks earlier was gone, and his muscles quickly warmed to the brisk pace set by Captain Lyman.

He adjusted his pack so it felt like a part of his body, its weight distributed between his shoulders and hips. The Springfield hung over his right shoulder. He grasped the sling with his right hand held at mid-chest height.

The morning was clear and cool, and a southwesterly wind pushed the dust away from the column. Birds sang, insects buzzed, and the sun warmed Rambling until he felt like breaking into song.

Apparently, he wasn't the only one who felt that way, for he heard someone in third squad start singing "When Johnny Comes Marching Home." It was one of the few military marching songs that didn't cause trouble, since it had been sung by both sides during the war. Other voices joined, including Rambling's tenor and Hitchcock's powerful basso-baritone. Soon the song spread to the other infantry companies, until the words rang out across the prairie.

As the last verse died away, a Southern boy started "Dixie." Some men grumbled, but the rest sang along with him with the same gusto as before. This was followed by the "Battle Hymn of the Republic"—only fair in Rambling's opinion. The songs continued from sacred to bawdy until Miles called for a halt.

Lieutenant Baird rode down the line, stopping at each section leader to speak briefly and salute before moving on.

Bristol turned in his saddle and bawled, "Company commanders, prepare for inspection!"

Each commander turned and repeated the order to his executive officer, who relayed it to the company first sergeant.

As soon as Lewis issued his order, Mitchell hurried forward. "Awright, men, fall in and dress yourselves!"

Each soldier quickly drew himself to attention and extended his right arm to check his interval to the man ahead of him. He then swung the arm to the right and readjusted his position again.

As soon as the shuffling stopped, Mitchell called, "Left . . . face!"

Rambling pivoted sharply on his left foot and brought the right back into position.

"Unsling . . . arms!"

The rifle came off his shoulder, and he lowered the butt to the ground next to his right foot.

"First rank, one step forward . . . third rank, one step back . . . march!"

Rambling lifted the Springfield three inches from the ground and stepped forward, then set it down again.

Mitchell executed an about-face, prepared to tell Lewis the men were ready, but there was no one to report to. All the infantry commanders and their executive officers were clustered around Baird's horse. Mitchell faced his men.

"At ease, lads, while we wait and see what their lordships intend."

Rambling relaxed, leaning against his rifle.

"Hey, Jim," Larsen muttered from the second rank, "what ya think they're doing?"

As Rambling shrugged, Mitchell glanced over his shoulder.

"No talkin' in the ranks!" he barked. "I said at ease, not rest."

The command meeting adjourned, and the officers headed back to their units. Lewis signaled Mitchell, who left at a run. The two men held a short conference, then Mitchell saluted and ran back to the company while Lewis followed Lyman over to Captain Bristol.

"This ain't to be no formal inspection," Mitchell said. "I'm to make sure you're looking sharp for the march through town."

Mitchell quickly walked through the ranks ordering various men to button their coats or adjust their hats. Finally, he returned to the front and faced the company, fists on his hips.

"We're less than half a mile from Dodge City, and the general is marchin' us right through the middle. Then it's across the bridge and down the Fort Sill highway." He paused and gazed from man to man. "I'll be expectin' every man-jack of ya to keep yer intervals and keep in step. That's goes double for you, Larsen. We're the best damn outfit in the whole bloody Army, an' that means the world! Do me proud, boyos, and I'll stand the first round of drinks at Sill. Ballocks it up . . ." He stopped and grinned wickedly. "Ballocks it up, and there'll be hell to pay."

The crowds started at the outskirts of town. By the time the column made Front Street, it seemed all of Dodge City had turned out to send them off. Men cheered and waved their hats; women laughed, silken hankies fluttering. Children laughed and screamed with delight, while the town dogs, caught up in the moment, ran up and down the streets, barking excitedly.

Near the turn for the toll bridge, Miles and his staff waited for the troops to pass in review. As the company neared, Lyman and Lewis saluted, while Smith lowered the guidon.

Mitchell bellowed, "Company I, eyes . . . right!"

First and Second Squads turned their heads forty-five degrees to the right simultaneously. Third Squad looked straight ahead.

After the company passed the waiting officers, Mitchell brought them back into line. "Company I, ready . . . front!"

Rambling faced front again and saw H Company make the turn for the bridge. The inner files slowed and pivoted while the outer ranks lengthened their strides. The whole company smoothly rounded the bend like a great snake sliding around a fencepost.

On the bridge, the steady tramping of feet set the wood to buzzing, tickling Rambling's feet. His heart pounded with joy and his chest swelled with pride. He found himself actually looking forward to the march ahead.

This is how it must have been for Daniel, he thought. *No wonder he willingly marched into the bowels of Hell.*

Rambling licked his lips and reached for his canteen. He removed the cork, letting it dangle by its chain, and took a sip. The water had grown tepid, with a metallic taste. He took another swallow and spat it on the ground. At least it got his mouth wet. Recorking the canteen, he glanced over at Larsen.

The private had his uniform unbuttoned, a dark red patch of sweat-soaked underwear showing. Like many of the other soldiers, he wore an 1872-model campaign hat made of black felt. It featured a high crown and broad brim patterned after civilian hats worn by cattlemen in New Mexico and Arizona. Unlike the fine hats made by Stetson, the campaign hats sometimes fell apart in the rain. Rambling preferred his forage cap.

The lower half of Larsen's uniform was covered in dust. Rambling cleared his throat. "How you holding up, Bill?"

Larsen tilted his head back and gazed out from under the hat brim, blinking rapidly to clear the sweat from his eyes. "All right." His voice was little more than a whisper. He worked up some spit, then swallowed. "All right, I reckon," he repeated, stronger. "You?"

Rambling shrugged. "Been worse, though it's a mite warm for a stroll."

Larsen nodded, the brim flapping like small black wings. "How far you think we've marched?"

"I don't know. Ten, maybe twelve miles."

"We'll be to water soon."

"How the hell would *you* know?" Hitchcock growled.

Larsen ignored him and addressed Rambling. "I gotta friend in Headquarters Company what showed me a map of the whole road to Fort Sill. If I recall, we're about to come on a place called Mulberry Creek. The next water hole's about ten miles further. It's called Bluff Creek or some such."

"Well, it's not too soon for me," Rambling said.

No sooner had he spoken than the order to halt came down the line. Bristol rode down from a hillock where'd he been in conference with Miles and the other officers. As he approached, Lyman walked out to him. First Sergeant Mitchell broke ranks and made his way toward the two officers, stopping about ten yards away.

Lyman saluted his commander, then walked over to Mitchell. The conversation was brief, and the first sergeant returned to his company.

"There's no water here," he said, "so we're continuing the march to the next water hole, but first we're to eat dinner. I want you men to fall out and eat quick. The water wagon will be by before we hit the road again. Fill up your canteens, understand?"

"We get coffee?" Larsen asked.

Mitchell frowned. "There'll be no coffee, no hot meal. It's hardtack and pork rations for all."

"Jesus Christ!" Hitchcock swore. "No coffee? That just ain't right."

"I ain't eatin' no hardtack nor rations," Ketzel said

angrily. "That shit'll make a man crazy for water. 'Sides goddamn pork rations ain't nothin' but salt and fat nohow."

"Amen, brother," Hitchcock said. "I got me some jerky back at Dodge I'll share."

Larsen slipped off his yoke. "I'll toss in some rock candy. How about you, Jim? Got anything special?"

"Yep," Rambling said with a smile. "I just happen to have two big cans of peaches packed in syrup."

Hitchcock laughed. "Boys, sounds like a deal to me." He glanced around. "Let's find a roost and enjoy this repast." He paused, then looked back at the third rank. "You too, Bailey. I know you're carrying apples."

Bailey's eyes went wide, and he looked around to see if anyone had heard Hitchcock. "I don't got enough for everybody!" he hissed.

"There's just the five of us," Hitchcock replied calmly. "Get out three. We'll cut one in half for Rambling and Larsen, another for Ketzel and me. You get a whole one to yourself."

Mollified, Bailey nodded. "All right, but only three."

"God help us all," Hitchcock said, rolling his eyes. "Let's eat before Johnny Appleseed there changes his mind."

As the day wore on, the oppressive heat took its toll on the soldiers. They marched slower, drank more, and complained louder. Some abandoned extra articles of clothing or blankets along the trail. Still others dropped out, too exhausted to continue, and were picked up by Surgeon Waters and his ambulance.

Rambling pulled off his neckerchief, splashed it

with some water from his canteen, and draped it over the back of his neck. He enjoyed the coolness for the few moments it lasted, then retied the neckerchief. His uniform jacket was unbuttoned, but that didn't stop the sweat from pouring down his sides. More sweat soaked his trousers, chafing the insides of his thighs. He could feel his feet sliding in his boots and knew he'd have blisters by nightfall. The next day's march would be miserable.

His head ached from the heat. Sweat stung his eyes, blurring his vision, and his mouth was dry, his lips starting to crack. He could not remember being more exhausted or footsore. His earlier enthusiasm had withered.

They marched past General Miles, who sat astride his horse, watching them. His dog, a setter named Jack, lay in the horse's shadow, panting heavily. As he walked by, Rambling saw one of the scouts approach the general. Then the scout rode for the head of the column at a gallop.

A cheer came from ahead, and Rambling looked up to see the same scout riding along the line. As he neared, he shouted, "Water's just ahead, boys!" Rambling waved and smiled.

Fifteen minutes later, the column topped a rise and the men saw a line of trees in the distance, marking the stream's course. The pace quickened almost immediately, unordered and unopposed. By the time the men reached Bluff Creek, many had broken into a ragged trot, partly running, partly staggering.

Rambling moved upstream, dropped his rifle, and plunged his head into the cool, clear water. He rinsed his mouth out, then took a long, slow drink. Finally, he dumped the warm water from his canteen and refilled it. Picking up his Springfield, he found a cot-

tonwood and sat in its shade, leaning against the
trunk.

Other infantrymen jumped into the water bodily,
laughing and splashing each other. Mitchell ran to
the bank.

"Get yer bloody carcasses outta there!" he shouted.
"Yer muckin' it up for the rest."

Cavalrymen and their horses lined the bank downstream. Some of the men drank alongside their
mounts. The teamsters unhitched their animals and
moved further downstream.

Soon, order was reestablished. Mitchell and the
other noncommissioned officers moved along the
creek, ordering the men to retrieve their shelter
halves from the supply wagons. The cooks and their
helpers worked briskly to set up camp and start supper. Rambling was among the privates sent scrambling
for firewood.

Supper was simple—beans, biscuits, and coffee—
but no one complained. The hot food was appreci-
ated after the day's march. Conversation was minimal.
Rambling declined offers for poker, and chose instead to sit under another cottonwood and watch the
sun go down. A dozen times he thought about starting
a letter home, deciding against it each time.

As the regimental trumpeter started Retreat and
the flag was struck, Rambling gained his feet, wincing.
Then Pope saluted the colors with his Parrot. By the
time Tattoo sounded, Rambling had already limped
to his tent. He slid off his boots and socks, and rubbed
his sore and swollen feet. He only found one blister
and counted himself lucky. He decided to check it
again in the morning. If it was small enough, he'd
ignore it; otherwise, he'd have to stand sick call and
get it lanced.

Rambling rolled a cigarette as the strains of Call to

Quarters drifted over the camp. He lit the cigarette, quietly enjoying his smoke in the cool night air.

Larsen appeared, looking worn out. He plopped on the ground next to Rambling. "I'm beat," he said. "Hell of a day, huh?"

Rambling nodded, grinding the cigarette out in the dirt. "Yessir, that it was."

Ten

Rambling sat up with the opening strains of First Call. He yawned and stretched, then pulled on his boots. Climbing out of the shelter, he stood and joined the others making their way to the slit trenches.

The cooks had brought their banked fires to life, and the smell of coffee drifted over the camp. Rambling breathed deeply, anticipating his first cup, laden with sugar. Soon biscuits would brown in Dutch ovens while bacon fried in iron skillets. But that was as close to a civilian breakfast as they'd get. No butter, milk, preserves, or eggs, just beans. Sometimes the cooks added molasses or ground chili peppers—or both. Rambling didn't care. He was hungry.

By the time he'd returned from the latrine, Larsen was awake and dressed.

"Mornin', Bill."

Larsen grinned. "Good morning, Jim," he said brightly. He took a deep breath and released it slowly. "Man, smell that coffee! I don't know 'bout you, but I'm starvin'."

"Me, too, but first I've got to check my feet."

"Sure, Jim," Larsen replied, frowning. "Meanwhile, I'm gonna take a leak."

Sliding the boot off his foot, Rambling nodded. "Sure, Bill. I'll see you at chow."

He heard Larsen move away, and quickly glanced back at him. Larsen walked with a pronounced limp. *What the hell?* "Hey, Bill!" he called. "Come on back."

Larsen turned and slowly returned to the tent, making an obvious effort to hide the limp.

"What's wrong?" Rambling asked, pointing at the other's feet.

Larsen stared at the ground. "Nothin'," he said curtly.

"Bullshit. Take your right boot off."

"Why? There ain't nothin' wrong with my foot."

"The boot's coming off, Bill," Rambling said, looking Larsen in the eye. "The only question is who's going to take it off."

Larsen sighed and sat on the ground. He gingerly pulled off the boot, wincing with the effort. Rambling gasped. The entire toe of Larsen's sock was encrusted with dried blood.

"My God, man!" he swore. "You've got to get to the doc."

"No, I don't. It don't even hurt—much." Larsen bent his toes, sucking in against the pain. "See? I can wiggle it."

"Jesus, Bill, if you don't get that fixed, you won't last a mile, and you know it." He paused and gave Larsen a closer look, eyes narrowing. "So why don't you want to stand sick call?"

Larsen licked his lips, and looked around to see if anyone was paying too much attention to the conversation. He leaned forward. "Surgeon Waters carries a pocket watch," he said in a hoarse whisper. Then he straightened. "Now do you understand?"

Rambling groaned and rubbed his face. "Aw, hell,

Bill." He looked up and spotted Mitchell. "First Sergeant Mitchell!" he called.

Mitchell altered his course and angled toward Rambling and Larsen. "What's on yer mind, soldier?" he growled.

"It's Larsen, sir. His foot's all bloody, and I can't get him to go to the doc."

"Let's see it, boyo," Mitchell said to Larsen with a wave of his fingers.

Scowling, Larsen raised his right foot.

"Good God, man!" Mitchell exclaimed, his face twisted by disgust and disbelief. "Have ye no sense about ya? Get your arse to the ambulance! Rambling, go with the sod, but make sure you're back by formation. Understood?"

Blisters forgotten, Rambling pulled on his boot and jumped to his feet. "Yes, sir, First Sergeant. Thank you, sir."

"Don't be thankin' me, boyo," Mitchell barked. "Get on with it!" The first sergeant turned on his heel and continued his rounds.

Rambling looked down at Larsen and grinned. "Don't be wasting time, boyo," he said, mimicking Mitchell's Irish accent. "Off yer arse!"

Larsen stretched out a hand and let Rambling pulled him to his feet. He balanced on one leg, draped an arm over Rambling's shoulders, and allowed himself to taken away. "If I don't survive this, will you write my ma and tell her the Masons got me?"

"Sure, Bill, whatever you say. Tell you what, I'll stay with you until Reveille."

Larsen's eyes widened. "You will? Really?"

"Why not? I don't think Waters will try anything with me watching. Do you?"

"Probably not," Larsen answered thoughtfully. "But you watch him real close just the same."

* * *

Rambling scrambled into position just as the last notes of Reveille faded away, earning withering glares from Mitchell and De Armond.

Lieutenant Baird stepped forward and called the formation to attention. He checked the ranks, then shouted, "Present . . . arms!"

As one, the command saluted.

The color guard pulled the lanyard, and the United States flag rose smartly up the pole. Lieutenant Pope ordered the cannon fired, and the buglers played To the Colors.

As the last note died, Baird shouted, "Order . . . arms!"

The men dropped their salutes and stood rigidly at attention.

Baird about-faced and saluted Miles. "Sir, the men are assembled."

Miles reciprocated. "Very good, Mr. Baird." He turned and addressed his staff. "Gentlemen, I return command of your units to you. Good morning."

The officers saluted and wished Miles a good morning as he quickly moved off the field. The company commanders left their first sergeants in charge and went to breakfast. Mitchell immediately dismissed Company I, admonishing them to waste no time in eating and preparing for the day's march.

Rambling headed back to the ambulance to check on Larsen. He was met halfway. Larsen grinned and waved and walked with almost no limp. As he drew nearer, Rambling noticed Larsen seemed to be having trouble focusing and his smile was a bit too loose.

"Well, Bill," he said, "you look fit."

"Fine as frog hair, Jimmy," Larsen replied through

his grin. "You know, I don't think Doc Waters is a Mason."

"Really? Why?"

Larsen draped an arm around Rambling's shoulders and turned toward the chow line. "He fixed me right up, that's why. He cleaned up my foot an' wrapped it in a nice clean bandage an' gave me a new, clean sock an'—"

"He give you something for pain?"

Larsen shook his head. "Nosir, just a little laudanum for m'nerves. You know, Jimmy, I was right nervous there at first. But I'm much better now."

Rambling laughed. "I can only imagine. Come on, soldier, let's get some Army food in your gut."

By nine A.M., the camp had been disassembled and stowed, and the first marching orders rolled over the plains.

The command moved off.

Rambling stood on the bank of the Cimarron River, staring through shimmering heat waves at the opposite side. Between the banks, the wide riverbed's sandy soil glowed red in the blazing sunlight and reflected the heat until he felt like he was standing next to a fire. What little water there was ran thick and red as old blood, and was as unfit to drink.

Nothing stirred except a few insects scurrying across the riverbed. No birds flew. *They've got enough sense to sit out the hottest part of the day,* Rambling mused. As the temperature rose over a hundred degrees, the insects disappeared as well, seeking respite from the heat.

Everything but us, Rambling thought sourly.

He made his way down the bank to the hard-packed sand and began the task of crossing the river. They'd marched continuously since morning, with only a short dinner break of jerky, hardtack, and water. Since then, the column had strung into a ragged line, with infantrymen falling by the side.

One of the victims was Larsen, whose limp had returned by dinner and who, an hour later, proclaimed he could not take another step. With much grumbling from Mitchell, he was allowed to climb onto one of the supply wagons.

As they crossed the river, some of the troops commented on the huge sinkholes they passed. Rambling stopped long enough to stare into one, and saw it dropped deeply into the earth. At the very bottom, water ran. It seemed even the river had hidden from the heat. He sighed and continued his trek.

Once across, the column stopped long enough for men to refill canteens and get the units reformed. Rambling and other members of Company I took the opportunity to rest in the shade of the ambulance and enjoy a smoke. Conversation was minimal, centering on the odds of anyone making it to camp that night alive.

The column marched another three hours before Miles called a halt for the night. There was a streambed, but no water. Many of the men groused earnestly about the hardships of the day made worse by a dry camp. Rambling was among those who stood on the banks of the dried-out creek, staring at its bed as though they could will water from the sand. Soon, though, he returned to his tent.

Larsen was back, his right foot heavily bandaged. He was sound asleep, no doubt helped by a healthy administration of laudanum by Surgeon Waters. Rambling reached into his valise, took out his spare boots, and set them by his tent mate.

Maybe they'd fit, maybe not. But they were bound

to be better than the shoddy boots the Army had issued. If Larsen didn't find new footgear soon, he'd be crippled before the campaign was over.

Rambling took a long, deep drink from his canteen, then soaked his neckerchief. He lay down in the shelter and draped the cloth over his face, savoring the coolness.

Five minutes, he thought. *I'll rest five minutes, then try to eat something.*

Moments later, his breathing deepened and the neckerchief slid off his face.

Eleven

The Kiowa left the plains and moved into the low, rolling hills that told them they were close to the fort the soldiers called Sill. Boytale had looked forward to seeing Striking Eagle and the others again, but Lone Wolf told him it was not to be.

"I want no one to know we've passed this way," Lone Wolf said. "After we have our food and blankets and our families are safe, we will visit the peace chiefs again. Maybe by then they will have tired of their white friends."

Since meeting with the Cheyenne, the days of travel had reminded Boytale of the stories the old ones told. The men rode ahead and scouted the trail. Buffalo were shot, and the women cut them up and packed the meat in the hides. Everyone's belly stayed full with fresh meat, berries, and roots. The ponies grew fat and lazy with day after day of all the sweet grass they could eat. The bands were happy, as though nothing had changed.

Yet the truth was constantly there in the worried faces of the women as they stared at every cloud of dust on the horizon. Was it soldiers or hunters or Navajos come to prey on them? At night, the men sat around the cookfires and talked of who had found tracks of shod horses or seen riders at a distance.

Once a group of soldiers had been seen, but they'd been allowed to pass unmolested. Lone Wolf forbade any attacks before the winter supplies were in hand.

Boytale and Tehan crested a small hill and saw a flat-top mountain in the distance. Boytale regarded the mesa thoughtfully. Four miles beyond lay the fort with its black soldiers. There also waited the Kiowa under the leadership of Striking Eagle, but he knew that he, like Lone Wolf and Mamanti, was not welcome. The war chief was right. It was better to come back when they were ready to fight.

Lone Wolf rode up beside them. "That is the signal mountain," he said, nodding at the plateau. "For years, all of the people living here used its top for signal fires, and to watch our enemies." He smiled wryly. "Now the soldiers sometimes sit up there and watch *us.*"

"Do we ride to the north and avoid it?" Tehan asked.

"We don't, but the families do." Lone Wolf pointed just south of the mountain. "On that side are many trees that we can hide in. We will ride there, then climb up and look around."

The scouting party rode over the top of the hill and through a series of low rolling hills. They were only six in number: Lone Wolf, Bear Mountain, Buffalo with Holes in His Ears, High Forehead, Tehan, and Boytale. Mamanti remained with the families and other warriors.

Riding single file and at a lope, they covered the ground quickly. Lone Wolf chose trails that would tire the horses the least. Riding at the rear of the party, Boytale had the responsibility of watching their back trail. All of the warriors glanced around them, looking for any sign of an enemy.

Lone Wolf slowed as he neared the mountain.

Then he stopped abruptly and signaled to the left. Without comment, the five warriors turned. Once inside a copse of trees, Lone Wolf stopped again.

"There is a white man in the trees by the signal mountain."

"Has he seen us?" Bear Mountain asked.

Lone Wolf shook his head. "I don't think so. I would not have seen him except the sun flashed on something shiny in his camp. When we rode closer, I saw his horse and smoke from a fire."

"Maybe he *has* seen us," High Forehead ventured. "Maybe he's hiding, ready to ambush us."

"Then we assume it is so. Bear Mountain, I want you and Buffalo with Holes in His Ears to circle to the north. We will wait a while, then ride the same trail as before. We will make sure the white man sees us. With so many, he will hide and watch. As he watches us, you take him."

The two warriors moved off.

In the ensuing silence, Boytale's lips were suddenly dry. He licked them and stole a glance at Tehan. Tehan looked over and grinned.

"That is long enough," Lone Wolf said. "Boytale and Tehan will ride in the rear. If the white-eye starts shooting, I don't want them hit. We ride at a slow, easy pace. Make lots of noise like the whites do when they travel."

The scouts moved their ponies out of the trees at a walk, and rode back along their original path. Boytale was nervous, waiting for the thunder of the rifle, the smack of the heavy bullet.

"So, Boytale," Tehan said loudly, "who will you dance with at the victory dance when the whites are all gone?"

Startled, Boytale looked around wildly, then stared at Tehan. "What?" he asked in a hoarse whisper.

"What's the matter, cousin? Can't you talk?"

"That's right, Boytale," High Forehead said, almost shouting. "The dance will be soon. There are some cute girls in Red Otter's family."

"Well, I—" Boytale started hesitantly. Everything he'd ever been taught told him to be quiet.

"Speak up," Lone Wolf said, grinning. "You know Bear Mountain has some of the prettiest cousins I've ever seen. Nice and fat. They'll keep you warm." He laughed.

Boytale shrugged. "I . . . I never really—"

"But if you're going to dance with them," High Forehead rejoined, "you'd better be thinking about a wife."

"Oh, no," Boytale said, shaking his head. "I'm not—"

"Truer words were never spoken," Lone Wolf said. "Bear Mountain guards those girls closely."

Boytale nodded vigorously. "I heard that—"

Tehan cut him off. "I'm not afraid of old Bear Mountain, but his sister's another matter."

"No argument here," High Forehead said.

"I heard she's as—"

"—big as he is."

"Yes, but-but-but—"

"—meaner."

"Somebody let me speak!" Boytale roared.

The others sat in stunned silence.

Then Lone Wolf spoke. "What did you want to say?" he asked quietly.

Boytale looked from face-to-face, then felt his face redden. "I don't remember," he mumbled.

Lone Wolf sighed. "Don't you know it's rude to interrupt others, especially if you have nothing to say?" He slowly shook his head. "I don't know, High Forehead, the way these children act nowadays."

Tehan rolled his eyes and laughed.

"There's Bear Mountain," Lone Wolf said. "It looks like he's trying to hold onto something."

He eased his mount into a lope, quickly followed by the others. Shortly, they arrived at the white man's campsite. Bear Mountain stood in the center of a small clearing holding a small man by the scruff of the neck.

"Look at him, Lone Wolf," the massive Kiowa said, shaking the captive. "He squirms like a puppy."

The prisoner looked up at Lone Wolf, his eyes wide with fear and brimming with tears.

"He's so skinny," the war chief muttered. "He looks like a fox late in winter who has not had enough mice to eat. I wonder how much medicine he can hold in that tiny body." He looked at Bear Mountain. "Was he hard to catch?"

"With all the noise you made?" He shook the prisoner again. "I could have ridden in here at full gallop, and he wouldn't have noticed me."

Lone Wolf stepped off his horse and stood looking over the camp. "Boytale, you and Tehan search the wagon. He has a coffeepot on the fire. Find the rest of it and his sugar. Also see if he has any other food we can take with us. Don't forget to look for guns and bullets." He waved toward the fire. "Strip him, and stake him over there. High Forehead, check his animals. If they are any good, we'll take them. If not, kill them."

Boytale found sugar and coffee beans in cotton sacks. He also found a white powder in another sack, but didn't know what was done with it. He had a faint memory of a woman, perhaps his mother, using something like this. He remembered small, white circles cooked on a rock, then stuffed with meats. But that was long ago and may have been nothing more than a dream. He emptied the sack on the ground.

Tehan shouted and held up a pistol and a box of ammunition. Bear Mountain found a bag that held bacon and jerky. Buffalo with Holes in His Ears gathered up the white man's rifle and knives. High Forehead returned leading a black horse. He said there was another, smaller, but it had tried to bite him, so he'd cut its throat.

The warriors gathered around the cookfire, poured coffee into two cups they'd found, and heaped in handfuls of sugar. They passed the cups around and discussed what to do next. Bear Mountain wasn't entirely comfortable with the situation, and said so.

Lone Wolf nodded. "I agree. High Forehead, take Boytale and climb to the top of the signal mountain before it gets dark. Look for anyone close by. I don't want to waste this white man's medicine unless I have to."

High Forehead led Boytale up the mountain, making his way through cuts and ravines.

"The soldiers built a lodge up on top," he said, "but it is on the other side."

"Why? Does someone live there?"

High Forehead shook his head. "Not that we've ever seen. Mamanti says the Owl told him the soldiers stay there while they watch for us. He says they use it to get out of the rain."

"How can they see us from inside a lodge?"

"They can't."

Boytale frowned. "They why go up there at all?"

"I don't know, but that's a white man for you."

Cresting the last ridge, the warriors stepped onto the flat, rocky summit. Boytale looked to the east and watched darkness creep over the land. He looked west into the red ball of the setting sun. The skies held shades of oranges and purples and reds, thin clouds in the distance painted by the fading light.

"From here we can see for miles in all directions," High Forehead said, sweeping his hand before him. "To the east is the fort called Sill. North and east is another fort they call Cobb. West and south is where the Tejanos live."

They crossed the plateau to the east and soon stood on its rim.

"Look there." High Forehead pointed to distant lights. "That is where Striking Eagle and the others are. The lights are from the fires the soldiers keep in their lodges." He gazed at Boytale. "You've seen the small fires they keep in the glass?"

Boytale nodded.

"When I was younger," High Forehead continued, "I held such a thing. I touched the glass, and it burned me, so I threw it down. The glass broke and released a beast made of flame that burned down the lodge I was in and set my clothes on fire." He crossed his arms and frowned. "I don't like those small fires."

They walked north along the edge of the mesa. Near the northwest corner High Forehead paused.

"Smell it?" he asked.

Boytale lifted his nose and sniffed. A slight breeze blew and he caught a scent, but it was gone before he could tell what it was. He closed his eyes, sniffed, and concentrated on what came to him. Another breath of wind.

"Smoke," he said. "And something else I don't know."

"White man's food," High Forehead replied. "Wood smoke, coffee, beans, all of it together. No Indian camp smells like that."

They cautiously made their way along the rim until a faint shape appeared. It was a small lodge built of stone. Yellow light peeked through where wood covered the openings, but inside they heard voices and the sounds of pots being moved.

High Forehead leaned close to Boytale. "Lone Wolf should know of this," he whispered. "Let's get back."

They crept away until they felt they were safe from detection, then sprinted across the mesa. Scrambling down the side, they hurried back to the other scouts.

The news caused a great deal of excitement.

"Are you sure there are only two?" Lone Wolf asked.

"We only heard two voices, but we saw no one," High Forehead answered.

"Then it is better that we wait until daylight to take them. There were no other camps close?"

"We saw nothing except the buffalo soldier fort."

"That is four miles away. They can hear nothing." Lone Wolf looked at their captive. "Then we should start. While you were gone, Tehan asked for the honor of taking the prisoner's medicine. High Forehead, you are older. Do you care if he takes the medicine?"

"No, Lone Wolf. I have many coups, and my medicine is strong."

Lone Wolf turned to Boytale. "You have no coups. Do you wish to strike the first blow?"

Boytale stared at the naked, squirming man staked to the ground like a fresh buffalo hide. Though he knew what was about to happen, he'd never witnessed it. Could he butcher a man and relish in his torment? He wasn't sure. He could kill in war, because he knew his enemy would kill him if he did not, but to slice another to pieces, to see how much pain he could inflict . . .

"Tehan is older than I am. He can have this one."

He grinned with a lightheartedness he did not feel. "Besides, there are two more nearby."

Tehan picked up the white man's knife and withdrew it from its scabbard. He walked to the captive, thumbing the blade's edge. Dropping to his knees, he laid the edge against the man's chest and drew downward to the stomach. Bright red blood welled up in the cut and a low moan escaped the white man.

Tehan looked back at the others. His eyes were wild with excitement. He turned back and made another cut across the man's chest, deeper. The prisoner grunted and squirmed to evade the blade, but did not cry out.

Lone Wolf stepped closer. "Tehan, you are now locked into a battle with this man. If he dies without crying out, he will take your medicine with him. You cannot allow that to happen. It will mean bad luck for us all, but it might mean your death!"

Tehan blinked rapidly, lower lip clenched in his teeth. He slashed across the man's thigh, cutting him to the bone. The captive grunted and gasped for breath. Again Tehan looked at the others. This time his eyes were wide with fear and panic. He turned back to his enemy and rocked back and forth while he stared at him.

Suddenly, he grabbed the man's right hand, and with a quick swing, severed his index finger at the second joint. The captive screamed, but it was short, almost a shout—an explosion of sound cut off as easily as the finger.

Lone Wolf stepped to the fire and laid a hand on Tehan's shoulder. "You have broken him and counted coup. Now let me gather all the medicine he has so all may share."

Tehan slowly rose and backed away. He turned and

walked to where Boytale waited. He was breathing heavily.

"That was nothing like I expected," he said breathlessly. "No joy. No excitement. I was afraid, Boytale, afraid he would kill me."

Boytale nodded as though he understood. He had known he would feel something, but the deep revulsion that ran through him was not what he'd expected. It was not what he wanted. If he was to be Kiowa, he had to learn to revel in the agony of his enemy.

Lone Wolf pulled the captive's hand free of the stake and thrust it in the fire. The man shrieked as his flesh caught flame. He flopped on the ground like a landed fish.

"The screams are the medicine leaving," Lone Wolf said. It took all his strength to hold on to the man's arm.

As the noise slackened, he pulled the charred hand from the flames. Bear Mountain knelt and cut away all the burned tissue. Then Lone Wolf again thrust the now-raw and bleeding flesh into the fire.

The shrieks rose in volume and pitch, sending shivers down Boytale's spine.

"Feel the medicine!" Lone Wolf bellowed, still wrestling with the white man. "Feel it course through your body!"

Boytale felt it. His whole being hummed like a plucked bowstring, the vibrations making his teeth ache. He was light-headed, giddy, almost delirious with the power passing into him.

"Yes!" he shouted, wrapped in ecstasy. "The power is mine! The power is mine!"

Twelve

The march on August 17 had been pure hell. At dinner, Rambling overheard two officers talking about the temperature reaching 110 degrees. Rumors spread through the company that the water wagons were running dry and rationing would start soon.

The morning of the eighteenth dawned cool and clear, but by noon, the sun seared the earth and the men who had to walk it. Fearing rationing, Rambling tried to save his water. Miles called a halt at noon, and to Rambling's surprise, the company was told they were to get their shelters.

Carrying his and Larsen's shelter halves, Rambling spotted Mitchell. "First Sergeant," he called, "why are we stopping for the day?"

Mitchell glared at Rambling. "What is the matter, Private, don't fancy an early camp?"

"No, sir," Rambling replied. "I was just curious."

Mitchell slowly shook his head. "Lord help me," he muttered, then walked toward Rambling. "Yer familiar with the cat and curiosity, ain't ye?" he asked, stopping in front of the private. "Do you suppose that if their lordships had wanted you to know, they'd've said so, and that mayhaps they have their own reasonin'?"

"Oh, I'm quite sure, First Sergeant, but with the wagons low on water and no river in sight and still half a day to march, I wondered, why stop now?"

Mitchell smiled. "Yer a bright one, lad, maybe a little too bright." He sighed. " 'Tis no great mystery. We're near enough to Supply to march in, but General Miles doesn't want us lookin' like stragglers, so he calls an early camp. Not only that, but it's to be hot meals and all the water you want. There's to be an inspection after chow in the morning. Then we march into Camp Supply fresh as daisies. See?"

Rambling nodded.

"Ah. Then you approve?"

Rambling nodded again, slower, his lips slightly pursed.

Mitchell placed a hand in the middle of his chest. "It does me heart good to know that. And I believe, no, I *know* that the officers will sleep all the better for it." He removed his forage cap and clasped it in both hands. "Now, is there anything else I can do?"

Rambling shook his head, afraid to utter a word.

"No?" Mitchell asked, his eyes wide. "Then I t'ank you, kind sir, for takin' the time to speak to me. An' if your lordship don't mind, I'll be on me way."

Mitchell took three steps back, turned, and walked off still clutching his cap. Rambling looked around him and saw the grins on the faces of soldiers who'd overheard the conversation. He replied with a shrug and trudged to the company campsite. As he arrived, he saw Larsen sitting on the ground.

"Well, hello, Bill," he said. "Doc turn you loose?"

Larsen shrugged. "More or less. He wants me to keep my foot out in fresh air. I figure I could do that as good here as in the ambulance. 'Sides, Mitchell's been at me. Says maybe I should wear a yellow stripe on my trousers since I'm ridin' so much." He frowned. "You know, Jim, he's got a way of making a man feel like a turd."

"Yes, sir, that he does," Rambling replied, dropping the shelter halves. "Let me get this put together, and we'll go see what's for dinner."

"Nickel to you, Bill," Rambling said around the cigarette that dangled from the corner of his mouth.

Larsen regarded his cards again in the yellow light from the lantern, then dropped them on the blanket. "I'm out."

Rambling nodded. "You, Seth?"

"I'll see that," Hitchcock answered with a grin. "And it'll cost you another nickel to see why."

The players looked at Bailey, who nervously licked his lips. Rambling almost felt sorry for him. He obviously had a good hand, but was afraid he'd offend Hitchcock by winning. Finally, he sighed and set his cards down.

"Too rich for me," he said with a nervous laugh. "You'll have to take his money, Seth."

Hitchcock grunted and fixed his gaze on Ketzel. The private picked up two nickels and dropped them on the blanket.

"Looks like it's up to you, hoss," Hitchcock said.

"Yep," Rambling said quietly. He took a final drag off his cigarette and flipped it out of the tent. Then he grabbed a coin. "I'll call."

Hitchcock showed his hand. "Aces and jacks, boys."

"Nice," Rambling replied. "All I got is deuces— three of 'em." He chuckled and reached for the pot.

"Hold on there, buddy." Ketzel laid his cards on the blanket and fanned out his hand. "Last I heard, full house still beats three of a kind."

"Shit!" Rambling swore. He gathered the cards and started shuffling the deck.

Hitchcock leaned over and looked at Larsen's foot. "Damn, that looks painful."

"Not really. Doc says it's healing up real nice."

"You gonna be able to march?"

"Hell, yes!" Larsen frowned. "Doc says we'll stop at the hospital at Camp Supply. He says maybe they got some new medicine or somethin' to make it heal better." He looked at Rambling. "He also says that the boots you gave me were real good, and I shouldn't have to worry about this happening again."

"Glad to be of help," Rambling said, dealing out cards.

Hitchcock stretched. "Man, I don't know about you boys, but I gonna get me a woman at Supply." He scratched his jaw. "Only question is whether it's gonna be a laundress or a whore at the hog ranch." He grinned. "I heard tell they got Mexican whores. Wildest thing you ever rode, I was told." He laughed. "Yes, sir, got to wear spurs to bed. Yee-haw!"

Rambling laughed and looked at his cards. "Damn. Five cards that bear no relationship to each other at all. Who dealt this shit hand?"

"I don't know," Hitchcock replied, pulling three cards from his hand and dropping them face-down on the blanket, "but hangin's too good for him."

Rambling dropped a penny in the pot; the others matched him. Then he picked up the deck and dealt Larsen two cards and Hitchcock three. Bailey took two, but Ketzel only wanted one. He grinned at Rambling like a ravenous wolf. Rambling took four cards, almost afraid to look at his new hand.

"How about you, Rambling?" Hitchcock asked.

"How 'bout me, what?" Rambling countered.

"You gonna loosen up? Maybe get your laundry cleaned?"

Rambling dropped his cards on the blanket. "Way my luck's going, I'm going to be too broke to poke."

"Leastways, you ain't like Sunshine there." Hitchcock chuckled and looked at Bailey. "He's so ugly, whores make him pay to jerk off." He faced Rambling. "So, how about it? You gettin' a old used-up laundress or a wild-ass Mexican whore?"

"I don't know. I figure to do a little shopping first."

The first strains of Call to Quarters drifted through the tent.

"Aw, hell," Hitchcock complained. "Just when I get a decent hand." He threw the cards down and retrieved his ante and penny bet. "Oh, well, tonight we sleep, tomorrow night we screw." He winked at Rambling. "You might want to stop at the chow wagon, Bailey, maybe get some lard for your big night on the town."

"Dammit, Seth, that ain't funny," Bailey whined. "Crap like that has a way of gettin' around camp."

Hitchcock waved at Rambling and Larsen, and walked off with Bailey and Ketzel. "You know what, Dennis? You ain't got a sense of humor. You know that?"

Bailey bristled. "Do, too."

"The hell you do."

Rambling watched the trio walk back to their camping area. As he turned in, he could still hear Bailey arguing.

As they approached Camp Supply from the north, the first thing Rambling saw was the tall, white flagpole flying the United States flag. The bottom ten feet of the pole was hidden behind a stockade fence with two fifteen-foot blockhouses set on the northwest and southeast corners. Log buildings, tents, and corrals surrounded the stockade.

They marched past long, low buildings that housed the post's soldiers. Laundresses could be seen standing over washtubs, piles of dirty clothing at their feet. Some stopped and raised soapy hands in greeting or shaded their eyes, oblivious to the water and suds dripping on them.

Soldiers, both visiting and stationed at Supply, lined the road and watched the column pass. Most just stared, but others called out or waved to men they knew.

Just outside the north gate flew the guidon for Compton's battalion. His cavalry troopers were housed in neat rows of tents. They also stood by the road, waving at the members of their sister units and ignoring the infantry altogether.

Rambling didn't mind. Fights between the infantry and cavalry were common. In fact, the only time they seemed to get along was when they shared a common enemy like the Indians or the Navy.

Miles brought the column to a stop. Word came down the line to stand easy.

"Man, am I glad to get here," Hitchcock said, yawning.

"Me, too," Rambling answered. "I'm looking forward to a little rest."

"Rest?" Hitchcock laughed. "Not me, brother. I'm horny'n a goat with two peckers. I gonna find me a hog ranch and drink whiskey and dance all night with a Mexican whore. If my ass ain't draggin' tomorrow, I'll not consider the night a success."

Rambling pushed open the door to the sutler's store and walked into the loud, crowded building.

Through smoky haze he saw walls lined with shelves covered by every item imaginable. More merchandise hung from the ceiling.

A rough plank bar stood along one wall. Behind it, a large man, who exhibited a nose broken more than once, served whiskey to soldiers and civilians alike. Behind the bartender, whiskey and gin bottles lined one shelf, while another held various types of wine and champagne. Several jugs of corn or potato liquor sat on the floor. One corner held a barrel of beer. Another barrel had been sawed in half and filled with spring water and bottled beer.

A few tables were scattered about, and Rambling spotted his comrades from Company I gathered around one of these. He made his way over to the table. Mitchell glanced up as he approached.

"Well, well, it's his lordship, come to grace us with his presence," he said, grinning. "So what's yer pleasure, Rambling? First drink's on me."

"Shot and beer all right?"

Mitchell slapped the table. "Done, boyo!" He waved at the bartender. "Sir, me young friend here wants a shot and a beer. Mind you, Irish whiskey only."

The barkeep nodded.

"Thanks, First Sergeant," Rambling said. "Let me return the favor."

"As you wish, m'lord."

Rambling walked to the bar. The bartender set a glass of whiskey in front of him.

"What kind of beer you want?" he asked in a rattling, guttural voice.

"I don't care. Whatever's been in the water the longest."

The bartender shrugged and turned away.

"Oh, and bring me another shot of whiskey, too."

"Sure."

Rambling quickly drank his whiskey, his eyes watering at the burn. He opened his beer and took a deep drink. Picking up Mitchell's shot, he returned to the table. He set his beer and the whiskey down, then grabbed a nearby chair and sat.

Mitchell raised the shot glass. "To your health, gentlemen." He tossed the liquor back, smiled, and licked his lips. "Nectar."

The men drank through the evening, listening to Mitchell's tales of fighting in the Civil War and against the Plains Indians. The sutler's store emptied as soldiers left to find other entertainment, until there were just two tables occupied, one by Mitchell and the men of Company I, and the other by half a dozen Sixth Cavalry troopers, playing cards.

The door swung open, and Sergeant Hay stumbled in. He stood a moment, gazing at the occupants, then staggered to the bar.

"Whiskey," he demanded. "Scotch. None o' that swill the Irish drink."

When the bartender brought over the bottle to fill Hay's glass, the sergeant took it. He made his way to the table and plopped in an empty chair. He removed the cork and drank deeply. Then he wiped his mouth on his sleeve and began to sing.

Oh, cruel is the snow that sweeps Glencoe,
And covers the grave of ol' Donald.
And cruel is the foe that raped Glencoe,
And mordered the house of MacDonald.

"That's an unusual song, Sergeant," Rambling said.

Hay looked at the private, blinking rapidly. "Ye'll be De Armond's boy," he muttered.

Rambling had to listen closely. Not only was Hay's

voice thick with liquor, his burr was very pronounced. He trilled his *r*'s like the Spanish. "Yes, sir. Private Rambling."

"And ye have nae heard o' the massacre at Glencoe?"

Rambling shook his head.

"Well," Hay said, straightening in the chair, "it's a history lesson ye'll be wantin'." He cleared his throat. " 'Twas in the year of Our Lord sixteen hundred and ninety-two." Hay stopped and frowned. "Ach, back up a year, 1691. Prince William took the throne of England. He had nae a care for Scotland, so he turns her over to a right bastard named Dalrymple, makes him Master of Stair."

"What's that?" someone asked.

"Eh?" Hay stared at the faces around him. "It's a political position. He was the king's man in Scotland. Anyway, Dalrymple told the king he must make all the Highlanders swear allegiance to him. All did, save one. That was Ian Maclain o' the house of MacDonald."

Hay took another drink and continued. "It wasn't that Maclain snubbed William of Orange. He tried to make his oath, but he was held prisoner by the Campbells until the deadline passed. The Master of Stair was delighted, for he had a particular hate for the Maclains. He said the entire sept—" Hay raised a hand. "That's like a branch o' the clan. Maclain of MacDonald. See?"

When no one spoke, Hay tipped the bottle again. "Now Dalrymple saw his chance, and he sent soldiers o' the Campbell clan to Glencoe, where they slaughtered the MacDonalds. It was nae the killin' that outraged Highlanders. It was the treachery, for these soldiers arrived as guests and stayed in the house and ate o' the food and slept in the beds o' their victims a fortnight before the killin'."

Hay paused and drank again. "The Indians are as bad at killin', but they don't have the black heart or cowardly ways of a Campbell."

"That's a load o' shite, Fred Hay!" a Scottish voice shouted.

Hay looked around him. "What? Who said that?"

"I did."

From the table of troopers, one stood. He was small with a dark blond mustache and ruddy face. His eyes burned brightly with anger and whiskey.

"I did," he repeated. "You're a liar. The MacDonalds were thieves and outlaws at best, and Robert Campbell was following his king's orders when he put the lot to the sword."

Hay laughed. "Yer a Campbell, for sure. Still spoutin' the same excuses for that blackguard. It was as the song said, 'Like morderin' foxes among helpless sheep, they slaughtered the house o' MacDonald.' "

"Aye, I'm a Campbell. But we nae be morderers, ye sot."

Hay stood, weaving. "And I say yer a coward like all yer kith and kin." He pulled his pistol from its holster and aimed at Campbell. "This world needs ye not!"

"NO!" Rambling shouted. He jumped to his feet and pushed Hay's arm upward.

The flash blinded Rambling and his ears rang. The concussion blew out half the lanterns in the store, plunging that section into darkness. Amid the general confusion and shouting, Rambling and Hay fell heavily to the floor. As the din eased, Campbell could be heard shouting.

"He tried to kill me! By God, he'll pay, or my name's not Colin Campbell!"

"Shut yer hole, Campbell!" Mitchell bellowed. "There'll be no report. And if you and this lot don't go, I'm of a mind to let him get in another shot."

"Come on, Col," a trooper said. "Let's get the hell out before he turns that crazy goddamn Scot loose."

"This nae be the end!" Campbell shouted as he was hustled to the door. "Do you hear me, Fred Hay? This nae be the end. I'll be seeing you again."

"Aye, ye will, you bastard," Hay muttered. "Now, will someone get this lummox off me?"

"Oh, sorry, Sergeant," Rambling said, gaining his feet. He held out his hand, which Hay grasped.

"I wasn't really going to kill him," Hay said, allowing himself to be helped to his feet. "I just planned to brand him."

Mitchell frowned. "You're a stupid bastard when on the whiskey, Hay. You'd be doin' good to hit the wall, but with my luck, you'd shoot him right between the eyes." He picked up Hay's hat and handed it to Rambling. "You get him home, boyo. Take the back door and the long way around." He fixed his gaze on Hay. "And you, mister, go home. If you give this young fella any grief, you'll answer to me. Understand?"

Hay sighed and nodded. "Aye, First Sergeant, I'll go peaceable."

Rambling led Hay from the sutler's store back to the company area. They met no one on the way and conversation was limited to a curt "good night" from the sergeant. Rambling nodded and started back to the store.

As he neared his destination, he heard a feminine voice address him from the shadows.

"Hello, soldier."

Rambling stopped and peered into the darkness.

Soon a figure emerged. He could see it was a woman, small and slender, her breasts the size of apples. Her face was still obscured until she moved into the light from the store windows.

"Evening, ma'am," he replied, taking off his cap.

"Going to the sutler's?" she asked.

Rambling's heart beat faster. Her voice was soft and a bit husky. The poor lighting showed just enough of her face that he could see she was young.

"Yes'm," he muttered.

She stepped past him and looked across the post to the prairie beyond. "It's such a lovely night," she said, her voice stronger.

Rambling gazed around them at the clear skies and thousands of stars. A crescent moon hung near the horizon. He nodded. "Yes, ma'am, it is."

"I'd hoped to take a turn around the post, but with the Indian trouble and all . . ."

"No, ma'am, I don't suppose that would be a good idea."

"Of course, in the company of a young, strong soldier, I guess I would be safe enough."

Rambling drew a deep breath and let it out slowly. His pulse raced; he could hear the blood rush through his veins. "Well, ma'am, I don't know about that."

She stepped closer and placed a hand on Rambling's sleeve. He felt the warmth of her touch; a delicate scent rose from her body. His knees trembled.

"Please. Surely you wouldn't want to be inside that smoky old saloon on such a glorious night." She leaned closer. "Besides, I'm cooped up all day. This is the only freedom I have."

Rambling breathed in her essence. He thought of the sutler's store, the heat, the cigar smoke and swearing men. Then he gazed at the young woman before him, as delicate and fragrant as a rose.

"You're right, ma'am. It *would* be a shame to waste such a night indoors."

"Wonderful!" she exclaimed, and slipped her arm through his. "Now, you just let me be the guide, and I'll show you our post."

Rambling grinned, foolishly happy to be in such fair company. He'd have followed her anywhere.

As they walked around Camp Supply, Rambling's companion pointed out the quartermaster's building, the hospital, the blacksmith shop, and the guardhouse. They crossed the parade ground, the great white flagpole empty, and passed down officers' row.

"This first house is Colonel Lewis's. He's the post commandant," she said, pointing at a white two-story structure. "Next to him lives his adjutant."

She continued to list the personnel in each house, what each officer did, his wife's name, and their children, if they had any. Finally, she stopped at the last house on the row, and walked behind it.

"This is where I live," she said, mounting the steps and swinging open the back door.

"Oh." Rambling was appalled. He'd been escorting an officer's wife. He could be shot for what he thought about her. "Then I shall wish you a good night," he said with a small bow.

"Why? Can't you come in for just a moment?"

"No, ma'am. I'd be in the stockade for just about forever if I was caught in your house. Besides, ma'am, your husband—"

"Is on patrol," she interrupted. "And when he's home, he not affectionate at all." She stepped closer and gripped his arm, hard. "Please. I don't want another night alone."

Rambling looked closely at the lady. She was pretty,

maybe beautiful, though he'd had only half glimpses of her face. What she proposed could ruin both their lives and land him in prison—or worse. Still, he'd wanted her since the first time she'd touched his arm.

He gently pulled loose from her grip, climbed the stairs, and stepped through the doorway into the kitchen. Turning back to her, he smiled and held out his hand. She quickly joined him.

"My name is James," he said.

"Etta."

Thirteen

August 20, 1874, started warm, with cloudless skies and the early promise of another hot day. But the men in Miles's column were in a good mood, though many were suffering the aftereffects of a late night of heavy drinking.

Rambling was exhausted, but it was a happy fatigue brought on by a night of the wildest passion he'd ever experienced. His back bore the marks of Etta's fervor as she dug in her nails, her legs locked around his waist. More than once Rambling would have sworn she'd cracked one of his ribs or torn away a chunk of his skin.

Between rounds of sex, she clung to him, weeping bitterly at her life and how the Army had reduced her to the level of consorting with enlisted men. Then her eyes would light with fire again, and she'd pull him down on her or climb atop him and ride him until both were spent. Rambling had managed to keep up with her, but the ache in his balls and back made him wonder if it had been worth it. Almost.

A false dawn had turned the sky royal blue before he managed to make good his escape. He ran past the barracks, ignoring the stares of the sentries, and arrived at his tent just as Reveille sounded. Larsen was already awake.

"Where in the hell have you been?"

Rambling shrugged.

"Do you have idea how worried I was? I thought for sure the Masons had figured out who you were."

"I was fine, Bill," Rambling answered curtly. Being worshiped was not always a good thing.

Larsen rose, grabbed Rambling's arm, and turned him around. "You got to take this more serious. Today we start the big campaign, the march into the wilderness. Soon, you'll be called upon to do your part."

Rambling pulled himself from Larsen's grip. "Look, Bill, what are you going to do if they never cast us out or desert us to the Indians or lead us to our deaths? Have you considered that?"

Larsen gazed at Rambling a moment, then scratched his head. "Well, I suppose I *could* be wrong," he said, frowning. "And I reckon if I was . . . if I was wrong, that is . . . well"—he grinned—"well, then all this preparation and caution would be for naught. But if I'm right, and I do believe I *am* right, then we can't let down our guard for one second. Why, that may be part of the plan, Jim." He nodded vigorously. "Yep, that's it. They *want* you to think nothing's going to happen. Then you won't be ready when it does. And besides, if it don't, then what harm is there in being ready for when it does?"

Rambling stared at the ground, then slowly lifted his head to gaze at Larsen. "Your logic defies explanation," he said. A slow smile spread across his face. "But you are right. We really can't allow ourselves to be fooled by the watch keepers, can we?"

Larsen beamed. "That's the spirit, son! I'd knew you'd come around. Course there's nothing to ashamed of. Every true savior has his moments of doubt, a time when he wonders if he can do what is expected of him." He paused and toed the dirt. "So, where were you?"

"With a woman, Bill," Rambling said, too tired to argue.

"Get your laundry cleaned?" Larsen chuckled.

"Yeah," Rambling lied. "My laundry's in good shape."

"Was she pretty? You know some of them laundresses look kinda muley."

Rambling bent and pulled up a tent stake. "Well, you tell me," he said, absently brushing dirt from the stake. "She had great big ol' titties and buckteeth."

Larsen guffawed. "Buckteeth? Do tell. And big ol' titties?"

"Yessir."

"Well, I don't suppose you'd kissed her."

"Just on the cheek to say good-bye."

Larsen dissolved into laughter. After a few moments, he moved to other side of the shelter and began to pull up stakes. Soon, he and Rambling had the tent down and folded, ready for storage in one of the wagons.

" 'Bout ready for chow?" Rambling asked.

"Sure, Jim." Larsen said, picking up his yoke. "Let me just get this on. I don't want Mitchell on my ass." He stopped. "That reminds me, you missed all the excitement last night."

"Yeah? Like what?"

"The captain came by with some cavalry officer and rousted Mitchell out of bed. This other officer says one of our men took a shot at one of his."

Rambling slowly gathered his gear. "Really? He say who?"

"Didn't mention no names, not that it mattered. Mitchell stands right up to him and says that whoever said that was a liar and a son-of-a-bitch for disparaging the fine reputation of the company and the infantry."

"No lie?" Rambling asked, eyes wide. "What did Lyman do?"

"The captain tells this pony soldier that he'll stand by the first sergeant, and if he says nothin' happened, nothin' happened. Well, then the cavalryman gets mad and stomps off."

"And that was it?"

Larsen shrugged. "Mostly. When they was alone, I heard the captain tell Mitchell that if nothing happened again, the first sergeant was going to be shoveling shit and digging slit trenches for a year."

Rambling grinned. "That I'd like to see." Then he motioned at Larsen. "Come on, Bill, let's eat."

"All right, all right. Man, I can't wait to tell the boys about your laundress."

"Why not?" Rambling said, his smile fading. "Big ol' titties."

"And buckteeth!" Larsen crowed.

The hot, swirling wind picked away at the sandy soil, laying bare the white gypsum that lay just underneath. Those powdery deposits in turn were scoured to dust, pulled aloft by the same searing breezes, until the particles filtered back to the surface. The water holes, though small and scarce, got their share. Where the water was not polluted by bitter gyp, it sported alkali beaches or a rim of salt. Undrinkable.

Elsewhere, where fresh water had seeped or slowed or stood in seasons past, there was only dry earth. Springs, streams, ponds, riverbeds, all held nothing but cracking, curling clay.

Rambling marched stoically, blinking against the sweat that dripped into his eyes. He licked his lips constantly, tasting the salt. His sweat-soaked uniform clung to him as though he'd been caught in a rainstorm. His yoke and rifle gained weight with each step, until he was ready to toss his equipment away.

"I am utterly convinced," Hitchcock said in a hoarse voice, "that there is a conspiracy among the officers to kill us all by walkin' us to death."

"Amen," Larsen said.

Rambling grinned. He wondered if Hitchcock knew just how much Larsen agreed with him. "How're the feet, Bill?" Rambling asked.

"I'm doing good, Jim. My new boots are like walking on clouds."

"How far you reckon we marched?" Bailey asked.

"I couldn't guess," Hitchcock replied. "Too far for me, but not far enough for the general."

Bailey hawked and spat. "Goddamn officers ride all day and let us sweat our balls off. They don't quit for nothin' and nobody. Pox on 'em! Every goddamn one of 'em."

" 'Cept ours," Rambling called out.

"Yeah," Hitchcock said. "Pox on all of 'em except the captain and Lieutenant Lewis."

They stared at the dry streambed. Swirls of dust blew in the breeze. Beetles scuttled across the red sand leaving delicate trails quickly filled in by flying grains.

"They call this oasis Wolf Creek," Larsen announced. "We marched twenty-six miles to get here."

"Jesus Christ," Hitchcock swore. "No wonder I'm so tired. There ain't shit for water here, so why not stop earlier?"

"I don't know, and I don't care," Rambling said. He leaned on his rifle and gazed across the parched land. Tall yellowed grass swayed in the wind. Stands of prickly pear and cholla cactus dotted the landscape. No animal stirred. A lifeless place.

As the sun dropped below the horizon, Rambling slid out of his boots. He rubbed his feet, trying to get some feeling back into them.

"And how far did we march today?" he asked Larsen.

"Eighteen miles. That gulch over yonder is Commission Creek."

Rambling shook his head. "We've only been out two days, and I feel like I've marched all the way to Georgia."

"Gonna get worse than that," Larsen said, crawling into their shelter. "According to my friend, we're looking to meet up with the scouts near someplace called Antelope Hills. He says it's almost forty miles away."

Rambling groaned. He crawled in beside Larsen. Lying on his stomach, he peered across the campsite at the flickering fires that competed with the stars. He thought about Etta and wondered if another soldier shared her bed tonight, and if she wept for him. Maybe she had a new lover every night. Maybe he was a link in a very long chain of blue uniforms. He shook his head. What sort of man would marry a woman like that?

"Bill, you asleep?"

"Not yet."

"That buddy you have in Headquarters Company, the one that sees the maps, he tell you where Miles plans to find the Indians?"

Larsen yawned. "Nope. That's why Miles hired all

those buffalo hunters and Indians. They're supposed to find them for us."

And when they do, Rambling thought, *we'll fight them. Then I'll know what Daniel felt. The only question is, am I man enough to face it?*

Fourteen

Boytale awoke chilled by a cool breeze from the north. He sat up and looked around the shambles of the camp.

Goods from the wagon were scattered over the campsite. Clothes no one wanted lay in piles. Boxes and crates had been smashed, their contents used or strewn about, depending on need or comprehension. The coffee, sugar, bacon, jerky, pistol, and ammunition were neatly stacked to one side.

The white man's body lay near the smoking fire, his hands almost completely burned away. Boytale remembered when the man had stopped screaming. Nothing they did made him utter another sound. Lone Wolf declared him drained of all medicine. Then he stretched out the man's tongue and sliced it off. He emasculated the prisoner, and stuffed his genitals into his gaping mouth, then cut his throat. But before the white man died, Lone Wolf told Tehan to take his scalp. After that, the scouts sat around the fire drinking coffee and talking about what they planned for the next day.

Boytale finally felt a part of his adopted people. Now he had to prove himself a warrior. He hoped he'd get his chance with a new prisoner.

Other warriors yawned, stretched, and got to their

feet. Bear Mountain stumbled by and grinned at Boytale. "Good morning, little one."

Lone Wolf arose and made his way to start the fire. He blew on the embers and added small bits of grass until flames appeared. After stacking new wood on the blaze, he sat back and gazed at Boytale.

"Did you feel the medicine last night?" he asked.

Boytale nodded. "It ran down my spine like trickles of ice-cold water."

"I have often wondered how someone who has no Kiowa blood can get the medicine. Perhaps anyone can get it."

"I don't know. I have never considered myself to be anything other than one of the People."

Lone Wolf nodded. "I suppose Tehan feels the same, but I sometimes worry that you young men will act foolishly to prove yourselves, especially those not born Kiowa."

"It is not easy to be me," Boytale said. "Even with Mamanti as my uncle, there are those who would spit on me, those who would not allow me to marry their daughters. But one day I will prove myself to all of them—no matter what it takes."

Lone Wolf smiled sadly. "Then a word of advice. Before you test your manhood, think about your parents and your uncle. I have lost a son and a nephew, and there is no pain sharper. To die a warrior is to die as a Kiowa, but to die a fool is the white man's way and brings shame on your lodge."

The scouts gathered what they could carry and rode for the other side of the mountain. Less than halfway there, they met another party of warriors riding toward them. They were a mixed group of Kiowa and Cheyenne.

"Hello, Lone Wolf," a warrior called. "It is good to see you."

"It is a good day, Elk Tongue. We have much medicine and more to gather."

"Then it *is* a good day. Do you want to smoke?"

Lone Wolf shook his head. "We are going to kill some white men on top of the mountain. Come with us, and we'll smoke later."

Elk Tongue smiled wryly. "We already killed one. Snake Head has the scalp. The rest of them are hiding in a stone lodge up there. They can shoot anyone on this side, and don't act like they are coming out soon."

"Then we will continue our original journey," Lone Wolf replied.

"Where are you going?"

"To the Wichita Agency. We have heard they have food and blankets, maybe even bullets for hunting."

"You will be in good company. Big Red Meat and his Naconi Comanches are there."

"We heard that."

"But you probably don't know that the Yapparika and Kotoseka bands are there, too. There has even been talk that the Quahadis are coming off the Llano Estacado."

Lone Wolf smiled. "It would be good to see Quanah again. I liked that Comanche." The smile faded. "What of the yellow paint prophet?"

Elk Tongue grinned. "Isatai doesn't ride with Quanah anymore. His tipi stands with those of Black Duck."

Lone Wolf grunted. "Better his tipi to burn down with him in it." He sighed. "It is time to be going. Will you ride with us?"

"No. We're going to look for more whites. Tomorrow is the day the food is given out. We will see you there."

The warriors waved and rode away. Lone Wolf

turned his men in the direction of the Wichita Agency. Boytale was unhappy with the outcome of the meeting. He'd desperately wanted the opportunity to prove himself. Swallowing his disappointment, he quickly joined the others.

The sun had crossed the middle of the sky before the scouts spotted the main party. They charged down a hill with wild cries, eager to display their trophies. Tehan had a scalp. Bear Mountain carried the sacks of coffee and sugar and the coffeepot. Boytale had the bag of bacon and jerky, and wore a red shirt he'd found among the white man's clothes. Buffalo with Holes in His Ears had a Bible, long noted for its ability to stop bullets, tucked behind his bone-pipe breastplate. Lone Wolf had the white man's rifle, which was in better condition than his own, and a box of shells. High Forehead brought up the rear, burdened with blankets, canteens, a cooking pot, and the pistol.

The combined bands cheered them as they rode past, then circled around. On their second pass, each scout broke away and rode to where his band and family waited. Boytale and Tehan made their way to Mamanti.

"So, what is this?" the Owl Prophet exclaimed. "Two boys go on a scout and count coup?"

Tehan held up the scalp. "It is true, Father. I broke the captive, made him cry aloud and release his medicine. Lone Wolf gave me the scalp."

"And so it should be," Mamanti said. He looked at Boytale. "And you, nephew, what did you do?"

Boytale shrugged. "Buffalo with Holes in His Ears and I found some men high on the signal mountain, but some other Kiowas killed one of them before we could go back, and the others hid."

"Do not worry. The Owl has told me many times that you will be remembered as a great warrior." He beamed at the boys. "Both of you." Mamanti turned his horse and started away. "You have brought me much happiness," he called over his shoulder.

Tehan gazed at the scalp, then looked at his cousin. "Father's right. One day you will have a scalp, and ponies, and other war honors. It will just take time."

"I know," Boytale answered with a sigh. "I just hope I'm still young enough to enjoy them."

The Kiowa continued their journey across the wide, flat plain until they came to a stand of trees along the banks of the Washita River. Once across the river, they broke into the open and saw tipis that were clearly Comanche in design. A second band of Comanche were camped near by. The agency houses and corrals stood in the distance, built against a tall bluff. Near the river was still another building, and up on a hill, almost a mile away, sat a large house.

Lone Wolf ordered the lodges to be set up along the river, then gathered his chiefs and rode to the Comanche camp. Though uninvited, Tehan and Boytale tagged along. As they entered the camp, a chieftain stepped from his tipi and awaited them.

"Big Red Meat, my old friend," Lone Wolf hailed.

The Comanche raised a hand in greeting. "Lone Wolf, it makes my heart sing to see you again. Too many moons have passed since we smoked. You and your men are welcome in my camp and my home."

The Kiowa accepted the invitation by dismounting and allowing their horses to be taken by Comanche warriors. Boytale gazed around the campsite. It was not unlike his own village.

Big Red Meat was a massive man with a chest that looked as big as a buffalo's. He had muscular arms and wide, heavy shoulders. His paint was an elaborate display of black, red, and white covering his face and chest. Boytale, with his two red stripes on each arm and lines under his eyes, felt naked in his presence.

The Comanche chief sent a runner out of camp, then ordered blankets to be spread on the ground. "I have sent for the others," he said. "There isn't enough room in the lodge for all of us."

Presently the runner returned, accompanied by five men. After they dismounted and joined the group, Big Red Meat made introductions.

"This is Tabananica of the Yapparika. Standing next to him is Isa-Rosa, also Yapparika. Then comes Mowway, who brought his Kotoseka here. Black Duck and Little Crow came with me and the Naconi."

"What of the Quahadi?" Lone Wolf asked. "We heard they had come off the plains."

Big Red Meat nodded. "We heard the same, but no one has seen them."

Lone Wolf nodded and stepped forward. "My name is Lone Wolf, war chief of all the Kiowa." He placed a hand on the shoulder of the man next to him. "This is Satanta. Next to him is Woman's Heart; then Double Vision; my brother, Red Otter; and Poor Buffalo. The last man is not a chief, but our Owl Prophet and medicine man, Mamanti."

The warriors sat in a large circle. The villagers gathered around, Boytale and Tehan at the front. Big Red Meat accepted a lit pipe, smoked, and passed it on. The ceremony continued in complete silence until the pipe was back in Big Red Meat's hands.

"Many things have changed for both our peoples," he said. "The Comanche are split between the Honey-Eaters and their wish for peace, and the rest, who just want what we always had."

"The same is true for the Kiowa." Lone Wolf indicated those around him. "The men who are here with me don't want to follow the white man's road. They

want to live free as we, and our friends the Comanches, have always done. Striking Eagle and his
peace chiefs would have us be slaves to the soldiers."

The silence stretched out as Lone Wolf's words
were considered. No one spoke while Big Red Meat
pondered, no one would speak again until he gave
his answer.

"Then you will fight?"

Lone Wolf nodded. "If we have to, but we have
come here for food and blankets for the winter. We
are not at war with any of these whites."

"That may not be so," Big Red Meat said with a
laugh. "You are here, that is true, but you have no
ration yet. You must make the agency man give you
what you came for, and that's not that easy."

Back at their own camp, Lone Wolf brooded over
Big Red Meat's words. Suddenly he rose and called
for Bear Mountain, Red Otter, and Mamanti. Boytale
heard the shouting and came running to see what
was happening. He was the last to arrive at Lone
Wolf's tipi.

"You have heard Big Red Meat's words," Lone Wolf
told the others. "If what he says is true, we may have
to take what we need. Bear Mountain and I are going
to the agency to ask for the ration. While we are gone,
I want the rest of you to move the camp to the other
side of the river."

When the meeting broke up, Boytale approached
the war chief.

"Will you let me ride with you to the agency?" he
asked.

Lone Wolf regarded him closely, then slowly nodded. "That might be a good idea. After all, who would
bring a child to a fight?"

The words stung. Lone Wolf did not even consider him a man. But then, what had he done to demonstrate his manhood?

The warriors mounted their ponies and trotted into the Wichita Agency. The agent stepped from his house, and upon seeing unfamiliar Indians, sent for the interpreter. As Lone Wolf spoke, the interpreter translated.

"We Kiowa have traveled many days to this place for the ration."

The agent replied through his interpreter. "The food, blankets, and other things here are for the Indians who have the peace paper."

"I will accept such a paper if it means my people will not starve or freeze this winter. If I let you count me, will you give me what I ask?"

"Come tomorrow when the sun is high overhead. You will get the paper then. Tell me your name, so it can be entered in the book."

Lone Wolf drew himself erect. "I am Lone Wolf, *onde* warrior and war chief of the Kiowa."

The agent's eyes widened, and he paled as the interpreter translated what had been said. The agent nodded and waved, then hurried inside his home.

Riding back to their camp, Lone Wolf was in a good mood. "Did you see the agency man? He was impressed when he heard who we were."

Bear Mountain chuckled. "I think he was terrified. Not that that is necessarily a bad thing."

Boytale glanced back at the agency. A rider burst into view and headed south at full gallop. "I wonder where he's going in such a hurry."

Bear Mountain turned and watched the rider fade into the distance. "To the fort. You were right to move the camp, Lone Wolf. Tomorrow the soldiers come."

Fifteen

Boytale gazed across the field at the agency, in anticipation of the ration. He had no idea what a "ration" was, but he had overheard enough to know it involved meat, blankets, and bullets.

On the other side of the field, the Indians who held the peace paper waited as well. He saw Wichita, Caddo, and Delaware, and a short distance away, the Comanche that Big Red Meat had called Honey-Eaters. Lone Wolf and his Comanche counterpart had kept their people away, unsure of their welcome since neither had the paper.

A man stood in a wagon and spoke to the gathered Indians. Boytale could not hear his words, but the man waved his hands about, pounded the air with his fist, and finally lifted both hands high over his head.

"Tehan," Boytale said, leaning toward his cousin, "you're a white man. What's he doing?"

The rangy youth shrugged. "Maybe he's praying."

Boytale nodded. He could understand that, because the Kiowa never did anything important without the blessing of a medicine man. Not only did it assure a good ending, it protected the People from evil spirits.

The man in the wagon waved an arm. Boytale heard whistles and men yelling, then the lowing of cattle. The waiting Indians parted and allowed a small herd to pass. The cattle were the scrawny breed from the land of the Tejanos, thin, with flat sides and massive horns. They were less than half the size of a buffalo, but Boytale had heard tales of hunters killed by them, gutted by the long horns or trampled in stampedes.

Boytale jumped as two shots cracked in the distance. The noise startled the cattle, who bolted. The peace Indians' hunters immediately gave chase, pulling arrows from their quivers. Lone Wolf and Big Red Meat signaled, and the combined Kiowa and Comanche hunters charged across the field.

One hunter leaned in close to loose an arrow. The targeted steer tilted his head sideways and slipped a horn between the horse's feet. The horse stumbled, dumping its rider. The longhorn never broke stride.

Boytale laughed and pointed out the animal to Tehan.

Another hunter approached, and the steer again attacked, but this hunter was more cautious than his comrade and quickly pulled away. A third hunter advanced and managed to get a shot off, but the steer seemed to stop and pivot instantly. The hunter missed him entirely.

Two Comanches flanked the steer, one slightly in the lead. As the lead hunter neared, the steer tilted his head, dipping the horn for a strike. The second hunter closed and fired an arrow. It was on target, between the longhorn's ribs and into its heart. The steer bellowed, then collapsed.

Kiowa and Comanche women and children surged forward. They quickly butchered the animal, packing the meat into the fresh hide. Then, as several dragged the load back, others moved on to the hunters' next kill, leaving what remained of the carcass to scavengers.

The women grunted as they pulled their load. Children, faces bloody from eating bites of fresh, still-warm liver, pushed from behind. The camp dogs ran alongside, hoping for a tidbit to fall from the hide.

Lone Wolf surveyed the scene and nodded. He turned to Big Red Meat. "I think I like this thing they call ration," he said with a smile.

Pots full of boiling water and beef hung over cookfires throughout the camp. Some fires also roasted meat skewered on green sticks and placed in the flames. The beef that was not immediately cooked was cut into long, thin strips and hung on drying racks. Later, this jerky would be packed away or pounded to pieces and mixed with tallow and berries to make pemmican.

Lone Wolf gathered his warriors around him, preparing to go to the agency and get the blankets and whatever else they could. Big Red Meat's men were mounted and ready, waiting for the Kiowa.

A rider approached the campsite at full gallop. He was a Delaware, wearing shirt and trousers, moccasins, and a tall black hat with a flat top. Reining in, he quickly made signs.

"Soldiers are coming."

Goose stepped forward and signed back. "Where? How many?"

"Many buffalo soldiers." The rider pointed at the southbound road.

"When?"

The Delaware gazed at the morning sun, thought a moment, then pointed straight up—two hours.

As the Delaware rode off to spread his message,

Big Red Meat stared at the Fort Sill road. He sighed and dismounted. "I think I will wait here until the soldiers arrive. With them so close, the agency man might not be as friendly as he was yesterday."

"I agree," Lone Wolf replied. "Besides, here we can move quickly into the trees or across the river if they attack." He faced his men. "I am going to make medicine and paint a war face. Those who will fight need to do the same."

Boytale turned to Tehan. "Are we going?"

The redhead grinned. "Of course we are! This time you'll get a scalp."

Boytale smiled and wondered if the sudden fluttering in his stomach was his medicine at work.

Stepping out of his tipi, Boytale looked into the sky. The appointed hour was close. He was shirtless, but wore the new vest his mother had given him after the Lost Valley fight. It was buckskin smoked to a pale yellow. Bright bars of blue, white, and green beads formed badges on either side of his chest. His hair was greased and plaited, the ends tied in trade cloth, a vermillion stripe painted down the part. Two red stripes, drawn in the shape he'd seen on the soldiers' uniforms, adorned each upper arm. Another two red stripes were painted under each eye, turning downward at the corner and tracing a curved line across his cheek to his chin like the horns of a buffalo. He wore a breechclout, fringed leggings, and quilled moccasins.

A single black feather adorned his scalp lock, awarded to him for counting coup on the captured white man. He was the third warrior to touch him while he was alive. Tehan had earned two feathers the same day, one for touching the prisoner, and the other for breaking him.

As Boytale stared to the south for signs of the soldiers, he saw Tehan come out of Mamanti's tipi. The youth wore nothing but a breechclout. His chest and back were painted with Owl Prophet medicine, a blue owl against a white background. One blue line ran under each eye. His mane of red hair hung free, tossing in the wind with bright, coppery glints. No white man would ever doubt that he was born of their kind, but as he drove his lance home, they would know he was now Kiowa.

Boytale heard a shout and looked back to the south. A thin column of dust rose in the distance. He hurried over to Mamanti and Tehan.

"They are coming," he said.

Mamanti nodded. "Yes, but see the dust trail. It is not from soldiers who gallop or even trot. These men are in no hurry."

"Maybe they're here to talk," Boytale said.

Tehan frowned. "I hope not. I don't want to be all dressed up for nothing."

"Warriors!" Lone Wolf called. "Get on your horses, in case they want a fight."

Boytale ran past the war chief, whose face was painted white with bright red diagonal slashes. He freed his horse from its ground stake and mounted. Riding up behind Lone Wolf and Big Red Meat, he was flanked by warriors from both tribes.

Comanche women and children fled north to the safety of the trees and nearby bluffs. Watching them scamper, Boytale was glad the Kiowa women and children had moved their tipis to Poor Buffalo's campsite. Though it meant he had to share his lodge with three other warriors, at least he had everything he needed close at hand.

Soon the soldiers were visible, their blue uniforms looking black in the distance. The agency man walked out of his lodge and spoke to the white man in front. Boytale assumed that he was the soldier chief. The conversation was brief; then the chief spoke to a white man next to him. The second man took off at a gallop and rode straight at the Kiowa and Comanche warriors.

As he neared, the rider slowed and raised a hand in greeting.

"I come from the soldiers," he called out in perfect Comanche. "I was sent here by my chief to ask Big Red Meat to talk."

Big Red Meat took a deep breath and let it out noisily. "What does the soldier chief want with me?"

"The agency man said you wanted the peace paper, that you were willing to put your name in the book and be counted. This is what the soldier chief wants, too. He says that before you get the paper, you have to talk to him, chief to chief."

"And my men?"

"You must come alone, though you may bring along one warrior who speaks my language. I offer this so that you know I do not lie."

Big Red Meat sat quietly for several moments, staring across the land but focusing on nothing. He nodded and turned to Lone Wolf. "I am going," he said.

Lone Wolf grunted. "Do you think it's wise? How do we know these soldiers will not kill you?"

"We don't. But if they do, my men will seek revenge. I am willing to trade my scalp for many of theirs. And we might yet get the paper and blankets we want. That means we will live through the winter."

He nodded toward the agency. "I can wait to kill these soldiers until spring, can't you?"

"I suppose," Lone Wolf conceded, "but I don't trust them."

"It isn't a matter of trust. It is a matter of surviving."

Big Red Meat kicked his horse into a trot and rode toward the agency, followed by the interpreter. Reaching the building, both men dismounted and walked inside.

The Comanche warriors grew restive as time passed and Big Red Meat did not reappear. Their nervousness infected the Kiowa, until all the men were jittery and short-tempered.

"We should ride down there and see what's happening," a Comanche warrior demanded. Others, including some Kiowa, murmured agreement.

"No," Lone Wolf said. "We must have a sign first. If he has been taken captive and we attack, they will kill him."

"Bah! I hate this waiting. Women wait, men fight."

Just then the agency door opened, and Big Red Meat stepped outside. He was closely followed by several white men, including the soldier chief, the agency man, and the interpreter. Big Red Meat mounted his pony and waved farewell. The soldier chief waved back, then signaled some of his buffalo soldiers, who followed the Comanche chieftain.

Two long columns of black soldiers crossed the field, following Big Red Meat, a white soldier, and the interpreter. Since they approached at a walk, with weapons put away, Boytale had no feeling of threat, but he was curious about the strange procession. They stopped in front of the gathered warriors, and Big Red Meat drew himself erect.

"In return for food and blankets, I have promised the soldier chief that the Naconi Comanche will give them their guns. We will not fight these white men today."

"What of the Kiowa?" Lone Wolf demanded.

Big Red Meat gazed levelly at the war chief. "I speak only for the Naconi. The other bands and our friends the Kiowa are free to do as they please."

"I will surrender nothing!"

The Comanche chief again addressed his men. "Bring me your rifles and pistols. Lay them before my horse."

The white soldier said something. The interpreter argued back, but was clearly overridden. Finally, he translated what he'd been told.

"You are to give up your bows, too."

"What?" Big Red Meat said, surprised at the order. "How will we hunt? How will we feed our families? We have never had to give up our bows."

"I know," the interpreter replied. "The Indian without his bow is like a bear with no claws. It saddens me that they would leave you defenseless."

"Can you not change their mind? Is this the will of the soldier chief, or this other white man?"

The interpreter shrugged.

"Then tell him we will not surrender the bows."

The translation caused another argument between the white men, which ended with a terse statement by the soldier. The interpreter turned back to Big Red Meat.

"He says he will take it all, the rifles, pistols, and bows, and that if you do not give them up, he will take knives and tomahawks, too."

Big Red Meat sat silently. As he thought of his reply, his men and the Kiowa spread out, forming lines on either side of the soldiers. The realignment was not lost on the buffalo soldiers or their leader. Several licked their lips nervously, eyes wide and alert.

"I have made my medicine," Big Red Meat said quietly. "I am ready to travel to the Happy Hunting Ground, to visit the lodge of the Great Spirit." He smiled grimly. "Are you?"

The interpreter raised both hands high. "Wait!" he cried. "Listen to me. Let me talk to the soldier chief. Maybe he will change the order. Will you wait until I return?"

Big Red Meat nodded curtly.

The interpreter said something to the white soldier, then rode off. The look on the white man's face said he was displeased. He barked a brief order, and two men rode forward flanking Big Red Meat. They held each side of the chief's bridle, so he couldn't ride off.

"You don't have to surrender anything," Lone Wolf called out. "You can fight them. We'll help you."

"No man would give up his bow," Bear Mountain said.

Tehan laughed. "Maybe they'll change his name to Big Red Woman."

Several warriors chuckled. Then the calls came quicker.

"Fight them!"

"Don't be a woman!"

"We'll help you!"

Big Red Meat screamed, flagged his blanket at the soldiers on his flanks, somersaulted off his horse, and disappeared into the bushes at the edge of the campsite. The buffalo soldiers shouted, unlimbered their rifles, and fired a volley into the brush. Immediately, the warriors scattered.

Those with rifles fired back at the soldiers while trying to regain control of their mounts. The buffalo soldiers wheeled their horses and shot at anything that moved, further adding to the confusion. Soon a thick blanket of white smoke covered the area.

Boytale and Tehan, neither armed, abandoned their horses and hid in some bushes near the fight.

"This is great!" Tehan shouted as bullets pinged, zipped, and buzzed around them.

Boytale thought his cousin was crazy. Any second he expected to be shot. With firing on all sides, he wasn't even sure who would shoot him.

"Let's see if we can find Lone Wolf and the others," he yelled.

Tehan nodded, and pair crawled through the brush to the riverside. They gained their feet and sprinted upstream into the trees. Then they spotted the Kiowa, mounted and ready to attack.

"Look who's here," Bear Mountain said.

Lone Wolf turned and stared at the boys. "You two keep to the trees and go to Poor Buffalo's camp."

"But we want to fight!" Tehan declared.

"With what?" Lone Wolf replied savagely. "You have no horse, no gun, no bow. What will you do? Spit on them? I have no time to watch children!"

Stung, Tehan fell silent. Then they heard shooting from the north. Bear Mountain rode through the trees and returned quickly.

"More soldiers," he said. "Coming from the place where they cut the trees up. We can't stay here, or we'll be caught in a cross fire."

"Then we will ride for the bluffs," Lone Wolf said. "We can defend the high ground easily, and regroup before attacking."

Mamanti rode up next to Tehan and held out his hand. "Come," he said.

Tehan grasped the hand and swung up behind his father.

Bear Mountain grinned at Boytale. "Will you ride, run, or fly, little one?"

Boytale climbed up behind Bear Mountain. The

huge Kiowa kicked his pony into a gallop, and the pair sped after Lone Wolf and the others.

As they drew near, Lone Wolf veered to the right. He led the warriors through the dense smoke, avoiding any shapes they encountered. Boytale had no idea where he was until he spotted the rails of an empty corral. Lone Wolf had taken them to the agency lodge across from Big Red Meat's camp.

The smoke cleared as they rounded the corner of the building. A small group of Kiowa warriors were hiding there. Lone Wolf pulled up short and dismounted.

"Why are we here?" Mamanti asked. "Shouldn't we be with our people on the bluffs."

"I remembered something from the fight with the hunters on the Canadian River," Lone Wolf said with a grin. "The whites never think to look behind them."

Silence finally fell across the battlefield. As his ears ceased ringing, Boytale heard only the wind and the sound of horses' shuffling hooves. It was as though no fight had occurred at all.

Boytale crept to the corner of the lodge and peeked around it. The soldiers were visible, the remaining smoke whipping through their horses' legs like morning fog. One soldier raised his arm, and the men walked their mounts forward, guns at the ready.

"The soldiers are moving toward the Comanche camp!" he hissed over his shoulder.

Lone Wolf and the others quickly joined him, lining up along the corral fence. Those with rifles rested the barrels on the fence's top rail. Those with bows stood on the bottom rail to ensure a clear shot. Boytale and Tehan could only stand and watch, frustration clearly written on Tehan's features.

The Indians opened fire, and two soldiers fell from their horses. Several of the mounts screamed in pain, and the whole line reared and danced about. Some of the soldiers fired back, but their aim was thrown off by their panicked animals.

Boytale again saw the soldier chief signal his men. They turned and charged at the Penateka village.

"Look!" Lone Wolf shouted gleefully. "They are so confused, they attack the peaceful Comanches."

"Why not?" Woman's Heart said with a frown. "Is that not what Yellow Hair did to the Cheyenne?"

"Cowards!" Bear Mountain screamed. "Come back and fight real warriors!"

As the soldiers drew near the village, a single rider rode out toward them.

"Who's that?" Tehan asked, pointing.

"It looks like old Tosawi, the Penateka chief," Woman's Heart replied. "He must be trying to remind the soldiers that they are friends."

Lone Wolf grunted. "Old fool is going to get himself shot. Whites know no loyalty."

"They are turning away, Lone Wolf," Boytale said.

The band of soldiers changed course and galloped north toward the trees, where the second group of soldiers had appeared.

"I never would have thought they'd do that," Bear Mountain said quietly.

Lone Wolf shook his head. "I keep forgetting these are not white men. They're buffalo soldiers. If we start to think they are like the whites, they'll beat us."

"So what do we do now?"

"I'm not sure. We need to get back to our people, and we—"

A volley of bullets smashed into the corral rail and the building, showering the warriors with splinters. The Kiowa scrambled for cover. Boytale ventured another peek around the corner.

"They are coming back on foot," he said.

"Then we will go," Lone Wolf said.

The warriors mounted their ponies and fled downstream, soon coming upon a farmhouse. Lone Wolf charged into the farmyard, ready to shoot anyone he saw, but the yard was quiet. The remaining Kiowa fanned out, dismounted, and entered the house and outbuildings.

"There is no one here at all," Bear Mountain said.

"Look what I found," Buffalo with Holes in His Ears announced as he emerged from the barn leading two horses. "No more two on one horse."

Boytale and Tehan raced to the animals. Tehan arrived first and took the gray stallion. Boytale's new horse was a sorrel mare, but he wasn't complaining; anything was better than walking. Besides, now Lone Wolf might let them fight.

The horses had bridles, but no saddles. Searching the barn further, Boytale found two blankets and brought them out.

"I think we'll wait here a while," Lone Wolf said. "Maybe there is food in the house or guns."

Woman's Heart shook his head. "I don't like it. The soldiers might come this way. We're moving further downstream, maybe go back to Poor Buffalo's camp."

"We will see you there then."

Tehan pulled Boytale aside. "Here's our chance," he said.

"For what?"

"They won't let us fight without weapons, right?"

Boytale frowned. "I'm not so sure they'd let us in any case."

"Then we must show them we're worthy warriors. Big Red Meat's camp is close, much closer than Poor Buffalo's. Besides, I want my horse back, my bow and arrows."

"So do I."

"Good, then we're agreed." Tehan grinned at Boytale. "Right, cousin?"

The sudden realization of what Tehan meant struck Boytale like a blow.

"We're going back?"

"Sh-h-h. If they hear, they might try to stop us."

"And well they should. Do you know what's going on back there? We might get shot by the soldiers or the Comanches or even our *own* people."

Tehan waved off the suggestion. "You worry too much. We have to go. Do you want Lone Wolf and the others treating us like children forever? When we get back, we'll have our horses, our weapons, our medicine intact. They'll have to let us fight."

Boytale nodded slowly. Tehan was right. Until they showed they were men, nothing would change.

"All right. I'll go."

The other warriors had disappeared into the farmhouse, from which came the sounds of smashing furniture and dishes accompanied by laughter and howls of delight. Tehan and Boytale led their horses behind the barn, where they draped the blankets over them and mounted.

To avoid the soldiers, they immediately forded the creek. Then they rode upstream until they reached the place they'd crossed the previous day. Again they forded the Washita, but this time with a great deal of caution. They slipped through the trees and into Big Red Meat's camp.

The scene was as unreal as anything Boytale could ever imagine. Cookfires still burned. Kettles and charred meat still hung in the flames. Strips of beef remained on drying racks. Here was a half-finished moccasin, abandoned. There was a buffalo skin, pegged, ready to work—but no workers. There was

no sound in the camp, yet he kept expecting a tipi
to open and someone to step out and tend to a meal.
It was a ghost village, and Boytale could all too easily
imagine the evil spirits that would reside in it, ready
to pounce on the unwary.

He and Tehan hurried to their tipis. Inside, Boytale
gathered his bow and arrows. He also found a tomahawk, which he slid under his girdle. Stepping back
outside, he looked for his war horse, but it had apparently fled with the others. He'd have to make do
with the mare from the farm. He squatted to wait for
Tehan and assess their situation.

He understood they would not be getting the peace
paper now. He wasn't sure what that meant. They had
beef, but no blankets. So did Lone Wolf plan to leave
or fight? He heard popping rifles all around him, but
nothing that sounded like a big fight. Was the fight
over?

"Ready?" Tehan asked.

Boytale glanced up and nodded.

They collected their horses and mounted, then
crossed the Washita and rode back toward the farmhouse. As they neared, a flurry of shots sounded in
front of them. They slowed, and picked their way
through the trees. More shots were fired, this time
from the direction of the farmhouse. Another volley
from the front.

They stayed hidden in the trees and peered around
the trunks. The farm was on their right, smoke coming from rifles fired through the windows. To the left,
they clearly saw the buffalo soldiers lying in the grass
and shooting back. Then several Kiowa warriors appeared at the back of the house, gathering horses.

Tehan pointed. "They're getting ready to leave."

Boytale kicked his mount into a gallop, Tehan at

his heels. They burst from the tree line and into the open field, heading straight for the farmhouse.

Boytale heard a shout behind them, then the familiar boom of rifles. Bullets sang past, thudding into tree trunks, clipping limbs and leaves. He swung to the side of his horse, hanging on with one leg, an arm around the animal's neck. More rifles fired. Bullets zipped by like angry hornets, striking more trees.

Then they were at the house, and he swung onto the horse's back again. The other warriors were just getting on their horses. He saw several startled faces as he and Tehan swept by. He could only imagine what they thought.

Had anyone asked him where he was going, his only reply would have been, "Anywhere but here."

Sixteen

Within a mile, the boys slowed their horses. Boytale glanced over his shoulder and saw the other warriors closing quickly. When all were together, Lone Wolf led the party further downstream following the fresh trail of a wagon. The sounds of shooting faded with distance until all that could be heard were the birds, bugs, and labored breathing of the horses.

They trotted past densely packed bushes, many with thorns. They had slowed to examine the tracks closer when three white riders burst from the brush. The riders passed within yards of the party before turning upstream and fleeing at full speed.

Lone Wolf jumped on his horse and led the chase. This time Boytale found himself in the middle of the pack instead of relegated to its rear. He pulled the tomahawk free, resolving to count coup on one of the men.

The white men stayed on the cleared path. One man led, two rode behind him. Boytale expected one of the men to turn and shoot, but they seemed determined to outrun the Kiowa.

"They are headed back to the farm," Lone Wolf called.

If the riders reached the farmhouse, not only would they escape the Kiowa, but the warriors would face the soldiers' rifles again. They drove their animals harder, slowly closing the gap.

One white man looked back and shouted to his companions. Within sight of the farm, they reined in and dismounted, prepared to fight the rest of the way on foot. After firing a volley at the charging Indians, the three took cover in a shallow ditch.

The Kiowa stopped and dropped to the ground. They hid behind trees and bushes and lay in the tall grass on either side of the trail. They returned fire and killed one of the white men's horses. Its owner crawled from the ditch to hide behind the body, only to be shot through the head.

The second member of the trio bolted for the farm. Lone Wolf signaled several warriors to give chase, Tehan among them, who moved back into the protection of the trees and skirted the remaining white man. Both parties stopped firing long enough to watch the scenario play itself out.

The white man ran straight down the trail, maximizing his speed. He was within a hundred yards of the farmhouse when he shouted and grabbed his side. A Kiowa arrow was buried between his ribs. He stumbled and fell. The pursuing warriors broke from cover and rushed the wounded man. Soon there was a shriek, then quiet.

"Hear that, white-eye?" Lone Wolf called. "Only you are left."

The trapped man may not have understood Lone Wolf's words, but his answer was plain enough. The gun he carried boomed, and half a tree trunk was blown away. The Kiowa hugged the ground.

"What was that?" Boytale asked.

"He must have one of those guns with the two barrels," Lone Wolf replied. "They shoot many small balls. I've seen them cut a man in half before."

"Aren't we going to charge him?" High Forehead demanded.

"You charge him," Lone Wolf said. "After he has scattered your body all over the trees, he'll have that many less bullets for the rest of us."

"What do want to do?" Bear Mountain asked.

"We have to get closer. Maybe we can put an arrow into him. He's trapped between us and the others."

"He moves!" High Forehead called.

The white man got to his feet holding the gun before him. He backed slowly away, never losing sight of any of the Kiowa. Lone Wolf signaled part of the men to circle around to one side. He indicated for the rest to circle the opposite way.

Boytale crept through the grass, using trees when possible for cover. They meant to encircle their prey, using the warriors who killed the second man to close the trap. If they could get him away from the trees, he could be easily shot down. Slowly they closed, pushing the man into the open.

Suddenly, the white man pivoted and let loose with his gun. Kiowa behind him scattered like quail. The white man ducked behind a slender tree long enough to reload. Then, taking advantage of the momentary panic by the Indians, he took off for the farm. He ran less than twenty yards, then he swung around and leveled the gun at Lone Wolf.

The war chief stopped and raised his hand. Those with him also stopped. Boytale continued his movement, creeping closer and closer to the white man. He had his tomahawk ready to strike. His heart and mind were prepared for combat.

The gun had two huge holes in the ends of equally large barrels, and now they pointed directly at him. The weapon was frightening enough, but what really scared the young Kiowa was the look in the white man's eyes. There was anger and resolution, but no fear. He would kill Boytale and as many more as he could before dying.

The white man continued his slow journey to safety. The Kiowa tried again to get behind him, but each time, he pointed the gun at whoever moved his way. One warrior raised his bow. The white man aimed at him and fired in one smooth movement. The warrior screamed and fell, writhing on the ground. The white man then swung the gun in the opposite direction. Kiowa disappeared into the grass and brush. The second barrel fired.

Running quickly through the grass, the white man opened the gun, tossed out the spent shells, and reloaded. Then he stopped and faced the Indians again.

Boytale was frustrated. Already two of the men they chased were dead, and this third man constantly faced them down. How was he to count coup? Angrily, he gained his feet and headed toward the white man. The massive barrels swung his way, and he heard the hammers click back. The white man slowly shook his head and moved away.

Shouting came from the farm, and the white man answered. The Kiowa were forced to seek cover as bullets filled the air around them. The white man turned on his heel and sprinted for the farmhouse. Boytale watched him run inside one of the buildings.

Lone Wolf stood and quietly regarded the farm. "Let's get our horses," he said. "There is still more of the fight left for us."

Disappointment wasn't a strong enough word for the way Boytale felt. Twice he'd been cheated of coups. Worse, his cousin now had two major coups to recount at the campfires. Turning, he trudged back through the grass to his horse.

Lone Wolf led his warriors west, then north, staying

well clear of the agency area. They rode through a series of low hills until they reached the crest of a small valley. A house stood on the other side, atop the ridge. Warriors covered the area in front of the house. Lone Wolf and his men watched many go in and come back out, arms laden with brightly colored objects.

"Maybe that is where we the blankets," Lone Wolf said.

He trotted his horse into the valley and up the far slope. Stopping near the house, he asked what was going on.

"This is the place where we trade buffalo hides for goods," a Comanche said. "Now we don't have to trade. Just take what you want."

"What about the soldiers?"

The Comanche jutted his chin south. "Down there, at the bottom. Some are closer, but they are few, and we're out of range."

Lone Wolf dismounted. "Then let's take a look."

The other warriors climbed off their horses and followed the Kiowa war chief into the store. The place was a shambles, with broken dishes scattered over the floor and other trade goods dumped out of boxes. Cloth was strung across the store, ripped or slashed off when each warrior had all he wanted. Smashed food containers oozed their contents over the counter and onto the floor.

As Boytale stared around him in awe, a warrior threw a black iron kettle through the only unbroken window. The glass shattered, showering the floor and ground with razor-sharp pieces. The pot landed outside with a hollow bong that reminded Boytale of the bells in the *padres'* lodge.

He paused a moment. How long had it been since he'd thought of that? He remembered those strange men in brown robes—white-eye shamans, priests to the god of the whites, who lived in a large house made of mud. They rang bells, black like the kettle, and people came to their house. Had he gone? He shook his head. That was too long ago, before he was Kiowa, before he was of the People.

Boytale rummaged through what remained, careful to avoid the occasional flying pot or trade rifle. He found several blankets on the counter. They were covered in molasses from a shattered jug on the floor. He picked up the top one, tossed it away, and took the two beneath.

He jumped the counter. This area was as big a mess as the rest of the store. Drawers had been pulled out, their contents piled on the counter or floor, and the shelves were empty. He was disappointed. It seemed everything worth having was gone.

Then he saw it. Directly under one of the molasses-covered blankets was a closed drawer, evidently overlooked. Boytale grinned as he slid it open, hoping for a new knife or maybe even a pistol. What he saw was another Indian staring back at him. His hair was black and worn like a Kiowa warrior's. He had a pointed chin and high cheekbones painted with red stripes. Dark brown eyes looked directly into Boytale's, unblinking.

He slammed the drawer shut. What sort of magic was this that a warrior was kept in a drawer? Had the whites a new weapon unknown to the Kiowa, unknown to all Plains Indians?

He slowly inched the drawer open again. The more it opened, the more he saw of the other Indian's face. He stared at the image. There was something familiar. . . .

Boytale raised his hand. So did the other.

He touched his face. So did the other.

Then he laughed and opened the drawer wide, reaching in and pulling out a large handheld mirror.

This was the first time he'd ever seen his whole face at one time. The tiny pieces of mirror they used to apply paint only showed an eye here, a cheek there, part of the hair, a glimpse of chin. Now he saw it all.

He admired the thin face and skin browned by years of sun. He saw why no one thought him a true-born Kiowa. He looked nothing like Lone Wolf, Bear Mountain, or his adoptive uncle, Mamanti. He was as different from the People as Tehan. Still, he liked what he saw.

He looked back in the drawer and took out three more mirrors, a treasure trove of goodwill to pass on to the women of the village. He had one for his mother, one for a favorite aunt, and one left over for a girl he'd had his eye on.

Gathering his blankets and mirrors, he cautiously made his way back through the store, then outside. He hurried back to his horse and set his burden down. Then he spread one blanket on the ground, carefully laid out the mirrors, and spread the other blanket over them.

"What did you find, Boytale?" Tehan asked.

Boytale glanced up at his cousin, who was sauntering from the ransacked store. Tehan's left hand was closed tight. "Some blankets and mirrors," Boytale replied. He nodded at Tehan's fist. "Did you find anything good?"

Tehan opened his hand and a silver cross on a delicate chain dropped, suspended on the youth's thumb. The cross sparkled and flashed in the sunlight and swung with a gentle motion.

Boytale was dumbfounded. "Where did you find that?"

"Where no one else looked," Tehan said, nonchalantly. "Too many of the others are in a hurry, but like fresh honey, you have to search for treasure."

Boytale folded his blankets, making sure each mirror was sandwiched between material. "Are you going to wear it?"

"I don't know," Tehan answered with a shrug. "Maybe."

As Boytale lifted his bundle, a warrior ran from the store trailing scarlet ribbon. He tied one end to his horse's tail, mounted, and galloped off into the valley, the ribbon streaming behind him. Another scout appeared carrying brightly colored cloth covered with small yellow flowers. He mounted, holding one end of the cloth, and tossed the rest in the air. Then he kicked his pony into a gallop and charged after his fellow warrior, the cloth fluttering and intertwining with the ribbon.

Boytale laughed as more Indians tied yards of ribbon and cloth to their horses' manes and tails. Then they pranced the animals in tight circles, the streamers flashing gaily in the sunlight. He pulled his rawhide rope loose and tied the blankets behind his saddle.

"This *is* fun," he said.

"What else would you expect?" Tehan asked. "We're Kiowa warriors. This is what we're meant to do." He grinned. "And this is just the beginning. Soon we'll take the fight to the soldiers. Then the real fun begins."

A sudden flurry of shots came from below the summit, and warriors scrambled for cover. Lone Wolf and Bear Mountain ran for the edge of the hill. Tehan looked at Boytale, whooped loudly, and followed them. Boytale decided that he wouldn't pass up another opportunity for war honors. He grabbed his tomahawk and gave chase.

The four Kiowa slowed at the edge of the valley and looked down. Below them, soldiers ran from rock to rock, slowly making their way up. As one group hurried to a new location, their comrades fired rifles and pistols up the hill. The pistols were still hopelessly out of range, but several rifle rounds came close enough to make Boytale uncomfortable.

"Do we fight?" Bear Mountain asked.

Lone Wolf shook his head. "Not now. It will be dark soon. Let's ride to Poor Buffalo's camp and make sure our families are safe. Tomorrow we'll come back."

The Kiowa ran to their mounts. As Lone Wolf climbed into the saddle, he ordered his warriors to hurry and leave. Kiowa poured out of the store, carrying what they could. They quickly mounted and galloped off as a group, leaving the Comanche, Wichita, and others behind.

They kept to the high ground as long as possible, giving the forest where the soldiers had hidden a wide berth. Then they forded the Washita and raced for Poor Buffalo's village.

Just outside the campsite, they stopped long enough to paint their faces black, the sign of victory in combat. Then they entered the village slowly, with dignity. The two scalps taken near the farm were prominently displayed. There would be a scalp dance that night to honor the warriors for their achievements. Coup stories, both old and new, would be recounted as each warrior talked of his part in the fight against the buffalo soldiers.

Boytale didn't feel much like dancing. He'd participated in virtually nothing that had happened. His coups were on blankets and mirrors. He'd only faced the one man, and that one got away. Suddenly, the mirrors seemed a small thing. He was never going to get the chance to prove himself more than just a Mexican captive. He blindly followed the other warriors until Lone Wolf drew aside and he was allowed to ride to his parents' lodge.

They ate their evening meal in silence, neither of his parents pressing him for details of the fight. His mother had exclaimed with delight when he presented her with the mirror, but his father just gazed at him.

Boytale had no idea what the man was thinking. Was he disappointed that this captive he had taken in as his own could offer nothing more than wool and glass? Did he wish Tehan was his son? The more Boytale brooded, the darker his mood became. Finally, wordlessly, he walked out of the tipi and into the night.

"Boytale," Tehan called from the darkness.

He pretended not to hear. The last thing he wanted was to hear of his cousin's accomplishments with his silver necklace and coup.

"Boytale, wait!"

Boytale stopped and Tehan jogged to his side. "Say, cousin, you going to the dance?"

"No."

"I thought not. Me neither."

Surprised, Boytale looked at Tehan with arched eyebrows.

The redhead nodded. "That's right. Look, why should we dance when we have no scalps? Sure, I've got one from the other day and I counted coup on those white men—but will that get me a wife?"

Boytale shrugged. "So, what do you want to do?"

"Let's go back to Big Red Meat's camp."

"What?"

Tehan leaned closer. "I heard some of the older men talking to the Comanche. Big Red Meat means to go back and get his lodges, buffalo skins, and the meat we left behind."

"What about the soldiers?"

"What will buffalo soldiers do with a tipi? What does the agency man want with our robes, clothes, and meat? He has plenty. You saw the store. Besides, if anyone is in the camp, we have another chance for a scalp."

Boytale nodded. It made sense. The whites had never had any interest in their lodges. All they wanted were buffalo skins and other pelts. "I'll go," he said. "When do we leave?"

"Soon. Go ahead and get ready. That way they can't leave us behind."

Boytale hurried home and saddled his horse. He and Tehan waited at the edge of the campsite until Lone Wolf came by with a small party of warriors. The Kiowa left Poor Buffalo's camp and joined a larger party of Comanche, following single file until they reached the Washita. Then they crossed in pairs. On the other side, they eased through the trees.

Boytale saw bright light ahead of them, and as they broke into the clear, the reason became painfully apparent. Big Red Meat's camp was engulfed in flame. Every tipi, meat rack, and robe burned where it had been stacked and set alight by the soldiers.

Many of the men groaned at the loss of their trophies, medicine shields, and spare bows and arrows. Boytale was sickened to think that everything he owned, except for what he wore, was gone. He was also angry.

Sounds came from upstream. Soldiers walked through the trees and bushes looking for berries and roots.

Lone Wolf slid his rifle from its scabbard and cocked it. The others followed suit, and the war party rode silently forward. The war chief fired at the first shape to emerge from the darkness. Screaming, the man dropped to the ground. The others with him fired back, but their shots went wild, since their targets were hidden by the darkness.

Boytale saw movement and fired his trade rifle. No shouting or yelling followed the shot, but there was a sound of running feet going through the brush.

"Let's go get them!" a Comanche shouted. "We'll make them pay for burning our homes."

Lone Wolf put the rifle away. "The Comanche can chase black soldiers into a black night if they wish. The Kiowa want nothing to do with an ambush—especially if we're the ones being ambushed." He turned his mount. "I think I got one, Bear Mountain."

"Perhaps," the giant Kiowa replied, "but I'm not going to check."

The war chief laughed. "Neither am I. Tomorrow we'll ride back to the agency and see if there is still a fight left."

Boytale felt good. Only he and Lone Wolf had fired on the enemy. It wasn't a scalp, but it would make a pretty good story, and sometimes that was enough.

Seventeen

Boytale awoke to a clear morning with crisp air that reminded him the time of the green grass was coming to an end. The leaves, yellow and frail, would fall from the trees, to be swept away by a wind turned bitterly cold. Winter was approaching—the hungry time, the time of crying babies.

But this morning soon warmed under a bright sun, and as he stretched sleep-tightened muscles, Boytale shuddered as though shaking off the hard times to come. He gazed back toward the agency, seeing nothing but clear sky, nothing to mark the burning of Big Red Meat's camp. He'd hoped for a sign, at least a smudge of smoke staining the sky, to fuel his anger against the whites.

His hope was in vain. The bright blue sky was free of clouds; the air was filled with birdcalls and the sounds of the Kiowa stirring around him. He felt good, happy to be a part of these people at this place. He returned to the tipi and retrieved his paints, then headed for the creek.

Boytale bathed in icy water, taking care to wash his hair and to remove all the old paint from his skin. Shivering, he moved into the sunlight, basking until he was dry and his skin free of chill bumps. Then he set out his paints and picked up the large mirror he'd found at the store.

He closely examined his face, looking for any hair that must be plucked out to maintain the clean features prided by the Kiowa warriors. Unlike his fellow tribesmen, Boytale's Mexican heritage had given him a full beard, but through constant removal, virtually all his facial hair was gone.

Regarding the colors before him, he pondered on what he could do to make his face particularly fearsome. Lone Wolf painted his face like the wolf. Others looked like mountain lions or bobcats. Some took the image of their medicine spirits—owls, buffalo, crows, and bears. Still others looked like they imagined the enemy to look after battle, bloodied, slashed with scarlet. But Boytale had another idea. He wanted to cause the soldiers to hesitate, to allow him to strike while they watched.

He dipped his fingers in the white paint and covered his face from ear to ear and forehead to chin. Then he applied black lines where his eyebrows had once grown. He drew another line across his upper lip, then one on each side of his face, along the chin line. After brushing his hair with a porcupine tail, he dipped into the red, painting small clusters of hair until his head was covered by a dark vermillion mane. He let the hair hang loose as Tehan had done, and looked at himself in the mirror.

What could cause a soldier to pause, to hesitate to shoot? What was more frightening than being attacked by an Indian? As he gazed at his white face with painted on eyebrows, mustache, and beard, Boytale knew the answer.

He packed his things away, dressed quickly, and walked back into Poor Buffalo's camp. He noted the stares and reactions of the people around him, and his chest swelled with pride. Tehan stopped before him, red curls loose to the wind, and stared. "Well, cousin," he said with a smile, "today they have two white men to shoot at."

Boytale grinned wickedly and made his way to the captured mare. He saddled her quickly and mounted.

He wore only a breechclout and leggings today, forgoing the war shirt. His bow and arrows were slung across his back, the trade rifle cradled in his arm. His wore his knife and tomahawk on his waist. Clean moccasins covered his feet.

Boytale joined the other men, including Poor Buffalo and his warriors. They were all eager to return to the agency for more goods or a fight, happy to entertain either option. The warriors were in high spirits as they sat astride their painted and decorated ponies. They joked and laughed and predicted the great feats they'd accomplish during the day. The horses danced and fidgeted, tossing their heads and blowing through their lips as though to say they were ready for a good fight, too.

Tehan and Mamanti rode up, both covered in Owl Prophet medicine. Tehan stopped next to Boytale, but the elder continued, joining the chiefs and old men.

Lone Wolf and Bear Mountain were the last to arrive. As principal war chief for all the Kiowa, Lone Wolf assumed leadership of the party. He rode to the front and started toward the agency.

The war party followed their leader single file through the trees and across the river. They rode through the ruined Comanche camp, many expressing dismay over the destruction and the spoiled meat. Pale smoke drifted from still-smoldering hides and lodge poles. Then they swung north, crossed to the hills, and returned to the site of the store.

Indians were already in the place, taking what they could, destroying the rest. Most were Caddo and Wichita, but a few Comanche and Delaware were among them. Poor Buffalo needed no invitation to participate. He and his men quickly dismounted and ran into the store. Lone Wolf hung back, looking down the hill at the agency below. Boytale had no wish to try to force his way back into the store, so he trailed the war chief to the edge of the hill.

Below them, the buffalo soldiers had dug a long line of holes in the ground. Their horses were in the corral where Boytale and the others had hidden the day before. The agency man stood outside his lodge, along with the white soldiers and some women and children. All were watching the Indians on the hill. What was left of Big Red Meat's camp was clearly visible, as was the camp of the Penateka.

Movement caught Boytale's eye, and he looked down the hill just as a soldier broke cover and ran to a pile of rocks. He tapped Lone Wolf on the arm and pointed. Another soldier made a dash for the safety of the rocks.

"Come," Lone Wolf said.

They turned away and rode back to the main party. Lone Wolf dismounted.

"Soldiers are coming up the hill," he said.

A volley of shots startled Boytale. The Indians in the store came flying out through the doors and broken windows.

"Get ready for a fight!" Lone Wolf shouted.

The warriors grabbed rifles and bows and arrows.

"What are you doing?" a voice called.

Boytale turned and stared as a fat Comanche rode up from the far side of the store on a large gray horse, doubtless the only animal that could carry his bulk.

"You better get over here, Chee-na-bony," Lone

Wolf called. "You're going to get shot. The buffalo soldiers are over there."

"Ha," the Comanche returned. "Get back on your horses. I saw them earlier. They are too far away to hit anyone. They just want to see you run like frightened children."

Another volley of fire brought rounds close to the Indians. Dirt sprayed into the air around Chee-na-bony's mount.

"See?" Lone Wolf called. "They moved!"

Chee-na-bony turned his mount and clearly saw the soldiers nearing the crest of the hill. His eyes widened. The situation *had* changed. As he wheeled his pony, a rifle cracked and a bullet hit him in the back of the head. Killed instantly, the Comanche chief tumbled from his horse.

"Let's get them!" a Comanche warrior screamed.

"Wait!" shouted Buffalo Good, a Wichita chief. "There has been enough killing. Now we must go."

"That's easy for you to say, Wichita," a Comanche sneered, "but that's not your chief lying out there."

"I would like to fight," Buffalo Good countered, "but you have forgotten the white man's singing wire. Already there may be more troops coming. We must leave now before we are trapped."

Lone Wolf nodded. "I agree. We have nothing to gain by fighting here. We will go downstream to Poor Buffalo's camp, then back to the plains."

"We will ride upstream," Buffalo Good said. "The soldiers cannot chase all of us."

The Kiowa galloped away, accompanied by most of the Comanche warriors. They swung wide of any area that may have contained soldiers, and soon reached Poor Buffalo's camp.

Poor Buffalo shouted orders, and a hurried evacuation took place. In less than an hour, the lodges were struck and travois packed and the village was on the move.

Lone Wolf took his warriors and rode back toward the agency. They stopped near Big Red Meat's camp and set fire to the grass. As the flames rose, the warriors followed Poor Buffalo's people. Bear Mountain, Boytale, and Tehan hung back to serve as a rear guard.

"What are they doing over there?" Tehan asked.

Boytale stared through the flames and heat waves. Soldiers ran about on the other side, some carrying torches.

"It looks like they are setting fire to the grass, too."

"That's right," Bear Mountain said. "When their fire meets ours, they will both go out."

"Isn't that bad?" Boytale asked.

Bear Mountain nodded. "Normally." He grinned. "But the soldiers did not check the wind."

The breeze that blew at the warriors' backs fanned the flames higher. On the other side, it drove the fire directly at the agency. Soldiers ran to and fro, then bolted away.

Bear Mountain laughed and turned his horse. "It is a good day when the soldiers do our work for us."

Eighteen

In the days since leaving Camp Supply, the troops of Nelson Miles's expeditionary force had traveled over land as desolate as any Rambling had ever seen. An endless expanse of waving, thigh-high grass did nothing to alter his opinion that this place called Indian Territory was unfit for man or beast.

Yet life was abundant. Each night the cooks prepared antelope, turkey, rabbit, quail, or other game. In fact, the only thing the Indian Territory lacked was Indians.

"It seems to me," observed First Sergeant Mitchell, "that the red man is as slippery as the leprechaun. He'll not be seen unless he takes a notion to let it happen."

But there'll be no gold at the end of that rainbow, Rambling thought sourly. *Just an arrow or a hatchet to the head.*

Death was nothing new to the men of the Fifth Infantry. There were enough veterans of the Civil War and past Indian fights to bring any starry-eyed new recruit to earth, but capture was another matter.

"I've heard tell," Hitchcock said during what was turning into a nightly poker game, "that the Comanches is the worst."

Larsen shrugged. "Maybe, but there's them that says it's the Cheyennes."

"They're all bad," Ketzel said, tossing cards onto the blanket. "Gimme two."

Bailey shifted nervously. "Can we talk about somethin' else? I got the willies."

"Not if the Comanches get to you, you won't," Hitchcock said with a laugh.

Rambling dealt cards to Ketzel, then himself. "You know, if you're caught during a battle, they'll probably just kill you outright. Maybe not even take your hair."

Hitchcock nodded. "That's true, but if they carry your sorry ass off . . ."

"Oh, hell!" Larsen cried. "I don't *even* want to think on it. Jesus, they cut off your nose, ears, fingers, whatever they fancy."

"They rip open your belly," Ketzel said, folding his hand. "Rip it open, and let your guts spill out. They say maggots can eat most of 'em up before you die." He shuddered. "Can you imagine it? Layin' there ripped to hell and back, holding your guts, and fighting off flies, ants, buzzards, and such." He shook his head.

"The worst is the balls," Hitchcock said softly.

Rambling nodded. "Amen to that, brother."

"The balls?" Bailey said, his voice shrill.

Hitchcock leaned forward. "Now this depends on who catches ya. See, you're all staked to the ground buck naked, so you can't do shit. There's them that will just cut a slit in the sack and *snik*"—he made a quick cutting motion—"you're down to one nut." He straightened. "And then there's others who'll just whack the whole package and stuff your pecker and balls right into your screaming mouth."

Bailey clapped his hands over his mouth.

"Yessir," Hitchcock continued, "I reckon it's something a sodomite might enjoy, but not this ol' boy."

Ketzel chuckled at Bailey's horror. "Tell him 'bout the squaws, Seth."

Hitchcock gazed at Bailey, eyes wide. "You ain't heard about the squaws?"

Bailey shook his head. "I don't want to neither."

"Horseshit, Dennis. You got to know about the enemy, son."

"No, I don't!" Bailey covered his ears. "No, I don't!"

Hitchcock pulled Bailey's hands down. "You listen to me! We're at war, and every redskin you see is the enemy—man, woman, or child. There ain't a one that wouldn't kill you at the drop of a hat. You got to be the same." He released Bailey and leaned back. "Some of these asshole officers think Injuns is mean and stupid, like buffalo. Well, he ain't. He's mean and *smart*. Any time you see one, you think about a wounded grizzly bear. You forget that, and you are dead."

The men in the tent fell silent, the game forgotten, each lost in thoughts of what the next days or weeks might bring. Finally, Bailey broke the silence.

"Seth?" he asked, quietly.

Hitchcock glanced up. "Yeah?"

"Them squaws, they all that bad?"

Hitchcock nodded. "Yeah, they're that bad. They take a man and skin him alive, taking a lot of time with his manhood. When they're mostly done, they'll take two rocks and *POW!*" He slapped his hands together, the explosive clap making the others jump. "Nothing left but grape jam."

"That's it!" Bailey cried, throwing his hands up. "I'm gettin' outta here."

"But what about the game?" Larsen asked.

"The hell with it! You can take the cards, money, and your goddamn Injuns, and just shove 'em up your butt." Bailey stormed from the tent.

"What'd I say?" Larsen asked. He looked at Rambling. "Did I do something wrong?"

"No, Bill. I guess he just didn't care for the conversation."

"I wonder," Hitchcock said, "if it has anything to with that Injun whore he humped back at Supply. He said she didn't say two words to him the whole night, just played with his balls."

"There they go," Larsen announced.

Rambling glanced to the front. In an increasingly dense cloud of dust, a long column of riders moved away from the command.

"It's like I said," Larsen continued. "Now we're hooked up with the scouts, things're going to start hopping. I heard Baldwin had a run-in with a shitpotful of Indians. His scouts think they were Cheyennes. Anyway, he killed one."

"One?" Bailey asked. "All them soldiers and sharpshooters and they got just one?"

"Mr. Bailey," Mitchell called from the head of the company column.

"Yes, sir, First Sergeant."

"Have ye ever faced the red man in battle?"

"No, sir."

"Then you cannot appreciate the difficulties. The Indian and his pony are as one. Shooting them is like shooting spooks."

"C'mon, First Sergeant, they're just Injuns. It ain't like—"

"And I beg to differ," Mitchell interrupted. "We had one bunch that came into our camp in the dead o' night and stole forty-three horses from under the noses of the guards. They can't be heard, and they come from downwind, so the horses can't smell 'em. I'll tell ye true, lads, I'd just as soon tangle with the Rebs again."

The Company I men marched silently, sobered by Mitchell's confession. Rambling was shaken. The first sergeant had always seemed invulnerable, impervious to the ways of man and nature, a bastion of flesh and bone that the company could hide behind. Those who did not admire him, feared him. It seemed almost a betrayal that he should be afraid of anything.

"Sweet Jesus," Ketzel muttered. "If they can steal that many horses, what's to stop them from cuttin' our throats?"

"Shut up, Gary!" Hitchcock snapped. "We got enough worries with the heat and all, without that kind of talk. When the time comes, we'll fight. Understand? Till then, just use that cakehole of yours to eat with."

Boytale had never seen the Kiowa in such a state. The chiefs argued among themselves about their next course of action. Some wanted to go back to the fort and surrender, but Lone Wolf insisted the soldiers were coming after them and that they would be cut down. Mamanti said the Owl had told him there was safe passage to Elk Creek, but they must leave immediately.

Finally, they reached a compromise. The bands would set out for Elk Creek. Then those who wanted to return could do so, taking a different route back, and claim they had never left the reservation.

They struck camp and quickly loaded the travois.

With the chiefs in the lead and warriors riding the flanks, the Kiowa rode upstream along the Washita.

Boytale gazed back down the trail. The sun was setting, and the land behind them grew dim. "I still don't see any dust," he said to Tehan.

The redhead nodded. "I thought as much. Those soldiers weren't going to chase us. We're having to do this for nothing." He grunted. "It's an insult to a warrior to run like a whipped dog."

Boytale kicked the mare into a lope. "Come on, Tehan, I have an idea."

They caught up to the chiefs and fell in beside Lone Wolf. The war chief gazed at the pair, his expression a mixture of surprise and irritation.

Boytale looked at Tehan, then back to Lone Wolf. "We haven't seen any sign of the soldiers," he said.

"Doesn't mean they're not there," Lone Wolf grumbled.

"That's right. We want to ride our back trail and see if we can find them."

"Nonsense. You boys have no need to find the enemy. They will find us soon enough."

"We think the soldiers are staying far behind, and letting scouting parties follow us. The moon is already rising, and it's nearly full. By the time the sun goes down, they could be close enough to attack. What better time? Right, Tehan?"

Tehan stared blankly at Boytale, then looked at the war chief and nodded vigorously.

Lone Wolf looked from one youth to the other. "So, what is this plan you have?"

Boytale answered. "We ride until the moon is directly overhead. If we have not found the enemy, we return."

"We will also return if we find him," Tehan added with a grin. "Only much faster."

Lone Wolf shook his head. "It is a waste of time. You have seen nothing."

"But as you said," Boytale countered, "just because it isn't seen, it doesn't mean it isn't there."

Behind them, Bear Mountain chuckled. "It seems that you have backed into your own lance, Lone Wolf."

The war chief smiled. "It is a sad day when children use an old man's words against him." He waved them off. "Go. Chase your soldiers."

"Do you think this is a good idea?" Mamanti asked.

"Let them go, Owl Prophet. At least they're headed in the right direction—toward the enemy."

Boytale grinned at Tehan, and the two wheeled their horses.

"Wait!" Lone Wolf shouted. When he had their attention, he continued. "Coming back, follow this river until it turns north. Then ride west. There lie the headwaters of Elk Creek."

With war whoops, the youths kicked their mounts into a gallop. They charged past the Kiowa caravan and east into the fading light.

Nineteen

The pair slowed to an easy lope when they could no longer see their tribesmen. Boytale's spirits were particularly high since this adventure was his idea. He'd taken great pleasure in seeing his cousin's face go from confusion to understanding to admiration as he grasped Boytale's intentions.

"So, what made you decide to do this?" Tehan asked.

Boytale shrugged. "I was bored, tired of always running away." He looked at Tehan. "You were no happier."

"That's true." Tehan slowed his mount to a walk. "What bothers me most is that we have had no real taste of battle. Look at what happened at the agency. They shoot a little, we shoot a little. Then we leave. What has happened to the fights our grandfathers talk about? What will we get to tell *our* children?"

What Tehan said was true. Boytale had seen his people change with the coming of the white man. More and more trade goods were used instead of those that were handmade. Some hunted buffalo for the hides, trading them for whiskey and guns.

He remembered a Comanchero with his wagon and its giant wheels. This man was a Mexican, but he spoke the People's tongue and that of the Comanche.

He carried knives and tomahawks and metal points for lances and arrows. He had pots of brass and large black kettles. Beads and colored feathers hung from the sides of the wagon. One side was draped with red and black woolen blankets. Sacks of coffee were available, and cones of hard, brown sugar. For those willing to pay the price, white sugar was offered.

And buried beneath it all was the whiskey.

The women gathered around his wagon, giggling like children and picking out what they wanted. The chiefs and old men laid blankets on the ground and offered the pipe to the trader. After all had smoked, the haggling began.

Before long, the Comanchero opened his store of whiskey. As the bottles were passed around, the haggling lessened until a price was finally agreed upon. Then the men staggered off and returned with beaver pelts, wolf skins, buffalo hides, and the fur from bobcats, otters, and rabbits. Each piled his offering next to the wagon and took his goods away. When all the trading was done, more whiskey appeared, and the men drank themselves unconscious.

Sometime during the night, the trader packed his wagon and quietly drove away. He slowly rolled past the prostrate Kiowa like a warrior leaving the scene of slaughter.

Boytale thought the Comanchero was victorious. He had come, traded his goods, and left the men helpless. Worse, the People had become dependent on what was offered. Some even complained that they could not live without the new pots, steel needles, and glass beads. Slowly, the People were changing, and they didn't even notice.

"What's that scowl?" Tehan said. "Are you mad at me?"

Reverie broken, Boytale shook his head. "I'm mad

at everyone. The white man has bought the Kiowa spirit with beads and whiskey."

"You sound like my father."

"Well, maybe he's right."

"Perhaps," Tehan replied, then changed the subject. "It's almost dark. Do you want to keep riding by the river?"

"I don't know. Maybe we should go out there a little way," he said, waving at an area off the path. "If the soldiers are following the trail, they won't see us over there."

"That's what I was thinking. You remember those bluffs we passed?"

Boytale nodded.

"We could just sit up there and wait. With this moon, we'd see anyone who passed by."

"That's a good idea," Boytale said, glad for the opportunity to dismount.

They prodded their horses back into a ground-eating lope. Soon tall, black shapes emerged from the gloom. Tehan in the lead, they rode up the back side of a butte and across its top until they could see the river below. Moonlight sparkled off its waters.

Tehan reined to a stop and climbed off his horse. "This looks like a good spot." He shivered as a northerly wind blew across the plateau. "I'm going to get my blanket."

The same breeze chilled Boytale and, as he dismounted, he pulled his blanket free, draping it around his shoulders.

They walked to the rim and sat, facing the river. The sky was black to the east, stars sparkling, the moon a bright white disc.

"We'll have a full moon in a couple of days," Boytale observed.

Tehan glanced up. "Clear skies and a full moon. Good traveling weather."

The sky overhead changed to a deep blue. Farther to the west, it still carried a bit of red and pink light as the sun lost its battle against night. Thin clouds drifted by, pushed by the north wind.

The breeze struck them full in the face, slipping past the edges of the blankets to find unprotected skin.

"I wish that wind would change direction," Tehan complained.

"Soon it will carry snow."

"But then we'll be in a warm tipi in a warm canyon."

The temperature continued to fall as the night wore on. More clouds flew by, but always high and thin. Sitting where they were, they could see shadows drift across the land.

Boytale wanted to build a fire, but knew better. Any flame could be seen for miles, and given their location, they could have called no more attention to themselves if they had stood and shouted.

As the hours passed, the moon continued its passage across the sky. Boytale and Tehan seemed to have the prairie to themselves. Only the howls of the coyotes and wolves, along with the occasional scream of a wildcat, gave any indication of life. The trail by the river remained stubbornly empty of soldiers.

Finally, Tehan stood. "Let's go."

Boytale nodded and got to his feet.

They gathered their horses and mounted, then walked across the mesa, and wound their way down its back. Swinging around the land mass, they rode to the river and followed the trail left by the passing Kiowa bands.

"How far ahead do you think they are?" Boytale asked.

"Can't be far. It was getting dark when we left. We should find them soon."

But Tehan was wrong. The boys rode through the night with no sign of a Kiowa camp. As dawn broke, they reached the place where the Washita turned north, but saw nothing other than the wide trail they followed.

With daylight, the north wind freshened, carrying heavier, lower clouds with it. Soon the sun was a pale disc in the midst of swirling, darkening clouds, but it shed enough light for the boys to move into a lope.

They rode across the flat, open land constantly scanning the horizon for some sign of their families. Finally, as they crested a low ridge, thin trails of white smoke could be seen in the distance. Urging their horses forward, the boys charged toward the encampment.

Boytale, for one, was relieved to see the tipis come into view. The cloudy day had kept the worst of the heat off him, but he was hungry and exhausted after the all night ride.

Then lightning split the sky, striking the ground so close to him that he smelled it, and with a tooth-jarring clap of thunder, the rains came.

"Rain would be nice," Larsen said as he fanned himself with his hat and leaned against a wagon wheel. "Don't you think so, Jim?"

Rambling, lying in the shade of the same vehicle, shrugged. "Hot and miserable, wet and miserable. What's the difference?"

"There's a hell of a lot of difference," De Armond growled. He stood, shoulder to the wagon's side, face bathed in sunlight. Sweat cut muddy trails through the dirt on his cheeks and neck. "When it's wet, your clothes rot, your shoes rot, your body rots. If you get chilled, you never get warm again. At least that's the way it feels. Then you got pneumonia or consumption. Bodies laying in the mud and rain bring cholera." He shuddered slightly. "Give me the heat any day. You just wait." He looked into the cloudless sky. "Won't be long before it's colder'n hell—and wet."

The column had stopped for dinner, but many of the men were sick from the heat and constant marching. Instead of eating, they sprawled under or behind the wagons, seeking respite from the sun.

"Hey, Sarge," Hitchcock called from under the wagon, "any word on when we tangle with the redskins?"

"Nah. Captain says that Baldwin's scouts cut sign of a big outfit. We're trailing them and the pony soldiers."

"Story of my life," Hitchcock complained. "Always did show up to supper too late to eat."

First Sergeant Mitchell stepped around the tail of the wagon and regarded his troops. "My, oh, my. Are we havin' a loverly tea?" He placed his fists on his hips. "Well, bloody tea time's over. Gather yer gear and make yer way to the water wagons."

De Armond straightened and shrugged his yoke back into place. "You heard the first sergeant. Move out!"

Rambling groaned and got to his feet. He picked up his yoke and slid it onto already sore shoulders. Then he took his canteen, uncorked it, and emptied what remained of the tepid, metallic tasting water over his head. He shivered with delight as the liquid coursed down the collar of his uniform coat. Following his squad, he waited his turn at the water wagon quietly. Once there, he refilled the canteen, took a deep drink, and topped off the container.

He was in the best shape of his life, and it was with no little pride that he joined his company formation. He had managed to endure mile upon mile of marching in intense heat and discomfort. Each night he rolled into bed exhausted, but by the next morning, he was ready to start again. Rambling finally felt like a soldier, but he knew his true test would come in battle.

Boytale and Tehan dashed through the sudden downpour and into the campsite. The Kiowa had been caught by surprise by the storm. Half-erected tipis were abandoned as the women and children grabbed buffalo robes and hid under them. The men turned their backs to the driving sheets of rain, covering their heads with their blankets.

Tehan jumped from his horse. He pulled off his saddle and blanket, draped the cloth over his head, and rushed to join the other warriors. Boytale did the same, flinching and ducking whenever lightning struck or thunder exploded overhead. Half-blinded by the rain, he stumbled to where the men waited, slipping several times in the mud.

Standing next to Tehan, he glanced up and saw Lone Wolf looking at him. The war chief raised a single eyebrow in query. Boytale shook his head, and Lone Wolf nodded before retreating into the folds of his blanket.

The storm continued to lash the Kiowa with rain and brisk winds. Thunder crackled and boomed from all directions while the air was filled with the smell of lightning. Ground strikes hit the earth, and the accompanying thunderclaps threatened to suck the wind out of lungs.

Boytale was wet, miserable, and frightened. He wanted nothing more than for the storm to go away. He peeked at Mamanti, huddled against the rain. Why had the Owl Prophet not foretold this storm? If things could befall the People and he did not know, what other surprises awaited the Kiowa?

How long the squall lasted, Boytale couldn't guess, but eventually the rain slowed and settled to a wind-blown mist. Thunder rumbled in the distance like some great animal held at bay growling its frustration.

The chiefs lowered their blankets and started shouting orders for the travois to be repacked lest the storm intensify. Shivering men, women, and children scrambled out from under robes, gathering tipi covers and personal items. They wasted no time in packing and securing their bundles.

The chiefs took the lead again, traveling upstream toward drier ground. Warriors fanned out beside the caravan, trying to find warmth from wet blankets and their mounts. Boytale's teeth chattered as he shifted his sodden blanket over his shoulders, sagging under the weight of soaked wool. Icy gusts chilled the mist and drove the cold deep into his bones, warning him of the coming of winter.

After a few miles, the mist lifted, and the black-bottomed rain clouds began to dissipate. The wind eased and the air warmed, though the sun was invisible in the slate-colored sky. Boytale lowered his blanket, draping it across the mare's back.

As the ground underfoot became drier, the pace was quickened. Scouts rode out, checking the trail before and behind them. Finally, Lone Wolf called a halt after spotting a small herd of buffalo grazing near the river. A hunt was quickly organized while the women erected the tipis.

No pretense at stealth was made. The warriors charged into the buffalo shooting arrows and stabbing with lances. Animal after animal fell until the terrified buffalo managed to stampede far enough away to escape further pursuit.

While the women butchered the kill, Lone Wolf and Mamanti called a council meeting to decide what to do next. The chiefs sat around a large fire, split into two groups. Satanta took up the cause of the peace faction.

He stood and regarded his peers. "I have no love of the white man," he began. "They took me from my people and put me in their prison, which is a cave with iron bars. My trapped spirit yearned for the freedom of our lands, and I became sickened. I called on the man from Washington and told him I must leave his prison or I would soon die."

He shifted his blanket, then dropped it to the ground. "Bah! That thing is useless."

Satanta then strode close to the fire, letting its heat warm him and dry out his clothes.

"Washington let me go," he continued, "but not before making me promise to never fight against the whites again. If they find me here, it will go hard with me, and I will go back to the prison and my death. So I want to return to the fort they call Sill and tell Striking Eagle that I have not taken the war road. Big Tree has told me he feels the same. For both of us, the war road only leads to a slow death."

"Satanta," Lone Wolf said, "what makes you think the white man will not imprison you anyway? Stay out here, at least for a while. There are no white men to see you—none living, that is."

The chiefs chuckled at Lone Wolf's joke. Even Satanta's dour expression lightened a bit.

"What you say is true, old friend, but I must return as soon as possible. The whites believe Striking Eagle. He is their friend, and he knows that one Indian looks like another to them. If he says that the Indian they saw at the agency fight was not me, they will believe him. But if I stay away too long, no one will believe any of us."

Lone Wolf pondered Satanta's reply, trying to think of a convincing argument to make him stay. Before he could formulate his answer, a crier ran through the camp announcing the arrival of riders.

The council members rose to their feet, turned, and watched as another Kiowa chieftain named Big Bow rode into camp with his band. Big Bow was widely admired for his skills as a hunter and warrior, but he was openly skeptical of Mamanti and his powers as an Owl Prophet. On several occasions he had publically opposed the medicine man, and many were afraid to stand too close to him.

"Big Bow, welcome," called Lone Wolf. "Welcome all to our camp. Come sit with us in council." He hoped the chief's hate for the whites would overrule any personal feelings he had about Mamanti. After all, the Owl Prophet was one of the People.

The new arrival dismounted and stepped to the council fire. He rubbed his hands briskly before the flames.

"We were rained on a while ago. I still feel the chill." He turned to face the others. "I have been to Striking Eagle's camp. The whites refused me the peace paper, so I have ridden to the south and west to come here. Along the edge of the Llano I have seen many scouting parties of the soldiers, so I would not ride that way."

"Then where?" Poor Buffalo asked.

"We must ride to the Llano and hide in the canyons along its edge," Lone Wolf said. "The Kiowa have always been safe there."

"But the soldiers are there now," said Big Bow. "They are riding the trail to Palo Duro Canyon."

Lone Wolf frowned. "We can sneak by them and hide under their noses. You did."

"We are a small band," Big Bow argued. "You have many families here. I say it is best to ride downstream to a canyon that lies east of the river and wait for the soldiers to leave. Then we can go to the Llano."

"Let the vote decide," Satanta said. "We will either go to the Llano or back downstream."

After the votes were cast, criers ran through the camp announcing that the Kiowa were to ride back to the south. Lone Wolf and his faction had lost.

Preparations were brief. As the women packed the camp, two scouts were sent far to the northwest to try to find the soldier scouts. Boytale and another young warrior named Blue Shield were told to remain behind and watch for pursuers.

Tree branches were tied to the horses' tails. The bands rode away, the trailing brush obscuring their tracks. Boytale yawned mightily as he watched the people leave. His eyes burned and were blurred with tiredness. He blinked rapidly to clear his vision, then wiped away the tears. He'd had no sleep the night before, and had been caught in the storm that afternoon. Every time he tried to rest, the council moved the tribe.

"This is pretty exciting," Blue Shield said. "Don't you think so?"

Boytale stared at his companion. Blue Shield was younger than he was, with the fine features of a full-blooded Kiowa. The youth had all the eagerness of a puppy. Boytale decided he didn't like him. "No."

"Oh." Blue Shield bit his lip, then tried again. "Do you think the soldiers will show up? Do you think we'll get a chance to fight?"

Boytale rubbed his face and yawned again. "No," he replied sullenly. "We waited all night for soldiers and none came. None will come now, so we'll just sit here until the sun goes down."

Conversation lapsed into silence as the boys watched the terrain around them, Blue Shield occasionally stealing glances at Boytale. Boytale knew he'd dampened the other's spirit, but he didn't care. Maybe after a decent night's sleep. . . .

Boytale's head snapped up. He looked around wildly, confused and a little frightened. The sun rode low on the horizon, and deep shadows covered the land to the east. All traces of the storm were gone. The few remaining clouds were dark purple smudges in a crimson sky. Remembering where he was, he looked for Blue Shield, and finally saw him sitting against a nearby tree.

"I fell asleep?" he asked, voice still thick.

Blue Shield nodded.

"Why didn't you wake me?" Boytale demanded.

Blue Shield shrugged. "Why? You were right. So far, I've seen two vultures, a coyote, and, I think, an eagle. No soldiers. No Indians. No people at all. Besides, you looked very tired."

"I was," Boytale said. Then he grinned sheepishly. "Thanks."

Blue Shield smiled back. "You're welcome. I'm bored. You think we can leave now?"

Boytale nodded and stretched.

The boys gathered their blankets and saddled their horses. They rode back down the river at an easy walk.

The water, high and moving swiftly, was the color of blood.

"Who'd think so much water could come from such a short rain?" Blue Shield said.

They continued until they reached the first ford, but there the water still ran deep, crashing along in white-foam madness.

"There'll be no crossing here," Boytale observed.

"Look," Blue Shield said, pointing at the ground. "The trail goes right by here. They must have crossed further downstream."

The pair rode on to the second ford. There the streambed widened, and though the water was still deep and fast, it had slowed enough to be crossed. Boytale's horse plunged into the water, and he slid off the mare's back, hanging onto his saddle while she swam the river. Once she gained purchase on the other side, he climbed back on, and they emerged dripping and covered in red silt from the water. Stopping, he turned and watched Blue Shield ford the river. Safely across, they continued their journey to the Kiowa campsite.

Daylight was almost gone when they first saw the light of campfires. They rode among the lodges, smelling the cooking food. Tehan appeared from the gloom and waved them to a stop.

"There's another council meeting," he said. "They're talking about moving again."

Boytale groaned. "Tonight?"

"In the morning maybe. That's what the argument's about."

"We'd better go see," Boytale said as he dismounted. He turned to Blue Shield. "You want to come?"

The other shook his head. "I'm going to bed."

Boytale waved good night, and he and Tehan made

their way to the council meeting. Big Bow stood near the fire.

"There is no reason to go to the Llano," he argued. "We know the soldiers are there. There may be many soldiers behind us from the agency or the fort. Here we are safe." He moved back to the circle and sat.

Poor Buffalo rose. "I agree. We have our families to think of. We can wait here until the soldiers leave the Llano or get tired of looking for us. There is still enough time before the snows come to go to the canyon."

As the chief sat, a low murmur of agreement ran through the council. Then Mamanti stood. The chiefs fell silent.

"There is something that you have all forgotten," he said, walking to the fire. He stopped and raised his right hand, on which was placed the Owl—the symbol of his power, the seer of his prophecies. Mamanti noted with satisfaction that some of the chiefs averted their eyes. Only Big Bow stared at him defiantly. "I have consulted the Owl," he continued. "And it has told me that we will be safe at Palo Duro Canyon. It says that we are to camp on the Red River there, and the canyon's high walls will protect us from the whites."

Big Bow laughed. "I believe it is most remarkable that the Owl chooses now to speak. Could it not have told us earlier and saved the journey here?"

"You dare to question the power of the Owl?" Mamanti hissed. "You would dare to defy its prophecy?"

"I defy nothing," Big Bow said with a snort, "other than a medicine man with his hand in a dead bird's butt."

Several men inhaled sharply, and Boytale was shocked at Big Bow's behavior. Near the fire, Mamanti paled, then reddened sharply.

"The Owl has the power to kill you, Big Bow. *I* have the power to make you die!"

"Then do it, shaman! Show me this death that you can cause."

Mamanti raised the Owl, then paused and lowered it again. "No," he said. "I will not do it. To cause your death by magic is to forfeit my own life. I have too much to do for the People to waste myself."

Big Bow stood and waved dismissively at the medicine man. "Now you sound like that yellow Comanche who told us we would be bullet-proof when we fought the hunters." He walked around the fire, looking each chief in the eyes. "You don't need this man and his bird to tell you how to think. If he is wrong, then we are taking a huge chance with the lives of our wives and children. There are no soldiers here. We can be safe. We *are* safe."

As he spoke, Big Bow noticed that many of his peers would not return his gaze. They looked at the ground or stared into the flames or straight ahead, but virtually none in his direction. Finally, he stopped and sighed, then addressed Mamanti.

"Now I will make a prophecy, bird man. I say that these men will vote with you, and we will move to the canyons on the Llano Estacado. They will go, not because it is wise or the right thing to do. They will go because they fear that thing on your hand. I also say that I will abide by the vote, and my band will join the others. And if you are wrong, and the soldiers come, my family will die like the rest. But then . . ." He paused and stared at Mamanti. His eyes narrowed, his lips tightened into a straight, hard line. "But then, Owl Prophet," he continued, "I want to see what that owl does for you when the long knives are hot on your trail."

* * *

Lounging outside their shelter, Rambling and Larsen enjoyed an after-supper smoke. The sun was a red ball, and as it descended, the temperature dropped accordingly.

"You ever been to the desert?" Larsen asked.

Rambling shook his head.

"I have." Larsen pointed around them with his cigar. "It's a lot like this. Hot during the day, but at night it's cold. Some nights, water freezes."

"Be a bear to march through."

Larsen nodded. "There's them that says it's a type of art to live in the desert."

"Well, sir, it's not an art form I'd care to learn." Rambling stubbed the cigarette out in the dirt.

"Jim, you mind if I ask you something personal?"

"Shoot, Bill."

"When you joined up, you weren't in trouble with the law or some gal's daddy, right?"

Rambling nodded.

"So, how do you like it?"

"What?"

"Bein' in the Army. We got men here just two steps ahead of the hangman. There's swindlers, debtors, runaway husbands and sons, thieves, and all manner of men. Then you got your lifers like De Armond and Mitchell and most of the officers. But along comes you, rich, from a good family, no worries to speak of. Most of us have got to stay, but you don't."

Rambling paused a moment to marshal his thoughts. Then he rolled another cigarette to buy more time. The problem was how much to tell Larsen. He'd just as soon his real reasons weren't spread through the camp.

"Well," he started, then stopped long enough to

light the smoke. "Well, it's not that simple," he continued, shaking out the match. "Everyone has something that he has to do with his life, you know? I could have stayed in Baltimore, worked for my father, and then owned the business. But what would I have built?"

Larsen laughed. "Built? Hell, Jim, I've had to fight for everything I ever had. If it'd been given to me, I'd have taken it."

"But that's just my point. You had nothing, so everything you do have is precious. Me? I was given everything you could imagine, yet had earned none of it. Even rich boys can be poor."

"Hmm. I don't see it," Larsen said with a shake of his head, "but then again, you're smarter'n me. So, now that you're in it, think you might stay?"

"You mean reenlist? Become a lifer?"

Larsen nodded. "Yep."

"I don't know." Rambling took a drag at his cigarette and let the smoke curl out of his nose. "Never really thought about it. You?"

"This is the best life I've known," Larsen answered softly. "I eat fair, sleep warm, and get paid to do it." His voice grew stronger. "Course I ain't forgot the Masons, but out here, the lines is a little blurry. I still believe you got a mission to fulfil, but after that, I'm just not sure."

Rambling lay back, cigarette in his lips, and stared at the darkening sky. Stars peeked through the velvet. He removed the smoke and stared at its glowing end.

"As far as I'm concerned, not being sure is good enough for now. You'll do all right, Bill."

"You really think so, Jim?"

"Yes, I do."

"Thanks. You're a good friend."

Rambling didn't answer. He just lay there, watching the stars.

Twenty

Rambling spooned a bite of beans into his mouth and chewed slowly, enjoying the slightly sweet taste of molasses. It was the only difference between the beans they ate at breakfast and those offered at supper. Dinner was usually jerky, hardtack, and on good days, coffee. The rest of the time they drank water. Meals had become so routine, the beans had lost all flavor but the hint of sweetness. The jerky was bland and chewy, the hardtack bland and rocklike.

Coffee was another matter. It was always hot, black as tar, and strong. Weak sisters added water. Most of the men heaped in sugar. Occasionally, a soldier opened a can of condensed milk he'd been saving, and his whole squad would indulge in what they called *café au lait* in New Orleans—coffee with sugar and milk. Hardtack soaked in this brew became pastry.

Still others flavored their coffee with a more potent substance. The enlisted men used rotgut whiskey, its pungent smell hovering over the cup. Officers usually had brandy, which lent a heady, fruit-filled aroma that hinted at fine meals and after-dinner cigars.

That was something Rambling instantly identified with. He remembered the lavish parties at his home. Only the best families in Baltimore were invited. Champagne and wine flowed easily before the meal, which was always sumptuous. Afterward, the men retired to the library for brandy and cigars while the ladies moved to the parlor to sip sherry.

In the Army, he'd experienced the military version of the social gathering. The place was usually a local watering hole that offered feminine companionship at a price. Champagne and wine flowed as freely as before, but the meal was meager at best, nonexistent as a rule. Afterward, the men retired to gaming tables for poker and cigars. The ladies offered kisses and dances for drinks, themselves for money. The night ended with the winners and ladies pairing off for another kind of sport, while the losers bellied up to the bar to drown their sorrows.

Rambling dropped his spoon into his empty plate, picked up and drained his coffee cup, then shook it dry. He scrubbed the plate and spoon with sand and packed the dishes away in his valise.

Larsen, who'd silently watched Rambling eat, waved his coffee cup. "You're sure quiet this morning."

"What's there to talk about?" Rambling replied with a shrug. "The changing scenery? The quality of the meals?"

Larsen sipped his coffee, then said, "I ran into that Headquarters buddy of mine going to the slit trenches. He says we ain't more'n a day or two from catching the Indians. Says the general's chompin' at the bit."

"Well, I'll believe it when I see it. At the rate we're going, we'll be back in Kansas before we see any Indians."

Boytale watched the last of his people ride away, the brush dragged behind the horses throwing dust into the air. Again, he and Blue Shield had been left as the rear guard.

"What shall we do today?" Blue Shield asked.

Boytale shook his head. "I have no idea. I just don't want to sit around. It just makes the day longer."

"You get to eat anything before they left?"

"No."

"Me neither. Everyone was in such a rush because the Owl said to hurry." Blue Shield stood. "Let's get a couple of rabbits or something. I can't go all day without eating. Besides, we both know there won't be any soldiers coming."

Boytale looked around them and saw nothing except empty land. He agreed with Blue Shield, but still worried that they might be wrong. After all, if the Owl Prophet could be caught by surprise, what chance did *he* have?

Blue Shield, sensing Boytale's hesitation, pressed on. "We can move over behind that low bluff," he said, pointing at a nearby ridge. "While you hunt, I'll watch. Then I'll cook, and you watch. At least we'll get to eat."

Boytale nodded his agreement and picked up his bow and arrows. Slipping the rawhide bowstring into place, he said, "Take the horses with you. I'll try not to take too long."

He slowly moved away through the tall grass, arrow nocked and ready. Several times he flushed birds, but no game. Then he saw long ears above the grass. The rabbit stood on its hind legs, searching the landscape for predators.

Boytale froze, knowing how keen the animal's eyesight was. He was close enough for a clean shot, so he slowly brought the bow up. As he drew the arrow back, the ears disappeared. Boytale relaxed and waited. His patience was rewarded when the ears reappeared a little closer. Apparently the rabbit had moved to a choicer grazing area.

He redrew the arrow, sighted, and let go. The bowstring popped and hummed. The missile shot through the grass, catching the rabbit just below the left foreleg and coming out the other side. It immediately dropped.

Boytale ran to the spot and found the rabbit on its side, one leg kicking spasmodically. The animal didn't lie flat, but was suspended at a slight angle by the arrow. Boytale picked up his kill and withdrew the arrow.

His luck held when another set of ears appeared not twenty yards away. Boytale grinned. This second rabbit had heard the commotion and maybe smelled blood or Boytale's scent. But rather than staying low, it too looked for the cause of its distress. Without taking a step, Boytale nocked, drew, and fired. In less time than it takes to raise a tipi, he had two rabbits ready for the cookfire.

Pleased, he jogged to his camp, carrying the animals by their ears. When he topped the ridge, Blue Shield was below him starting the fire.

"I watched you shoot those two," he said, "so I thought I'd better get the fire going."

Boytale set his bow and quiver on the ground. "I'm going up to the top to clean these. Call me when you're ready."

Leaving Blue Shield to his job, Boytale walked to the top of the low bluff. He sat and quickly skinned and gutted the rabbits, wrapping the meat loosely in the pelts. After wiping his knife and hands on tufts of grass, he gazed into the distance.

All signs of the Kiowa were gone, except perhaps a trace of dust far in the distance. Boytale knew that if he was unsure, then anyone who didn't know where to look would assume it was haze. For that matter, it may have been. He looked back to the east, then to the south, and finally behind him to the north. Nothing was there except the open prairie and the small canyon where they'd slept last night.

"Ready?" Blue Shield asked.

Boytale nodded and handed the rabbits over.

Blue Shield grinned. "These are going to taste great! I'll call you when they're cooked."

Boytale watched his companion run back down the hill. He wondered how much longer they'd be able to live like this, free of walls, forts, the white man. Already, powerful warriors like Striking Eagle, Satanta, and Big Tree were willing to surrender. Thankfully, men like Lone Wolf realized that in the hands of the whites, the Kiowa would vanish.

Exactly when he'd come to that conclusion, Boytale didn't know. But as he gazed over the land they'd once ruled, and now had to hide in, he decided never to surrender, never to give his spirit to the enemy, and never to allow the Kiowa to die.

The scene before Rambling was surreal. Brass buckets, iron kettles, blankets, bolts of trade cloth, bits and pieces of shattered pottery, unfinished bows, and a myriad of smaller items littered the landscape. Fire pits, flames dead, cold ashes scattered by the wind, dotted the area, marking the locations of Indian lodges.

Captain Bristol rode from company to company, ordering the commanders to disperse their men and search the campsite for weapons, bodies, or white prisoners that may have been left behind.

When he mentioned white prisoners, Rambling knew he had in mind the German sisters. As Larsen told the story, the German family had been traveling west from Georgia when they were attacked by Cheyenne. Everyone was killed except four of the girls, who were carried off. What Indian bucks did to white women was common knowledge, and many lurid tales had been written of beatings, rape, and torture. It had always struck Rambling as odd that the very people who denounced these books as exploitation of the victims always knew every title and the most intimate details contained between their covers.

Whether the stories of captive women were true, or mere yarns intended to titillate bored Easterners, was of no concern to Rambling. What he knew was true was that most Indians killed their prisoners, rather than let them return to white men's hands. As he scanned the flat, featureless prairie before them, he was certain they were looking for bodies, period.

First Sergeant Mitchell saluted Captain Lyman, then turned toward the company. "All right, lads, you heard the cap'n. Each squad leader take yer men and spread out. Sing out if you find anything important, and fer Christ's sake, don't gather more booty than you can carry. Questions?"

"We get to scalp any dead Injuns?" Hitchcock called out.

Mitchell's face reddened, and a vein pulsed on the side of his throat.

"There'll be no takin' hair or ears or any part o' any body found!" he bellowed. "Trust me, any manjack I see with a trophy like that"——he clenched his fist before his face—"I'll have his ballocks, and I won't be takin' 'em quick, neither." He lowered the fist, took a deep breath, then continued. "You pick up bows 'n arrows an' such. If you find a person, sing out." Mitchell's glare centered on Hitchcock. "Is that clear enow fer you, mister?"

"Yes, sir, First Sergeant!"

Mitchell pivoted and stalked away. "Goddamn jackals!" he muttered.

De Armond slowly turned and gazed at Hitchcock. His expression was unreadable, but the glint in his eyes told volumes. "I ought to kick your sorry ass," he growled.

"What the hell I do?" Hitchcock protested. "Jesus, goddam redskins take and pollute our women, scalp little kids and old men. What are we supposed to do? Bury 'em, maybe read the Good Book over 'em?"

"Not all the captives are killed," De Armond replied. "Some go Injun. The children they keep, they dress like their own. You get me yet, boy? It's always some cracker like you who hates all Indians that comes along and kills a white kid gone Injun. You do that, and I wouldn't give two cents for your life." He looked at Rambling. "You're his buddy, understand? He don't piss unless you hold it for him."

Rambling nodded. "Yes, sir."

De Armond returned his gaze to Hitchcock. "You give this private any grief, we're gonna have a little talk behind the tent!"

The squad moved out, Hitchcock taking a line that would put as much distance between him and the sergeants as possible.

"Goddammit!" he swore. "They had no cause to roust me like that."

"I don't figure it was you, Seth."

Hitchcock glanced sharply at Rambling. "How you reckon that?"

"If I had to guess, Mitchell was loaded for bear before he said anything. It just happened you asked the question on everyone else's mind, so you got the brunt of it. It could have been me, Larsen, anyone."

"Yeah. Well, it wasn't. Was it?"

The two walked slowly across the campsite, kicking over pails, lifting buffalo robes and blankets. At one point, Hitchcock stopped and bent over. He stood with a bag in his hand.

"Well, looky here," he said, with a grin. "Some Injun went and dropped his possibles bag."

Rambling gazed at the leather container. "Is it of any value?"

"Hell, I don't know." Hitchcock turned the object over in his hands. "Look at this beadwork. I can cut this part out and sell it for a pretty penny to some greenhorn recruit."

Rambling stared at the intricately sewn rows of tiny glass beads in shades of white, yellow, red, blue, and black. "I don't know, Seth. I think I'd keep it, something to pass on to your children."

"You think?" Hitchcock rolled up the beaded leather. "I'll just tuck it away while I study on it."

They continued their slow journey across the ground, the silence only interrupted by an occasional shout as a soldier found something he thought worth mentioning. Coming close to the edge of the camp, Rambling noticed a wide trail leading west. He was just about to mention it to Hitchcock when Larsen trotted over.

"You fellows see that trail?" he asked breathlessly. "You see how wide it is?"

Rambling nodded. "We've seen it. I was wondering how many Indians it would take to cut sign like that."

"Well," Larsen answered. "You figure we got about seven hundred men in this here outfit, and we don't make nearly as wide a track. So I reckon there must be two, three times our number ahead. And if you think about it, they ain't even tryin' to cover their trail. They must have enough bucks to put up one hell of a fight."

"Damned it you ain't just a potful of good news," Hitchcock complained. "I don't mind fightin', but if we're going against maybe three thousand of them son-of-a-bitches, I'd just as soon head home."

The column reformed on the western edge of the Indian campsite. No bodies had been found. Two rifles, a pistol, and a cavalry sword were discovered among the piles of personal items, but the weapons were ruined, the sword rusted to its scabbard.

Excitement ran high among the rank and file, but was quickly squelched by the noncommissioned officers. With a battery of orders and a snap and pop of the bullwhips, the combined infantry, artillery, and supply-wagon train column moved out.

"I am *so* bored," Blue Shield complained.

"Mmm," Boytale replied sleepily. His stomach was full, and the afternoon sun felt good on his bare back.

The young warriors lazed on the top of the ridge, in a warm, gentle breeze blowing from the southwest. Insects whirred and chirped, birds called to each other, and the overall feeling was one of peace and contentment.

Boytale resisted the urge to sleep, and slowly opened one eye. "No soldiers," he muttered.

"No nothing! We might as well be the only two Kiowa on the whole Llano."

"All right," Boytale said, sitting up. "What do you want to do?"

Blue Shield shrugged. "I don't know. Let's see if anyone's following us."

Boytale stood and walked down the hill, Blue Shield on his heels. They saddled and mounted their horses, walking them around the bluff they'd been on. Kicking his mare into a lope, Boytale rode for the stream.

"We'll ride upstream," he called to his companion. "I'm thirsty, and maybe we can find some berries."

They followed the trail left by the Kiowa bands along Elk Creek. This was the third time the Kiowa had crossed the same land. The bushes were picked clean of fruit, the creek muddied by the passage of many people and animals. All grass within reach of the horse herd was cropped to the ground. After several miles, the trail veered away from the stream and turned west toward the Red River. Boytale kept his horse headed upstream, looking forward to a cool drink.

A pool had formed near the headwaters of the creek, surrounded by a stand of trees and sheltered on one side by a low mesa. The boys approached slowly, wary of predators. They dismounted and hobbled their horses before allowing themselves to enjoy the water.

Suddenly, Boytale straightened. He cocked his head to one side and listened carefully.

Blue Shield looked around them. "What?"

"Listen," Boytale said quietly.

They heard a jingle, then another. A long drawn-out creak followed.

Blue Shield crept through the trees, then came running back. "Riders!" he said.

The youths freed their horses, mounted, and rode out of the oasis. They rounded the mesa and waited. Soon the sounds of harnesses and groaning wagon wheels grew louder. Then they heard voices.

Boytale climbed off the mare and handed his reins to Blue Shield. Crouching, he peeked around the edge of the butte.

Two large wagons rolled in view, pulled by four

oxen each. Seeing the two large wooden wheels, he guessed they were Comancheros. The wagons' three occupants wore wide-brim hats and white shirts and pants. They spoke rapidly and laughed loudly, teeth gleaming in sun-browned faces.

"Who are they?" Blue Shield whispered from behind him.

Boytale jerked around as though shot. Instantly angry, he hissed, "What are you doing here?"

"I want to see, too." Blue Shield said. Then he chuckled. "You should have seen your face."

"You surprised me," Boytale said, his gaze fixed on the ground.

"Surprised? You almost jumped out of your breechclout."

"Did not!"

Blue Shield stepped past Boytale. "Did, too," he said as he leaned out for a look. A moment later, he moved back. "They look like Mexicans."

Boytale nodded. "They're probably Comancheros. I heard one talking about trading with the Comanches."

"You understand them?"

"Some. Enough to know what's going on."

The boys peeked back around the end of the mesa. The traders had unyoked their oxen and led them a short distance downstream to water. They settled near the pool, one man starting a fire.

Boytale whispered, "The one talking now says that they are going to visit the Cheyenne next."

A second trader spoke. Then the first answered, pointing west.

"The other man asked where they were going, and the first one says west to Palo Duro Canyon."

"But that is where we are headed," Blue Shield said.

The third member of the team broke into an animated discourse. He was closely questioned by the first, who listened carefully, then threw his arms up, anger in his voice.

Boytale stepped back to the shelter of the rock, frowning.

"What did they say?" Blue Shield asked. "Why was that fellow so mad?"

"One of the Comancheros talked to a Comanche scout who told him that many soldiers have come from the east and are riding west."

"The ones from the agency?"

Boytale shrugged. "Who knows? What is important is that they are moving west to the Llano. He also said they found sign of many Indians ahead of the soldiers. That is why the other one is angry. With the soldiers between them and the Indians, they can't trade."

Blue Shield pondered what he'd heard, then said, "These Indians that the soldiers chase, could they be Kiowa?"

"I don't know. Maybe us, maybe Cheyenne, maybe even Comanche."

"Then I think we should leave. The council will want to know."

"I agree," Boytale replied. "The sooner we are among our people, the better I'll feel."

Twenty-one

"Now, that's different," Rambling commented.

"What?" Hitchcock asked. His gaze swept the wide trail littered with Indian goods. "You mean all this Injun shit? Hell, that ain't new. We saw it all yesterday."

"Actually," Rambling countered, "what we saw was a camp. This stuff has been cast off en route."

"You mean like they're shedding weight to move faster?"

"My thoughts exactly."

"Pew-wee!" exclaimed Bailey. "What is that stink?"

"If you'd look around," Ketzel said, "you'd see all them dead buffalo we been passin'."

Bailey stared at the huge brown shapes scattered across the countryside. "They ain't even been skint. Injuns always skin buffalo, don't they?"

A rider dressed in civilian clothes passed the unit at a trot.

"Hey, mister!" Hitchcock called.

The rider slowed, allowing the column to catch up. Then he turned in the saddle. "Yes, sir?"

"You're one of them scouts, ain'tcha?"

The civilian nodded, long brown hair sweeping his shoulders.

"You know how close we are to the Injuns?"

The scout smiled, teeth showing under his bushy mustache. "Close enough to spit. We'll tangle with 'em tomorrow, next day latest."

"You know how many we're facin'?"

"Not really. Best guess is two, maybe three thousand, if you count women and kids and old people. Fightin' men, maybe five hundred, not that you can turn your back on any of the rest."

Hitchcock nodded. "Amen to that, brother. I heard what the Comanches done in San Antone."

"Jesus," Ketzel swore. "That was back in '40. Why the hell you want to remember something like that?"

"You're friend's right," the scout said to Ketzel. "Everyone expected the bucks to fight, but the twelve-year-old that killed that soldier surprised 'em. You forget that, and some pimply-faced redskin'll put a arrow in you."

"Say, mister, you a hide man?" Bailey asked.

The scout's eyes narrowed, and his expression hardened.

"I've hunted buffalo," he replied evenly.

"You and your friends kill these?"

"Nope. Cheyenne did. They're ripping out the bellies and bladders for water sacks. That's how we know we're real close. They're not hauling anything to slow them down." He gazed into the distance. "They're running now, but we'll catch 'em." He shook his head, looked back at the troops, and grinned. "I got to git, messages for the general and all. I reckon we'll see you boys directly."

The scout spurred his horse, waving his hat as he rode away.

The column recombined that night for the first time since leaving Camp Supply. The camp was divided by branch, cavalry in one area, infantry and artillery in another. The wagon train was corralled to one side, and Lieutenant Baldwin and his scouts kept to themselves near the river.

Sergeant De Armond and his squad sat around a fire in the middle of Company I's campsite. The mesquite fire crackled and popped, tinting the men's faces red-orange as though they faced the setting sun. Beyond it, the night was black until another fire came into view, another pinprick of light to hold off the darkness.

"Man, I couldn't believe what all I saw today," Larsen said, "what with the dead buffalo and all."

"I've seen it before," De Armond said. "Back in '61." He looked at his audience, faces expectant. It suddenly occurred to him that many of these soldiers had been children during the Insurrection. He pulled a cigar from his coat pocket, lit it off the campfire, then leaned back.

"July 1861, I was a young pup like you boys, wet behind the ears, full of piss and vinegar. The South had seceded starting with Georgia that January. By the middle of April, Fort Sumpter was in Confederate hands, and we were at war. Lincoln called on us to help 'preserve the Union,' as he said it, and we came."

He gazed toward the stars, but what he saw lay thirteen years in the past. "Yes, sir, it was a grand sight to behold, all of us new recruits marching through the streets of Washington." He looked at his men. "It's not like now. Back then we had a cause, we were righteous with a mission and knew God was on *our* side." He smiled wryly. "Sounds kind of silly now, I know. But I believed it then."

De Armond drew on his cigar, its glowing tip briefly softening the shadows of his face.

"General McDowell had over thirty thousand men under him, and we were marchin' to Richmond. We would seize the capital of the breakaway states and end the rebellion. We were so green we spent the first day picking blackberries along the road. Couple days before the fight, we reached Centreville. About five miles ahead of us was Bull Run Creek and twenty thousand Rebels."

De Armond shifted his position for comfort. "We weren't the only ones looking the Rebels over. Politicians of every flavor, their wives and children, townspeople, newspapermen, just about anybody who could, showed up. I remember seeing the buggies parked along a ridgeline. The women had them fancy little umbrellas from France.

"Anyway, McDowell spent the next day or two trying to get around the Rebs, but every move we made, they checked. By that time, ten thousand more Southerners joined the fray. On the morning of the twenty-first, the main column moved to the Confederate left flank while a smaller force attacked the front to get their attention. The trick didn't work, and the Rebs reinforced their lines at Matthews Hill. We had to pound them all morning, but they finally broke and ran until Stonewall Jackson rallied them.

"Come noon, McDowell decides to call off the attack and regroup. Only problem was, the Rebels got to do the same, so when we start up again, they're ready, and we get to fighting over a place called Henry Hill."

"Why?" Larsen asked.

De Armond frowned. "Hell, I don't know. In those days, you just did what you were told. No one asked fool questions like 'Why?' " He paused. "Where was I?"

"Henry Hill," Rambling said.

"Right. We push them off, then they'd come back and push us off. It was like that all afternoon. On the way up, we'd pass dead Rebs. On the way back down, we'd pass dead Yanks. By late in the day, the bodies were all jumbled together. I saw men shot through the head, the face, in the eye, in the throat, gut-shot, lung-shot. Some men took it in the balls, and some looked like they died of fright.

"And the noise was unbelievable. Cannon, rifles, attacking soldiers screaming, the howls and moans of the wounded. Orders came from every direction, but you were really on your own. Whenever everyone charged, you charged. When they ran, you ran, too.

"Then about four o'clock, fresh Rebel troops hit our right flank. We were whipped. Of all I saw and heard that day, the thing I remember best was the sound of Retreat. That bugle call cut through it all and sounded heavenly to me. All them politicians spooked and bolted. Seeing our fearless leaders cut and run panicked the units."

De Armond paused and gazed into the fire. "We ran, every goddamn one of us. Men threw down their weapons, their packs, any gear that slowed them down. We ran all the way back to Washington and hid." He glanced around. "That's what it looked like today. Manassas."

"Well, hell, Sarge," Hitchcock said cheerily, "if we got the Injuns on the run, then we oughtta be able to spank 'em good come tomorrow."

De Armond took another puff of his cigar, then faced Hitchcock. "Let me tell you something about Indians, boy. They'll run, all right. They'll keep running until they're ready to fight. Then they'll climb all over you like a stink on shit."

The silence stretched a few moments. Long, uncomfortable moments for Rambling. Like Hitchcock, he'd thought De Armond's story was about an easy time to be had with the Indians. The idea that they were being led into an ambush frightened him.

De Armond stood. "I'm to bed," he announced. "Rambling, you best get what sleep you can. You have the midnight-to-four watch."

Rambling walked his post, pivoted, and walked back. He was nervous. Several nights before, Indians had walked into camp and stolen four horses, one off the cavalry's remuda. The poor guard had almost been drawn and quartered the next day by the cavalry officer who owned it. Fortunately, Rambling's post was along the back side of the infantry camp. There wasn't anything worth stealing nearby.

He spun as he heard a sound, and saw two shapes in the moonlight. The moon had been full just three days before and was almost directly overhead.

"Halt!" he barked. "Who goes there?"

"It's Billy Dixon and Amos Chapman. We're a couple of Baldwin's scouts."

"Advance and be recognized."

The shadows moved closer until Rambling could discern substance. They looked strangely alike. Neither man was tall. Both sported long hair. One had a full beard, the other just a mustache. In the darkness, their clothes were little more than rumpled shapes. The scout with the mustache moved closer.

"We're taking a little look-see up ahead," he said. "We should only be gone two, maybe three hours."

"What's your name?" the other asked.

"Jim Rambling."

"Well, Jim, just off to the right there is an arroyo. When we leave, that's where we're gonna start. When we come back, it'll be up through there again. Understand?"

Rambling nodded, then realized it was useless in the dark. "Yes," he said.

The bearded scout chuckled. "Good to hear that. Now, you be watchin' for us. We'll holler when we're close."

"You do that," Rambling said. "Make sure you holler loud."

"Don't worry, son, I got no intention of gettin' shot by no trigger-happy soldier."

The men walked on and were swallowed up by the night. Rambling never heard a sound. He tried to imagine what it would be like to creep along behind enemy lines. Even with two of them, it must be a lonely business, especially knowing the consequences of capture. What joy they must feel when they finally return to the safety of the camp.

Rambling continued to walk his post. The night was filled with the sounds of the plains. He heard crickets, wolves, and coyotes. Occasionally, there would be the sound of running or the sharp squeal of a small animal caught by its predator.

Finally, he grew used to the sounds and ignored them. Stars sparkled, but were dimmed by the bright moon. By avoiding looking at the campfires, his eyes adjusted to the dark. He saw how moonlight bathed the prairie in cool, blue light. He could make out brush and cactus between long stretches of grass that swayed slowly in the breeze. He even managed to see the gully the scouts had mentioned.

He turned around again for what seemed the hundredth time. As he gazed across the land, he thought he saw movement near the arroyo.

"Jim?" a voice called. "Jim Rambling?"

Rambling waved. He recognized the voice as the scout with the mustache. "Come forward."

The men seemed to peel themselves from the ground. They trotted straight to him, then slowed.

"Howdy, son," the bearded scout said. "Good to see you again."

"You, too. Any luck?"

A quick flash of white in the dark beard was all Rambling saw of a smile.

"You might say so."

The scouts hurried away, leaving Rambling to wonder whether good luck meant finding the Indians or not finding them. His question was soon answered, as he saw a man run across to General Miles's tent. Within moments, a light flared inside. He saw the silhouettes of men bent over something. Then a third man joined them.

One of the men left the tent and ran to where the scouts slept. Another of the trio walked out, and in the light of the open tent flap, Rambling saw he wore red long-handles. The man hurried to where Headquarters Company camped. The light in the general's tent stayed on.

Something was up—something big.

Reveille rang through the camp, and half-asleep soldiers stumbled from tents and shelters. The man in his underwear stopped at the tents of the company commanders and shouted something through the doorways. As he passed Rambling, he stopped.

"You there!" he shouted.

Rambling snapped to attention; he didn't need to see braid to know this man was an officer. "Yes, sir."

"Report back to your company and pack. We strike camp within the hour."

"Yes, sir!"

Rambling ran back to Company I's site. The others

were up, many tripping over themselves in the dark. Curses floated on the air like wood ash, but above it all was the ring of Mitchell's voice.

"Listen up, boyos! Pack yer gear, stow the shelters, and form up on me. We'll not be waitin' for the wagons and artillery today. As soon as the companies are ready, we leave. So tarry not, me lads."

Rambling quickly packed his valise and shrugged the yoke over his shoulders. He tore down the shelter, and had it rolled up before Larsen was completely dressed. Leaving his rifle in Larsen's care, he hurried to one of the supply wagons and threw the shelter halves in, then ran back.

The company had already formed, and as Rambling slipped into position, Larsen handed him his rifle. Captain Lyman appeared on horseback, called a quick "forward march," and the men moved out. In the light of a false dawn, Rambling was pleased to see that they were the second unit out.

The sun had just started its ascent when a rider galloped by the company. Moments later, he galloped back followed by the artillery detachment, whose horses strained to keep up. The Parrot and Gatling guns bounced along the trail. The caissons rattled and clanked as they rumbled by, several times tipping precariously on one wheel, only to drop back down.

Then Rambling heard the distinctive pop of many rifles being fired. Lyman called for a quick march, and the company jogged toward the shots. Suddenly, the rifle fire was augmented by the steady pop-pop-pop of the Gatlings, followed by a roar that had to be the Parrot.

"Aw, shit!" Hitchcock swore between gasps for air. "They've done gone and started without us."

Twenty-two

The first thing Rambling noticed as they neared the battlefield was the acrid smell of burnt gunpowder. White smoke drifted over the company, stinging his nose and leaving a sulphurous taste on his tongue.

The land before them was broken and strewn with rocks. The Indians held the high ground, smoke from their rifles betraying where they hid among the boulders and scrub. At the base of the first ridge, the horse soldiers had taken both flanks, dismounting and taking shelter where available. There was activity on the far left flank as the scouts scurried up the hill.

Company E arrived first and was immediately moved to support the artillery. When Lyman approached Lieutenant Baird, Miles's Adjutant, he was directed toward the artillery as well.

"Son of a bitch!" De Armond swore.

"What's the matter, Sarge?" Rambling asked.

"Ten to one we're in reserve."

"What's that mean?"

"It means," De Armond said, turning to gaze at Rambling, "that we sit here on our asses and watch everybody else fight."

"What?" Hitchcock yelled. "You mean we run all the way here for nothin'?"

"You heard me, boy," De Armond replied. "Now, shut up! The cap'n's comin'."

Lyman stopped in front of his company and said nothing. His cheeks were red. He scowled, a deep furrow between his eyes like an ax wound.

"Gentlemen," he said, his voice tight, the words clipped. "Gentlemen, we are to wait in reserve. I share your disappointment, but fear not, for soon we will test our mettle on the field. We shall remain behind Company E. Should they be called forward, we will assume the support role for Lieutenant Pope and his artillery. If any of you wish to aid the surgeon or the armorer, do so. However, do stay in earshot. If the opportunity presents itself, I shall not hesitate to move forward. First Sergeant?"

Mitchell snapped to attention. "Yes, sir!"

"Dismiss the men."

Mitchell saluted and pivoted sharply on his heel. "Company I . . . attention! Dismissed!" As the men broke ranks, he called, "Mind the captain's orders and stick close by. I'll not be chasin' you down if we get to fight."

Rambling wandered to the Parrot's limber, dropped his pack and rifle, and sat, his back against one of the wheels. Larsen, Hitchcock, and Bailey joined him, forming a small circle.

"Aren't we one shy?" Rambling asked.

Hitchcock shrugged. "Gary's off seeing if he can help Waters. Seems he's taken an interest in doctoring."

They all looked up as the fire from the Indians increased dramatically. It was quickly returned by the Gatlings, their ten barrels spitting out lead at an incredible speed. As soon as they stopped, the Parrot fired, a thunderclap that set ears to ringing.

"My God," Larsen cried, clapping his hands over

his ears. "Why don't they warn a fellow first?" He caught the loader's eye. "Why don't you let us know before you shoot that thing?"

The loader looked blank, then squinted. "What?" he shouted.

"I said," Larsen shouted back, "why don't your warn—?"

"What?" the loader repeated.

He slapped the shoulder of the man next to him, who held the long swab for sponging out the barrel. When the sponger turned, the loader pointed at Larsen.

"Why don't you—?"

"What?" the sponger asked.

"What?" echoed the loader.

Larsen rubbed his hand over his face. "God, grant me strength!" he muttered to himself.

The sponger tossed a pebble at one of his compatriots on the other side of the gun. As the man turned, the sponger nodded toward the limber. The third cannoneer, the gunner, was a corporal in charge of the piece. He glanced at Larsen.

This time Larsen was taking no chances. He screamed at the top of his lungs, *"WHY DON'T YOU ASSHOLES WARN US BEFORE YOU SHOOT?"*

The corporal's expression remained neutral. He gazed at the distraught private for a moment. "There's no need to shout," he said mildly, "or be rude. A simple request would have sufficed."

Larsen's mouth dropped open, then closed again, only to reopen.

Hitchcock chuckled. "Damn, if you don't look like a fish outta water!"

Larsen ignored Hitchcock and continued to stare at the gunner, who silently turned away. He then shifted his attention to the loader, who gave him a slow wink. Larsen's face reddened. "I've been had."

Rambling and the rest laughed. The cannoneers soon joined in. Then the corporal turned and a slow grin spread across his face.

"Don't worry, Private," the gunner said in that same calm voice, "we'll let you know before we let loose again."

Companies C and D had marched by while the men were distracted, but Rambling now saw them nearing the base of the hill. They had been positioned in the center and spread out to fill the space between the cavalry units.

The regimental bugler sounded Charge, and the units inched their way up the hill. The scouts took the lead early, and soon were far ahead of the rest of the column.

The Gatlings opened up again, firing along the ridgeline. General Miles rode up and shouted at Lieutenant Pope. One of the guns suddenly fell silent, and the crew scrambled to fix it. The first soldier jerked the magazine from the top of the weapon. The second grabbed his bayonet and poked inside the breech. The third member of the team slowly turned the crank back and forth. The second gun continued to fire until Pope signaled the gunner to stop. Miles's voice carried well in the silence.

"Mr. Pope, be prepared to move quickly. Captain Ewers!"

"Yes, sir, General," Ewers called, running to Miles's side.

"You will take your company and go right up the middle of the command. I intend to use your troops to force a breech in the Indians' line.

"Captain Lyman!"

Ewers saluted and ran off, shouting orders. Lyman marched briskly to Miles, stopped, and saluted.

"Sir!"

"You will now support Pope and his artillery. If this detachment moves, follow it."

Lyman saluted again. "Sir!" He turned away from Miles and bellowed, "Mitchell!"

"I heard, sir," the first sergeant called back. "All right, squad leaders, gather yer men and relieve the boyos from E."

De Armond stepped around the end of the caisson. "Hitchcock, you and Rambling fall in on me. Larsen and Bailey, find your squad leaders."

"How do we support the artillery, Sergeant?" Rambling asked.

"By staying out of the way," De Armond replied. He pointed at a group of soldiers near one of the Gatlings. "You men, move over here."

As the company reformed, Ketzel trotted over from the surgeon's ambulance.

"You learnin' anything?" Hitchcock asked.

Ketzel frowned. "Hell, no. All this damn shootin', and nary a soul shot—red or white. Nothin' but a big waste of my time."

Company E quick-marched across the plain. They split into squads at the base of the breaks and moved uphill, each squad moving under an umbrella of protective fire from the remaining two. Return fire from the Indians was sporadic, and Ewers and his men climbed steadily past the units flanking them, until they reached the ridge crest.

One soldier stood at the summit and waved his hat before disappearing over the top. All shooting from the Indians stopped, and the column quickly finished its ascent.

Miles charged past the Parrot, his horse wheeling

to avoid the cannon. "Mr. Pope!" he yelled, wrestling his mount back under control. "Get your artillery on top of that first ridge immediately!"

Pope threw a hasty salute. "Yes, sir, General Miles! Right away, sir!" He faced the guns. "Load up! Bring up the teams!"

The gun crew quickly closed up the caissons and hung the cannon on its pintle. The horses were brought forward and hitched to the limbers, and the men mounted, ready to ride. The Gatlings' crews prepared their weapons with the same efficiency.

Rambling watched closely, fascinated. He imagined himself trying to remember whether he was supposed to ride this wagon or that or which horse went where.

Pope had managed to find and saddle his horse before the artillery detachment could get under way. He quickly assumed the lead position.

"Detachment . . . forward!" he shouted.

The artillery pieces rumbled away in a cloud of dust.

Lyman wasted no time. "Sergeant Mitchell, prepare to move."

"Yes, sir," Mitchell replied, then faced the company. "You heard the cap'n. Company I . . . attention!"

At Lyman's order, the troops moved off at a brisk march. They followed the trail of Pope and his artillery, keeping far enough behind to avoid the bulk of the flying dirt. At the base of the first ridge, Lyman took his men up at an angle away from Pope. They faced no opposition. In fact, they saw no one at all, except Miles, who was above them. Cresting the ridge, they crowded forward, trying to see what was happening.

Cavalry and infantry soldiers ran down the far side. Ahead of them, small figures darted among the boulders and vegetation, disappearing shortly after reaching the top of the next hill.

"Hey, Bill," Rambling said, nudging Larsen. "Those must be Indians."

"Where? Where?"

"Look along the ridgeline. You can see them pop up just before they head down the other side."

Larsen stared across the valley. Then he grabbed Rambling's arm. "There's one, Jim!" he shouted and pointed. "There's an Injun! An honest-to-God redskin." He paused. "Looks kinda puny, y'know?"

Miles's arrival in their midst on foot stopped further conversation. Mitchell, caught by surprise, screamed "Attention!" but the general waved him off.

"At ease, men," he said around a cigar stuck in the corner of his mouth. "Captain Lyman, have your men assist Pope any way they can."

"Yes, sir, General."

Miles turned toward Pope. "Lieutenant, there are Indians atop that high bluff behind you, intent on impeding our progress. Clear them off, sir."

Before Pope could reply, Miles turned and left. Shortly, he reappeared mounted on his stallion, Adjutant Baird at his side.

"Must be nice," Hitchcock mumbled, wiping sweat off his face with his hand.

"What?" Rambling asked.

Hitchcock dried his hand on his uniform blouse. "The way the general and his buddies ride around like it was a goddamn Sunday social while we sweat our asses off."

"I wouldn't trade places with him."

"Really? Rich boy like you? I figured you was natural officer material."

Rambling grinned. "Talk like that might get your nose broke again."

Hitchcock rubbed the bridge of his nose and chuckled. "It just might, hoss, at that." He nodded toward Miles. "So why wouldn't you trade?"

"We just do what we're told, but men like Miles have to send us in, knowing some will die. I don't know if I could live like that."

"That why you run off from your old man's business? Afraid to make a decision that might get a man killed?"

Rambling shrugged. "Maybe. Part of it anyway."

Hitchcock clapped Rambling on the shoulder. "Tell you what, son. When this enlistment's up, you and me'll go back to Baltimore and tell your old man I ain't afraid to make the hard decisions. Then you can work for me."

"Hey, you soldiers!" the Parrot's gunner called. "We're fixin' to let loose. Wouldn't want to scare any of you children now." He placed his hands over his ears. "Fire!"

Flame and smoke belched from the Parrot's barrel. Rambling jumped in spite of the gunner's warning, and cursed under his breath when he saw the smiles on the gun crew's faces. Standing almost behind the gun, he could see the shell arc across the valley and slam into the side of the bluff.

"I saw that!" Rambling said. "I actually saw the cannonball fly through the air."

The corporal grinned. "Same thing I said when I first saw it. Remarkable, ain't it?" He turned back to his men. "Before you prime it, let's bring up the elevation. General wants the shells on top."

The artillery pieces had been arranged differently here than at the base of the hills. The Gatlings remained attached to their limbers. With no real targets to shoot at, their crews waited until the next move.

While the Parrot had been taken off its hook, the horses remained hitched to the limber.

The Parrot fired off three more rounds, leaving the top of the bluff covered by smoke and dust. Then Baird returned to instruct Pope to take the guns to the next ridge. Once again the cannon was lowered onto the limber's pintle, and the weapons rattled down one side of the valley and up the other.

No Indians were in sight. Only a few straggling soldiers showed the direction the battle had taken. Pope sighed and announced he wasn't wasting time preparing to fire if they were just going to move again. He ordered the artillery forward.

Chest heaving from the run and drenched in sweat, Rambling stared at the lieutenant, then at his squad leader.

De Armond removed his headgear and slowly shook his head. "Well, Sarge?" he asked Mitchell.

Mitchell looked for a Company I officer and found none. He was de facto in charge. Cursing under his breath, he faced his command. "Men, our orders are to support the artillery. With no one here to say otherwise, we've got to go. But there's no rule says we have to run. It's walking we'll do, and if Pope gets himself lost, so be it. Stay in your squads."

Mitchell turned and walked down the slope through the dust kicked up by the limbers. The squads fell into line behind him. Company I followed Pope through the broken land, occasionally catching glimpses of the horses. The sounds of shooting were rare, as the battle seemed to have become a chase.

Hitchcock was plainly disappointed at being relegated to a noncombative role, and said so, but Rambling enjoyed the opportunity to catch his breath and cool off. He shook his canteen. It sounded about a quarter full.

Throughout the afternoon, they continued the pursuit. Rambling's canteen was dry, and his lips were starting to crack.

They crested a hill to look down into a wide riverbed. The rest of the column had stretched along its sandy banks, Pope and his guns in the center. Soldiers sat or lay in what shade they could find.

"All right, boyos," Mitchell said. "Let's look lively now. Make your way to Pope. I'll look for the cap'n."

Rambling sighed. "Any of you boys see the water wagons?"

"I don't see nothing," Hitchcock said. "I reckon they're back behind us trying to pick their way through this shit."

"You think there's water down there?" Rambling asked, pointing at the riverbed.

Hitchcock snorted. "None fit to drink, I'd bet. I ain't seen water worth a damn since Supply."

The troops marched down through tall grass and cactus, stopping behind the artillery detachment and exchanging greetings with the gun crews. Company I members scattered among the guns.

Rambling sat with his back to one of the limber's wheel. He dozed, images of Baltimore flashing behind his eyes. He saw the brick streets, the warehouses near the harbor, his father's tall ships. He heard seagulls cry and smelled the water. It was a world far different from the hot, dry plains, and now seemed as alien as the Moon.

A toe nudged him. He opened one eye and slowly focused on Mitchell.

"Up with ya, lad," the first sergeant said. "There's work to be done."

Rambling nodded, and slowly gained his feet. He stared around him at the shuffling, bleary-eyed men who'd also fallen asleep. He licked cracked lips and reached for his canteen.

Empty.

Again he looked around for signs of the wagon train, but saw nothing but prairie and the cloudless blue sky.

Mitchell walked to the middle of the men and waved them forward. "Gather round," he ordered. When he was satisfied all could hear, he continued. "Soon now, there will come the order to open fire across the river. You'll be shootin' at anything that moves on that side. While we're makin' noise, one company is going to cross." He pointed at a tall bluff on the other side. "There's Indians posted up there, and these gentlemen are going to persuade them to leave. Once we have the high ground, the general himself will lead the final charge."

He paused and looked at the tired faces around him. "They've got their backs against the wall, boyos, so look for a hard fight. Any questions?"

"Who's crossing the river?" Larsen asked.

"Pony soldiers on foot." Mitchell smiled. "Should be quite the sight."

The group laughed and separated into squads, moving to either side of the artillery pieces. Rambling checked his rifle, making sure the Springfield's action was free of dirt. He then sat on the bank and waited.

He'd heard this river called the Salt Fork of the Red River. It was a half-mile-wide expanse of red sand. There was no cover, nothing to hide behind or under. Nothing moved in the heat; even the wind had stilled as though in anticipation of the coming battle.

The firing started near Miles and rippled down the command. Pope's Parrot boomed, and a cloud of dust and debris rose over the top of the bluff. Rambling heard a bugle sound Charge, and saw the cavalry troop start across the sand. They began well enough, but soon strung out as their boots sank into the soft river bottom.

Between rounds, Rambling watched the charging soldiers. He saw no Indians on the other bank. He saw no signs of life at all, so while he watched the floundering troops, he amused himself trying to hit various target he picked at random. Then Cease Fire was called, and the guns fell silent.

Rambling saw little troop movement near the base of the bluff, but he soon heard the boom of a cavalry Sharps carbine, then another, followed quickly by return fire from lighter-caliber rifles.

Then silence. The tension was palpable, and most of the soldiers jumped when the firing resumed with a flurry of shots, ending with the distinctive pop of a pistol.

"Damn," Hitchcock said quietly. "I wonder who won."

A figure walked to the edge of the bluff and began waving a stick. When the cavalry ensign unfurled, the soldiers along the riverbank cheered. Miles rode his stallion onto the sand. He unsheathed his sword, swung it over his head, and pointed to the bluff, the blade glinting in the sunlight. Bugles sounded Charge, each bugler playing at his own tempo, their asynchronous melody all but lost in the roar of hundreds of screaming men who plunged into the riverbed and rushed toward the enemy.

Rambling was caught up in the excitement. He yelled a war cry and ran for the opposite bank. When he left the hard-packed sand near the edge and hit the soft bottom of the riverbed, he felt the distance had doubled. He quit screaming and concentrated on running as his boots sank, then slipped, in the red sand.

His breath came in ragged gasps. His equipment weighed tons. He needed a drink so badly, he would have killed for it.

Two thirds of the way across, officers suddenly appeared, herding the troops to the left while encouraging them to keep up the pace.

Rambling lurched onto solid ground again, the soil feeling strange after the soft, shifting sand. He scrambled up the riverbank and stopped, chest heaving.

The land before him was broken and covered in scrub and cactus. In the distance, he saw tall, almost mountainous bluffs.

Larsen stopped next to Rambling and bent over, gasping for air. "Those rocks," he said between gasps. "Those rocks are what they call the Escarpment." He stood and took a deep breath. "Whew! That was a run." He grinned. "Better, son?"

Rambling nodded.

Larsen pulled his neckerchief loose and mopped his face. "Like I was sayin', these breaks lead to a canyon that'll take you up on the Llano Estacado. That's Spanish for Staked Plains. If the Indians get there, they're gone for sure. The officers think we got 'em bottled up in the canyon, but most of the old-timers say they'll get away."

"How do you know all this stuff?"

Larsen shrugged. "I keep my ear to he ground, talk to a few people I know. Like I know the reason we took that bluff back there. There's two canyons here with that bluff in the middle. No one knew which canyon the Indians'd head for, so Miles said to take the high ground and see."

"I don't suppose you know where the water wagons are, do you?" Rambling asked, running his tongue over his cracked lips.

"Nope. No one knows, not even the general. You about ready to move?"

Rambling nodded, and the pair trotted over the first low hill. Miles's command was scattered through the breaks in small, unorganized units. Some men ran toward the canyon, others walked, and still others sat, too tired to continue. The noncommissioned officers begged, cajoled, or threatened their men—anything to keep them moving. Slowly, the soldiers made their way out of the breaks. A brief rally occurred when word came that the Indians had been spotted near the back of the canyon, but it was brief and halfhearted.

By the time Rambling reached the main contingent, there was no one to see but soldiers in various states of fatigue. Most sat or lay in small groups. Many had wrists wrapped in neckerchiefs. Rambling wondered what had caused the injuries until he saw a trooper cut his wrist and suck at the blood as it welled up.

"I don't think I could get that thirsty," he said to Larsen.

"Amen to that."

They located the rest of their company gathered near a stand of stunted cedar trees. Hitchcock and Ketzel sat together. Bailey lay nearby, his left wrist wrapped in cloth. Rambling walked over to them, dropped his yoke, and sank to a sitting position.

"How's Bailey?" he asked.

"Bad," Hitchcock replied. "He's almost crazy for water. You know what he *done*?"

Rambling nodded. "I've seen others." He glanced around. "You see any of the sergeants?"

Hitchcock waved his hand. "Out there. Lookin' for officers, any officers." He offered a lopsided grin. "Hell of way to fight a war, huh?"

Twenty-three

The news Boytale and Blue Shield brought about
the Comancheros caused a sensation, and a council
meeting was called early the next morning. Again,
the chiefs were divided over whether to stay or continue.

"Now it is more important than ever that we remain here," Big Bow argued. "We know the soldiers
are somewhere between us and the canyon. But the
do not know we're here. Why take the chance?"

"The Owl has said that we are safe in the canyon,"
Mamanti replied. "The sooner we get there, the better."

Big Bow snorted. "Yes, but has your owl said that
the way there is safe? I agree that we have spent many
winters protected by the walls of Palo Duro, and that
no white man has discovered our campsites, but the
path is not protected. I say wait until the whites leave
the area."

Poor Buffalo cleared his throat. "Does the Owl say
when we should arrive at the canyon?"

"No," Mamanti said. "Only that we hurry."

"And you, Lone Wolf, as principal war chief for the
Kiowa, what say you of this new information?"

"I respect the power of the Owl Prophet. His wis-
dom has led to victory on many raids. But I fear for

my family. If the soldiers catch us out here, we will be slaughtered. The boys tell us that the Comanchero will not ride to Palo Duro until the soldiers leave. I think this is wise.

"I say we send warriors to find the traders and learn more of what they saw. We should also send men to the canyon and in every direction to search for the whites or their scouts. Even if we move on, we cannot be safe without knowing where our enemy waits."

"I agree," Poor Buffalo said. "Mamanti, I speak for my band, Lone Wolf for his, and Big Bow for his. I ask you to make it unanimous that we wait. With you beside us, we can make all the chiefs understand what has to be done."

Mamanti looked at the men around him. He sighed and shrugged. "Who am I to question matters of war? I am but a poor prophet who deals with the spirits. If you wish to stay, I will not argue the point. Tonight I will consult the Owl again and seek protection for us here and on our journey to Palo Duro."

Poor Buffalo smiled. "That is a very good idea." He rose. "Summon the criers! Have them spread the news that we wait here."

Boytale, Tehan, and Blue Shield left the council meeting and walked back through the campsite. It already looked like a proper village: tipis erect, drying racks set up, new buffalo hides staked out to dry, and the horses gathered together in a single herd again.

"What do you think of this waiting?" Boytale asked no one in particular.

Blue Shield shrugged. "It doesn't matter to me."

"Well, it matters to me!" Tehan cried. "I think my father's right. No good will come of staying here. He will have to work twice as hard to protect us out here."

Boytale asked, "Do you think we should go on?"

"Of course, but then no one asked me."

"Me either," Boytale replied.

Blue Shield glanced at his comrades. "I think it's a shame that the council didn't talk to the three wisest warriors before reaching their decision."

Boytale laughed. "Or to us."

Rambling ran his thickened tongue over his rough, dry, cracked lips. He'd give almost anything for a drink. Even the warm, metallic taste of day-old water in a canteen sounded like nectar.

General Miles was within fifty feet of the Company I troops. He looked haggard, his features drooping as if they had melted in the heat. Still, he sat ramrod straight in the saddle and gazed back across the river.

Rambling knew the look. He'd seen it on his father's face when a ship was lost or some other catastrophic event occurred. It was the face of responsibility. Whatever the outcome of the battle, Miles now sat there and looked at his command. He had caused their plight and would have to live with it. Men like Miles and Rambling, Sr., shouldered the load and persevered, but it was the sheer terror of failure that made Rambling shudder.

Could he ask men to die for him? Could he look a dying man in the eyes, knowing he had ordered him to go? Maybe that was the real reason he'd joined the Army. It wasn't to help his brother, it was to escape responsibility. How much easier to follow orders, to blame what happened on his superiors.

He heard a faint clink, almost like a coin dropped on bricks. He looked at Miles and knew the general had heard the same. Another clink followed—then a tinkling like small silver bells. Miles stood in his stirrups, and stared across the Red River.

"Hear that, boys?" Miles shouted hoarsely. "It's Baird and the water wagons!"

A weak cheer worked its way through the ranks.

Miles sat again and wheeled his horse. "Buck up, men," he called. "As soon as they get here, there'll be plenty of water for all." He rode to a small group of officers near the edge of the makeshift camp.

Rambling slowly stood on shaky legs. He looked down at Larsen, who stared back stupidly.

"C'mon, Bill," he said gently. "Let's get a drink."

Larsen turned his gaze to Bailey, still lying where he'd fallen earlier.

"We'll bring back some water for him," Rambling said.

He held out his hand, and Larsen grasped it, allowing Rambling to pull him to his feet. Then Rambling turned to Hitchcock and held out his hand again.

"Seth? You coming?"

Hitchcock shook his head. "I'm all right. I'll just sit here with Dennis." He pulled his canteen strap over his head. "I'd appreciate some water, though."

Rambling nodded and took the canteen. He watched as Ketzel struggled to stand. "You need a hand?"

Ketzel shook his head. "Hell, no! M'legs just went to sleep." He struck himself in the thigh. "Damn, I just hate that! Like thousands of pins stuck in me." He looked at Hitchcock. "I'm going to fetch Doc Waters. Bailey don't look so good."

The wagons were close enough for the soldiers to see the drivers. Their arrival brought a more enthusiastic, if still ragged, cheer from the men. Miles ordered the wagons spread out to allow as many men access as possible. He rode next to Baird, tapped him on the shoulder, and pointed to a group of men lying on the ground.

"Take one wagon, and help those men. No one walking gets near here. No one with straps on his shoulders gets a drink until the last enlisted man gets his fill. Understood?"

Baird nodded and saluted. "Perfectly, General."

The three privates skirted the wagon designated for the critically ill, and made their way to the next. A long line of soldiers had already formed. Rambling and Larsen moved to the end of the line. Ketzel left to find the surgeon.

No one talked. The stillness was interrupted only by the sound of shuffling footsteps and the occasional cough.

A noise caught Rambling's attention. He leaned out from the line and gazed forward. Near the wagon, two men struggled over a water dipper.

"Gimme it!" a cavalry private shouted. "You've had your fill."

"It's mine, goddammit!" an infantry private blasted back. "You can have it when I'm damn well through."

"Bullshit!"

The infantryman lost his grip on the dipper and crashed into the men behind him. A third soldier grabbed him, spun him around, and smashed him in the mouth, then made a mad grab for the dipper still clutched by the pony soldier.

Hands caught the third private from behind, and he was tossed aside, landing in a heap on the ground. A melee broke out, soldiers beating each other senseless for the opportunity to attack the frightened private and take his dipper. While they struggled, the cavalryman drank and drank.

BOOM!

The soldiers froze, some in mid-swing. The dipper

dropped to the ground unnoticed. All eyes turned toward Miles and his smoking revolver.

"I once served under a colonel who believed that each morning should start with Reveille, To the Colors, and the shooting of a private. He said there tended to be less insubordination. While I've never subscribed to the notion, it's still not too late to try."

Contritely, the men separated and helped fallen comrades to their feet. The soldier who dropped the dipper picked it up, wiped dirt off the bowl, and handed it to next man in line.

The soldier stared at the dipper, then nodded. "Thank you, James."

"Think nothing of it, Hiram. I reckon it's your turn."

Miles smiled and holstered his weapon. He rode over to where Baird ministered to the sickest men, not ten feet from Rambling.

"I see you managed to calm the men, sir," the lieutenant said.

"Yes, sir," Miles replied. "It's one of the tenets of command, George. There is nothing that cannot be accomplished when you use compassion, kindness, and an 1861 Navy Colt."

Larsen started to giggle, and Rambling punched him in the back. "Shut up, Bill, before you get us shot."

The line continued to move without further incident. Rambling filled his and Hitchcock's canteens, then accompanied Larsen back to their campsite.

Bailey was sitting up. He looked pale and weak.

"You gonna live?" Larsen asked.

Bailey managed a weak grin. " 'Fraid so. Leastways, Doc says so."

"We're to keep him cool and wet," Hitchcock said, "and let him drink his fill, long as he don't puke."

Rambling sat, uncorked his canteen, and took a long drink. "Well, then, I suppose we'll just wait here till chow. How about a hand of poker?"

Twenty-four

The following morning the camp bustled with activity. Baldwin and his scouts left early to find a way to the top of the canyon walls. Miles had ordered hot meals with plenty of coffee for all the troops. Then the cavalry recovered their horses and began to establish their own campsite. Company I stayed close to Headquarters Company, constantly sending Larsen over for the latest gossip.

Word had come down at breakfast that the command would spend a few days here resting from the battle and waiting for the scouts to find the Cheyenne again. With nothing better to do, Rambling decided to clean his rifle thoroughly. He laid out his blanket and disassembled the Springfield. As Rambling inspected the barrel, Hitchcock ambled over with his bayonet and a whetstone.

"Mind some company?"

Rambling shook his head. "Have a seat. How's Bailey this morning?"

"He'll be all right. He's still in the tent, but says he might eat a little dinner."

"That romp yesterday sure fagged him."

Hitchcock nodded. "Yep. I reckon the little shit learned to put water in his canteen."

"Ketzel go back to the ambulance?" Rambling asked, running a patch through the barrel.

"Yeah." Hitchcock spat on the stone and began moving the blade slowly over it. He paused. "Y'know, he's really takin' to that doctorin' stuff. Said he might put in for orderly duty." He shook his head. "First thing I've ever known him to show an interest in." He resumed sharpening.

Rambling shrugged as he wiped at the grit in the rifle's breech. "I suppose each man finds what he's looking for at some time."

"I reckon." Hitchcock glanced up and stopped sharpening. "Here comes your buddy," he said, pointing with the bayonet.

Rambling turned and saw Larsen weaving his way through the company lines. He moved quickly, almost breaking into a run as he came into Company I's campsite.

"You boys ain't gonna believe this," he said breathlessly. He stopped and looked around, then leaned closer. "Word is Miles is going to put together a wagon train."

"Why?" Rambling asked, the rifle forgotten.

" 'Cause we're low on supplies. There's supposed to be a train coming from Supply, but it's late, so Miles is sending back half the wagons to meet them along the trail. He's also sending a troop of cavalry and one infantry company."

"Could be us," Hitchcock said. "We were kept in reserve, didn't fight a lick." He pointed the blade in the direction of Headquarters Company. "Leastways as far as they're concerned."

"What about it, Bill?" Rambling asked.

Larsen shook his head. "They're real tight-lipped about who. I damn near wasn't told what little I know."

"Well, there's something happening," Hitchcock said. "The cap'n and Lieutenant Lewis just took off for the general's tent."

Rambling sighed and picked up the Springfield's bolt. "In that case, I guess we better start packing."

"Listen up!" Mitchell barked. "This here fine gentleman standing to me right is Mr. Sandford. He's the assistant wagon master, and he'll be explainin' the rules."

Sandford was a large man with wide shoulders and a deep chest from years of driving wagons. Dusty blond hair peeked from beneath his brown felt, wide-brimmed hat. He sported three days' growth of beard on his sunburned face.

"Thanks, Sergeant," he said in a whiskey-hoarse voice. "I ain't much on flowery talk, so I'll spell it out clear. We got to cover a hundred and twenty miles as quick as we can. That's one way. It means that you men will be riding in the box with the drivers. Since you're armed, I guess you might call it ridin' shotgun. While you're in the wagon, the driver's the boss. He says git off, you git. Now, I ain't gonna ask none of ya to help with the teams, but extra hands is always welcome.

"Wagon Master Callahan runs the train. I back him up. He says when we start and stop, and which way we go. We run into Injuns, Captain Lyman takes over." He shrugged and turned back to Mitchell. "I reckon I've had my say. I'll be seein' ya."

"Yes, sir, Mr. Sandford." Mitchell replied with a small bow. He faced his men. "Toss your gear into the wagons. Keep rifles at the ready and your canteens handy. If we run into trouble, you're to stay with your wagon unless ordered otherwise."

Company I quickly moved to the wagons. Rambling found his, threw his gear into the bed, grabbed the seat rail, and clambered up next to the driver in the box. He set the Springfield's butt against the dash next to the driver's rifle.

"Good morning," he said cheerily. He stuck out his hand. "I'm Jim Rambling."

The driver appraised him carefully with one eye closed and the other in a squint. He had long, shaggy, black hair, was in need of a shave, and his thick mustache hid his upper lip. The one eye Rambling could see was emerald green and flashed malice. The driver chewed tobacco deliberately as though enjoying a fine steak. Finally, he leaned to one side and spat.

"You're a gawdammed Bluebelly, ain't ya?" he drawled.

Rambling dropped the hand. "Actually, I was ten during the Rebellion."

The driver spat again. "You mean the War for the Confederacy?"

"As you wish."

"As you wish," the driver mimicked, then laughed at his own joke. "What kind of namby-pamby, Nancy-boy talk is that?" He drove his opinion home by spitting right between the soldier's feet.

Rambling reacted with aplomb, quickly unsheathing his bayonet and placing the freshly sharpened point just under the driver's spittle-covered chin. He leaned in close enough to smell the man's breath. "You, sir, are a most unpleasant gentleman," he said calmly. "If you wish to spit, please avoid hitting me or my gear."

The driver's head nodded a fraction.

"Good," Rambling continued, smiling. "Further, the war is over. I was not in it; however, if you wish to renew hostilities, I am glad to oblige."

The driver's eyes went wide.

"Mr. Rambling," said a familiar Irish voice, "if ye be cuttin' the man's throat, I can no save ye from the stockade."

The driver quickly recovered his composure and glowered at the private. "You seen it, soldier-boy. This here gawdammed Yankee is trying to kill me! I want him shot or hung!"

Mitchell nodded. "First, I have to know why he's committing this crime."

Rambling looked down at Mitchell. "Well, First Sergeant, he was saying some pretty bad things about the Fifth. He also had a few opinions about the Irish— none good."

"That's a lie!" the driver shouted. "I never said no such-a thing!"

"So, it's the Irish that ye defamed. The Army, I can forgive, but me home . . ."

"I'm tellin—" The driver shut up as the blade dug deeper.

". . . is somethin' else." Mitchell glanced at Rambling. "You know, son, that cuttin' the miserable son-of-a-bitch's throat is thirty days hard labor."

"Thirty days?"

"Aye."

Rambling lowered the bayonet. "It's not worth it."

"Good choice, Private." Mitchell looked up at the driver. "I'd be watching what I say, boyo. Young Rambling here is known for his short temper and quick knife."

As Mitchell walked away, the driver ran a hand over his throat, then checked for blood. "You'd really cut my throat?"

Rambling smiled. "If you piss me off."

The driver stared at the soldier a moment, then chuckled. "You got balls, sonny." He stuck out his hand. "Name's John Joseph McNally, but folks call me Greeny."

Rambling shook McNally's hand. "Because of your eyes?"

"Nope." The driver grinned. " 'Cause of my teeth."

That night, as the teamsters gathered around their cookfires, McNally retold the story of the morning's events. When he mentioned Rambling's lie about him insulting the Irish, the other drivers roared.

"I'm tellin' ya," McNally said, eyes wide. "He had that frog sticker stuck in my throat, and told the gawdamnedest lies about me to that big Mick sergeant, and him believin' it." He lowered his voice. "He's a cold one, that Rambling is. Man's got nerves of steel, a born killer." He leaned back. "And he's in *my* wagon."

Larsen moved away from the fire to where Rambling stood his post. "They're talking about you, Jim."

"I heard."

"Yes, sir, they are making you out to be some fearsome warrior. It's just like I told you that day in the barracks. You're special. You got a calling to protect us from the Masons. Greeny sees it. I see it. Hell, even the first sergeant sees it."

Rambling glanced at Larsen. "What do you mean?"

"De Armond wanted to kick your ass this morning, but Mitchell told him to let it be. He said sometimes a man just has to act like a man."

"Jesus, Bill, that's all I need."

"Cheer up," Larsen said. "This is your due. We may even be in the wilderness now. Think about it. How is it we got picked to guard this train? Why would we be sent back through Injun country when we know there's another wagon train coming from Supply? Then that thing this morning? Was that normal for you?" Larsen snorted. "Hell, no. It's that God-given ability of yours starting to show. You *are* the deliverer, and you *will* deliver us from the wilderness and drive the Masons from the land. I *know* it!" Larsen paused. "Sorry, Jim, I know you want to keep this quiet and all."

Rambling sighed. Larsen had no idea just how true that statement was. "Yes, well we'll see," Rambling said. "You better get some rest. I heard you got the last guard duty."

"All right. Good night, Jim."

Rambling waved. "Good night, Bill."

"Jim?"

"Yeah, Bill."

"Keep the faith. You're a legend in the making."

Legend, Rambling thought. *And what happens to the legend if I fall apart at the first shot? Who will lead us from the wilderness then?*

Greeny leaned to the left and sprayed tobacco juice onto the ground. "That there is Oasis Creek," he announced, straightening. "Not bad. Hundred and twenty miles in five days. Not bad at all."

Rambling gazed ahead. There was a thin green line that marked the passage of the stream, but nothing that reminded him of an oasis.

"Is this where we meet the train from Camp Supply?" he asked.

"Yep. They should be here. Callahan's gonna be pissed if we have to wait on 'em."

The wagon train clanked to a halt. Lyman rode down from the head of the column with Callahan and Sandford and stopped halfway. He signaled a meeting. Lewis, Mitchell, the other infantry non-commissioned officers, and Lieutenant West joined him.

The meeting was brief. West rode back to his unit, chose five men, and headed down the trail. Lyman and the rest spread out among the wagons. De Armond approached Rambling and Greeny.

"You can tell that the relief aren't here. The captain wants to keep moving, so we'll water the mules and top the kegs."

The stop lasted an hour; then the train moved north along the trail. The afternoon sun was hot. Rambling felt lazy and content like an old dog on a summer's day, and dozed when he could. But Greeny had decided he liked the young man who'd threatened to cut his throat a week earlier, and kept waking him with stories and comments. If the old teamster was quiet, he generally managed to hit a rut or run over a rock that would almost toss Rambling over the side.

"Greeny, you fought for the South, right?"

"Yes, sir. Fit alongside Jeb Stuart hisself till the day he died."

"What was the worst?"

Greeny thought a moment, then gazed at Rambling. " 'Pends on what you call worst. If'n you mean what hurt the most, that was watching my general die at Yella Tavern. Every man there cried, not a one ashamed to admit it now." He took a deep breath and let it out slowly.

"Course, if'n it's what was hardest to take, I'd say Vicksburg. I was laid up there with a bullet in my leg when the Yankees arrived. We had guns everywhere, no way was the Bluebellies comin' in. So they laid siege, said they'd let us starve or surrender, didn't make no nevermind to them. Weren't long afore they started shellin'. Day and night them cannonballs rained on us." He shook his head. "A man can fight in a field or woods or even in the desert, but we was trapped at Vicksburg. No enemy to see. No enemy to kill, just them cannonballs. Hell, you never knowed when one was comin'. It was just bang, one dead Johnny. Some soldiers went crazy. Lotta civilians did."

Rambling was confused. His brother had been wounded on the battlefield. He'd suffered nothing like the people at Vicksburg. "So it was being trapped that was so bad?" he asked.

"It was the fear that done it, boy. Every minute of every day you just sit there skeert to death." Greeny tapped the side of his head. "Plays with a man's mind, it does."

They spent the night next to a water hole and left at daybreak, arriving at Commission Creek later that morning. Lyman decided to wait there until he received word from his dispatched riders. Camp was set up under cloudy skies. A brisk southwest wind cooled the men, but stirred up dust and dirt.

By noon, one of West's men rode into camp and announced the relief train from Camp Supply would arrive the next day. Lyman took six of his men and rode ahead to make arrangements for the transferral of the cargo. Lieutenant Lewis was left in charge of the train.

Late in the afternoon, a shot rang out from the east. A small group of Indians were seen riding off at a gallop. Lewis, shocked by the presence of the enemy where none was expected, immediately gathered his troops and set up defensive lines. Then one of the teamsters said a driver named Moore was missing. Upon further investigation, it was learned he'd decided to go hunting.

"Goddammit," Lewis swore. "Didn't he know better than to leave the train, especially alone?"

Callahan shrugged. "I reckon he figured there wasn't no Injuns around, like the rest of us."

"Well, he was wrong, wasn't he?" Lewis beckoned at De Armond. "Sergeant, take your men and look around."

De Armond saluted. "Yes, sir."

The squad moved quickly into the brush. De Armond split the squad into two smaller units and had them march east fifty yards apart. Within minutes, the body was discovered, and the squad converged on the spot.

Moore had been shot one time, a bloody stain on his chest. His face was a mask of blood, where the Indians had taken his scalp. No other injuries could be seen.

"At least they didn't get his balls," Hitchcock said. "Huh, Dennis?"

Bailey stared at the body, a grimace on his face. "Oh, shit. I think I'm gonna puke." He turned away.

"Then get your ass away from me!" De Armond said as he pushed the private away. "That goes for the rest of you, too. If you feel sick, move away. Get your business done and come back. This ain't the last body you'll see, so get used to it." He tossed a blanket to Rambling. "You look healthy enough. You and Hitchcock wrap him in this. Larsen, fetch a wagon."

Rambling spread the blanket on the ground. Hitchcock took the shoulders, and Rambling the feet, and they lifted the body and set it in the center of the cloth. They then draped the edges over. When Larsen returned, Moore was loaded into the wagon bed.

Back at the camp, Lewis rifled Moore's pockets.

"Thirty-two cents and a pocket watch. I guess these

will go to his nearest kin," he said, handing the items to Callahan.

The wagon master nodded. "If we can find any," he replied, slipping the watch in a vest pocket.

They dug the grave well away from the trail and creek. After Moore was laid to rest, Lewis read passages from a Bible he carried for just such purposes. Then the men sang a couple of verses of "Amazing Grace," and the hole was filled in. Rocks were placed on top to discourage scavengers.

Lewis ordered the wagons moved into a defensive corral. After they'd been fed and watered, the horses and mules were placed inside. He stationed guards around the inside perimeter of the corral, and they waited for nightfall.

Twenty-five

The next morning dawned gray and damp. Driven by a northwest wind, heavy clouds tumbled across the sky, blotting out the sun and casting a colorless pall on the prairie. The air almost dripped with humidity, and a strong breeze chilled Rambling to the bone.

He huddled behind a wagon and breathed in the musty, wet smell of rain. Glancing skyward for signs of a storm, he saw nothing except shifting swatches of pewter.

When his relief arrived, he hurried to the cookfires and poured himself a cup of coffee. He wrapped his hands around the hot cup and held his face in the steam rising from the top. He relished the smell of fresh coffee. On a cold and blustery day, nothing tasted finer.

Larsen stumbled to the fire, bleary-eyed, his hair askew. He wore only his trousers, long underwear, and boots. His galluses hung limply at his sides.

"What happened to the heat?" he asked, shivering.

"Maybe you should finish dressing."

"Suppose you're so much warmer?" Larsen tried to still his shaking hand as he filled his cup.

Rambling shrugged. The hot coffee had taken the edge off his chill. "Sure was quiet last night."

"Maybe so," Larsen replied, sipping at his cup,

"but I didn't sleep a wink. Every little noise was some Injun come to cut my throat. One fellow farted, and I liked to jump clean out of my skin."

Rambling chuckled.

"Oh, I know what you're thinkin'," Larsen said; then he started to laugh at the memory. "This was no ordinary fart. It was a ripper. Sounded like the man must of blown off a cheek."

Rambling laughed.

"And it weren't just me either. Soon as it got quiet again, I heard giggling. Then Hitchcock starts saying stuff like, 'It ain't that funny,' and, 'Hell, I was asleep! How'd I know what it was?' But that just seem to make things worse."

"It's not like Seth to let someone laugh at him."

"Brother, ain't that the truth. He got riled, said he was fixin' to kick someone's butt. Then the other fellow starts laughing, and I realize it's Ketzel. The whole time he'd been giggling like a schoolgirl."

Rambling tried to picture the large, dour man lost in the paroxysms of laughter. It didn't work. "So what happened? They fight?"

"Nah. Hitchcock fussed and fumed. The last words I heard were 'Oh, shut up!' "

Hitchcock approached the fire, arms wrapped around himself. He stopped when he saw Rambling and Larsen watching him.

"Mornin'," he mumbled.

"Mornin', Seth," Rambling said cheerfully. "Rough night?"

Hitchcock regarded the other two through squinted eyes, his gaze shifting from one to the other and back. "Why? What'd you hear?"

Rambling turned to the fire to hide his smile. "Why, nothing at all, son." He filled a coffee cup, turned back, and held it out. "You just look beat."

Larsen cut off a laugh, choked, and broke into a coughing jag.

Keeping his eye on Larsen, Hitchcock took the cup and sipped. "Do tell," he said. He looked at Rambling. "As a matter of fact, I didn't sleep good. All this Injun business, I reckon."

"I suppose." Rambling kept his expression neutral.

"Good coffee," Hitchcock said, draining the cup. "I wonder what's for chow."

Rambling smiled. "Beans, I think."

Larsen performed a quick about-face and walked away.

By mid-morning, Lieutenant Lewis had decided the death of the teamster had been an isolated incident. He ordered the wagon train brought back into a single file. A rider appeared an hour later with news of the resupply train's imminent arrival. Lewis ordered the men to lower the tailgates and prepare to move the cargo.

Lyman and the wagons from Camp Supply arrived with the storm front. Dust raised by the mules' hooves and wagon wheels was swept away before it could rise. Shouting his orders, Lyman had the relief train pull alongside his wagons, and the transfer began.

Gale-force winds brought fat raindrops that slammed into the troopers. The icy water struck with such force, several men cried out in pain. As the front passed and the winds diminished, the rain gained strength.

Then lightning sizzled across the sky, and the real downpour began.

It came in wind-driven sheets. Soldiers and teamsters, soaked to the skin, struggled to move the boxes from one wagon to another. Men fell in the mud, their burdens dropped and momentarily forgotten as they tried to regain their feet. Fifty-pound sacks of feed soaked up rain, almost doubling in weight. Lyman walked from wagon to wagon shouting encouragement and lending a hand when needed.

When the last of the cargo had been moved, the men clambered into the wagons and huddled under the canvas tops. Bottles of whiskey, gin, and rye appeared and were passed around. Lyman shared space with Mitchell, Rambling, and the teamster Greeny.

Rambling shook so hard, his teeth rattled. Lyman reached into his uniform coat and retrieved a silver flask. He opened it and handed it to Rambling, who nodded his thanks. The first sip of the fiery brandy cut like a razor and threatened to take his breath away as it ripped down his throat and slammed into his gut. The second slid down the path cut by its predecessor and landed gently, sending warming waves through his system. He passed the bottle to Greeny.

The teamster took a healthy swallow and smacked his lips. "That's right tasty, Captain." He leaned out from under the canvas and picked up a bottle under the seat. "Now, this is a real drink," he said, pulling the cork. He handed the vessel to Mitchell.

The first sergeant sniffed the bottle, took a small sip, then a deep draught. He sighed. "I can taste the shamrocks," he said. Then he offered the bottle to Lyman. "Sir, it would please me to no end if you'd take a taste."

Greeny grinned. "That's from the old country, Captain. From Bushmills County itself. I've got an uncle who works at the distillery."

"I only hope," Mitchell said softly, "that when I die, I pass through Erin ere I see the Pearly Gates."

Lyman accepted the bottle and raised it in toast. "May you have warm words on a cold evening, a full moon on a dark night, and the road downhill all the way to your door." He grinned. "I've drunk with the Irish before."

The rain finally slowed to a drizzle, then stopped altogether. The men emerged from their hiding places, peering upward like prairie dogs checking for hawks. Then they climbed, stumbled, or fell from the wagons—depending on how much they'd had to drink.

Lyman quickly reestablished order. He had rocks laid in the mud to use as fire pits; he ordered the cooks to make coffee and start supper. He then pulled Lewis to one side.

Rambling felt warm and friendly with just enough brandy and whiskey in him to make him feel immune to the cold. He wandered to the wagon that held the shelter halves and gathered his and Larsen's. He stomped on the ground until he found a patch that, though wet, felt firm. He unrolled his groundsheet, spread it out, and sat, waiting for Larsen. When he appeared, they set up their tent.

Rambling sat in the tent and rolled a cigarette. The effects of the alcohol were wearing off, and his hand shook slightly. Striking a match, he lit up and drew deeply as though the smoke would warm him. He looked at Larsen. "Are you as cold as I am?"

"Colder."

"Grab your blanket."

They walked to the closest fire and stripped to their long underwear. They draped their uniforms on sticks near the flames to dry, then wrapped up in their blankets. As they watched the flames, De Armond walked by and stopped.

"You remember when you were grousing about the heat?" he asked Rambling. "What do you think now?"

Twenty-six

By breakfast, the morning sun had dried out most of the camp. Any predawn chill had been burned away, and the drivers readied their teams for the journey back to Miles's column. Rambling packed his gear and made his way to Greeny's wagon. The teamster already had the mules harnessed and hitched to the doubletree. He motioned for Rambling to climb aboard.

With cracking whips and shouted curses and farewells, the two trains separated and began their return journeys. Lieutenant West split his command, and the cavalry troops rode along the flanks, spread from one end of the train to the other. Lyman, Lieutenant Lewis, and the wagon master, Callahan, led.

Rambling grabbed the wagon seat and held on tightly as the vehicle bounced and jarred over the trail. They seemed to move at a snail's pace.

"Don't be thinkin' of getting home anytime soon," Greeny said. "We're runnin' heavy. This ain't gonna be no four day romp like comin' out here."

"How long then?"

Greeny shrugged. "I don't know. Most of it depends on the wagons. The mules'll hold up, but I reckon we'll have us some busted axles or wheels before we're through."

Once they left the area around Commission Creek, the land flattened back into the featureless prairie Rambling had come to know so well. The bouncing wagon rolled smoother, and he let go of the seat. Soon he dozed in the warm sunlight, content as an old dog in a sunbeam.

He roused himself, shaking his head to clear the cobwebs. Then he took a drink of tepid water from his canteen, and rolled a cigarette.

"Well, we're off to an exciting start," he said, striking a match under the seat and lighting the smoke.

Greeny nodded.

Rambling shook the match out and pointed to the plodding mules. "This as fast as we're going to go?"

"Most likely. Unless you want we should pass the captain, that is."

Just after the noon hour, Lyman called for a halt for dinner and to rest the mules. Rather than waste time trying to cook a meal, they left the camp cold, the meal consisting of jerky and hardtack.

Rambling was restless. They'd been on the trail six days with only Moore's killing to relieve the monotony. He was ready for something to happen—anything.

Since the last council meeting, the camp had grown quiet. Mamanti still made predictions of dire events to come, but the sky was clear, the sun warm, and game plentiful. The People hunted and ate their fill. They bathed in the creek and performed the hundreds of small tasks that made up everyday life.

Boytale wandered aimlessly through the camp. Like the rest of his people, he waited for the scouts to return with word of the soldiers' whereabouts. He saw Tehan in the distance and hailed him.

"What are you doing?" Boytale asked.

"Some colts left the herd. I get to find them. Do you want to go, too?"

Boytale frowned. "No, and I don't think you should either."

"Why not? My mother wants her horses back. Besides, aren't *you* bored?"

"Yes, but what if the whites catch you?"

Tehan laughed and grabbed his hair. "Look at me. I have their skin, their hair. I can still speak the language. Don't worry about me. I'll be able to talk my way out of anything."

Boytale shook his head, unconvinced. "I still wouldn't go."

"It's your choice, cousin," Tehan said with a shrug. "But don't blame me if you go crazy sitting here."

Boytale walked back toward his tipi. Even sitting on the mesas and looking for white men was more exciting than this. He longed for the open prairie, the endless expanse of land and sky. Mostly, he wanted to be away from the village. Every day, the lodges seemed to grow closer together.

On impulse, he saddled his horse and rode away, quickly losing the sights and sounds of the camp. He headed back down the trail they'd followed earlier. He knew no white men waited there.

The warm sun baked him as he walked his horse across the prairie. The sky was clear above him, but he saw storm clouds building in the west. The wind usually kept the rain away, but winds change, and he was powerless to stop them.

And it was just this feeling of powerlessness that bothered the Kiowa warrior. He knew the People had no wish to live among the whites. They didn't want the whites' food, their clothes, or their wooden lodges. They avoided their villages and forts. Yet, for all that, the Kiowa used glass beads instead of porcupine quills and cooked in metal pots. Boytale thought the white man was like a sickness that spread through all the Indians changing them like the rain reshapes the hills.

He turned south, remembering a stream where he could get a drink. His only company was a hawk, circling in the sky. Insects hummed and buzzed unseen in the tall grass that swayed in the breeze. It was still a good time to live on the plains. It was a good time to be Kiowa.

As the creek came into sight, he stopped. Something was different. He kneed his horse and cautiously moved forward. Closer, he saw signs of many horses and wagons. Deep ruts were cut into the ground. The remains of cooking fires blackened the earth. Looking further, he noticed the tracks left the creek in two directions.

He decided the trail leading southwest was from when the soldiers had passed through there earlier. The northeast trail might be them leaving again. Perhaps his people were hiding on the plains for nothing. Maybe the enemy had already gone back to his fort.

He started to follow the northern trail, then paused. He was not white or redheaded. If the soldiers caught him, what chance did he stand of escape? Who would tell the others?

Boytale stared at the remains of the soldiers' camp a last time before he wheeled his horse and galloped for home.

The rain had given them fair warning. It started as clouds building up in the west, then announced its intention as it moved across the plains on a southwest wind. Rambling had watched the squalls deliver their cargo and had grabbed his groundsheet.

Now, he and Greeny huddled together under the rubberized canvas as the rains lashed them. The storm turned the hard soil into oozing mud that refused the mules purchase while sucking the wagon wheels to a halt. The only good thing about the weather was that it offered Rambling another opportunity to sample Greeny's exceptional Irish whiskey.

"Whoa!" Greeny yelled, pulling back on the reins.

Rambling stared ahead, but he could barely see the wagon ahead of them through the sheets of water.

"What's happening?" he shouted over the storm.

Greeny shrugged. "Hell if I know. They stop, I stop."

A figure approached them through the rain. As it drew nearer, Rambling recognized De Armond.

"We gotta wagon stuck up yonder," the sergeant yelled. He pointed to the head of the column and moved to the next wagon.

Rambling sighed. "I guess I better go, hunh?"

"I reckon so." Greeny handed over the bottle. "It might be us stuck next time."

The private took a deep drink and passed the vessel back. Then he pulled off the groundsheet and jumped into the mud.

"Don't you worry none," Greeny called after him. "I'll take right good care of this here cloth."

Rambling waved and ran through the rain. He came upon a wagon surrounded by soldiers. As Mitchell yelled "Heave," they pushed, and the vehicle rocked forward, then rolled back. Rambling took his place among his comrades and again they shoved. The routine continued until with one massive effort, they rolled the wagon free. A half-dozen men fell face-first into the mud, but Rambling held on and allowed himself to be dragged free. Standing in the rain, he looked down at his legs, covered to the knee in thick, red mud.

The next wagon was waved around the hole that had trapped the first. The line slowly rolled by until the column had cleared the area. Then the wagons stopped again to allow the soldiers to regain their seats.

Rambling clambered into the box and pulled the groundsheet over him. Greeny handed him the bottle again, and he drank, the glass rattling on his chattering teeth.

"Th-th-thanks," he stammered through quivering lips. "You-you-you r-really should have b-brought a b-b-bigger bottle!"

Boytale stormed into the village, his horse in a lather. He slid to a stop and looked for his father, Mamanti, Lone Wolf, or any chief to tell what he had seen. He noticed that all the men had gathered at Mamanti's lodge.

He jumped off his horse and hurried to the men. As he approached, they fell silent and parted to let him pass.

"Boytale!" Mamanti cried. "You are here!"

"Of course, I'm here. I bring—"

"You did not go with Tehan?"

"No. He rode toward the soldiers. I went the other way." Boytale frowned. "Why?" he asked, impatient to tell them his news.

"He has not returned. We thought the two of you rode together."

"Where can he be?" Boytale asked frantically. "Do the whites have him?"

"Calm yourself," Lone Wolf said sternly. "We don't

know anything yet. He may be lost or injured. His horse may have gone lame and he is afoot."

"But we must search for him," Boytale insisted.

"We will," Lone Wolf replied. "And we'll find him."

"If the soldiers don't catch him first," Mamanti said, the reproof clear in his voice.

Lone Wolf regarded the Owl Prophet closely, but said nothing. Then he looked back at Boytale. "There are some men already looking. Others will go out soon."

Boytale spun on his heel and ran to the horse herd. He caught his war pony. Back at his tipi, he stripped his horse and quickly saddled the pony.

Once aboard, he kicked the animal into a fast lope and raced toward the white men.

The rain stopped suddenly, blown away by the same winds that chilled the soaked soldiers. The clouds broke up and sunshine streamed through in thick golden shafts. Rambling stripped off his uniform coat and spread it across the canvas covering the cargo.

While the whiskey was good, he longed for a hot cup of coffee. He wanted something warm to wrap his hands around and a good fire to thaw his bones.

The train reached Oasis Creek late in the day. No rain had fallen there, and the ground was dry and firm.

Camp was established quickly. The cooks built their fires with ample help from the rest of the men, who insisted that coffee be made first.

Rambling stripped to his underwear and laid his trousers across the back of the wagon next to his coat. He walked to the nearest fire and basked in the heat of the flames.

After supper, full and finally warm, he turned in early since he had the last watch. Sleep came easy.

Boytale tossed and turned under the buffalo robe. He'd spent the rest of the day searching for Tehan's trail and had failed to find it. Returning home, he'd eaten in silence and gone to bed intent on an early start. Sleep wouldn't come.

A thunderstorm swept through the village, then settled into a steady rain. As he lay listening to the downpour, he heard a horse blow through its lips. Hoping it was Tehan, he pulled aside the door flap and peered outside.

Five riders passed by in the darkness, more shadow than substance. They slowly walked their horses along, the men's heads covered in blankets. Boytale couldn't tell who they were, but decided they must be searchers coming back home.

He eased the flap back into position and lay down. Tomorrow he would start at dawn and not rest again until his cousin was found.

Rambling yawned and gazed out across the land. He kept his back to the firelight that would rob him of his night vision. It was quiet except for the insects and a lone coyote singing for a mate.

A noise caught his attention. Something faint, yet foreign to the night. Ears attuned, he watched carefully for movement.

Two men approached, riding abreast.

"Halt! Who goes there?" Rambling shouted.

"I'm First Lieutenant Frank Baldwin, Fifth Infantry, riding dispatches for General Miles. These men with me are couriers as well."

"Advance, and be recognized."

The men rode forward. Rambling moved in closer. There were five men altogether. Four rode in pairs. The fifth walked. Rambling saw a rope lead from one of the riders to the fifth man, who he suddenly realized was an Indian.

"He's a prisoner, son," Baldwin said.

Rambling nodded, came to attention, and saluted. "Go on in, sir."

"Thank you," Baldwin replied with a casual wave.

As they rode by, Rambling saw Baldwin's face clearly. The man looked exhausted. His eyes were sunken and deep lines creased his haggard face. The other white men seemed to be in no better condition.

The Indian was another matter. He glared defiantly at Rambling.

"Oh, my God!" Rambling said.

In the dim campfire light, the hair glinted red. Baldwin's Indian prisoner was white.

Twenty-seven

Awakening before sunrise, Boytale ate a quick breakfast of buffalo jerky and water. He collected his bow and arrows and knife, but left the trade rifle behind. He gathered enough dried meat to last the day, saddled his horse, and as the sun broke the horizon, rode north out of the village.

He rode alone, not wanting idle conversation to distract him as he searched for Tehan's tracks. Boytale remembered a series of breaks near the edge of the plains, full of arroyos and dry washes. It was the only place he thought Tehan might have run into the kind of trouble that would keep him out all night.

Of course, he could have come across a party of Navajo or Pawnee. That was something Boytale preferred not to think about.

About two hours into his search, he spotted three riders in the distance. He recognized them as Kiowa from the village and waved.

They approached him slowly, as though they had no particular place to go. There was an old man and two younger warriors. Boytale didn't know them.

"Have you seen any sign of my cousin?" he asked when the trio arrived.

The old warrior nodded. "We followed his trail to

the breaks. Where two arroyos meet, his tracks were mixed in with those of shod horses."

"Soldiers?" Boytale asked sharply.

The warrior shrugged. "Soldiers, scouts, who knows? They were white men, and who are the only whites near here?"

Boytale stared at the warriors, dumbfounded. Finally, he found his voice. "You did not follow them?"

"And do what?" The warrior thumped his chest. "There are three of us, and we counted four whites. Maybe there were more nearby. What good would it have done for us to be captured as well? He's in the hands of the whites. There is no more we can do."

"Well, I won't give up."

The old man shook his head, then pointed north. "Follow our trail, and you will find the tracks. When we get back to the camp, I will tell Big Bow what we found and where you have gone."

As Boytale wheeled his horse, the warrior cautioned, "Be careful, young man. I don't want to have to look for you, too."

Boytale kicked his pony into a gallop and raced across the plain. Near an opening in the breaks, two more Kiowa warriors rode slowly in his direction. More strangers from his village. He closed the gap quickly.

"I was told Tehan's tracks and those of white men are near here."

The first warrior nodded slowly as they rode by. "We saw them."

Boytale turned in his saddle. "Did you follow them?" he called.

The second warrior looked back, then pointed at a nearby ridge. "Up there," he said. "Ride up there, and take a look."

Boytale stared after the departing warriors, mystified at their odd behavior. Perhaps they weren't interested in finding Tehan because they didn't know him. Still, he was the son of the Owl Prophet.

Boytale continued to the hill. As he started toward its crest, two warriors from his band joined him, Saiausain and Antelope Feet. Reaching the top, they stayed behind sparse mesquite trees, peering between the branches.

A mile and a half away they could see a wagon train guarded by soldiers.

"How many wagons do you think there are?" Boytale asked Saiausain.

"Twenty, maybe thirty. See, they are in two rows."

"I can see almost as many walking soldiers," Antelope Feet added.

"And there are long knives riding near the wagons," Saiausain said, "but not so many."

"Could that be where Tehan is?" Boytale asked.

Saiausain shrugged. "They are the only white men I've seen." He turned to Boytale. "You need to go back to camp. Tell the chiefs what we've found, and have them bring up a big crowd of warriors."

Boytale turned his mount and rode back down the hill. Then he kicked the animal hard, and it sprinted across the prairie. His initial surge of excitement subsided, and he slowed the pony to a lope. The whites were moving slowly, and there was no need to kill his war horse to deliver the news.

He quickly retraced his trail and rode into camp, heralding what he'd seen. He reined in at Lone Wolf's tipi.

"Soldiers!" he called. "Soldiers and many wagons!"

The war chief stepped out of his lodge and held up a hand for silence. "Calm down, young man. Then tell me what you saw."

Boytale took a couple of deep breaths and willed his heart to slow. He turned and pointed back to the north. "There, near the breaks, we saw a wagon train." He faced Lone Wolf again. "It had as many as thirty wagons. Walking soldiers were on either side, and the yellowlegs rode in front."

Poor Buffalo trotted up to the pair. He was accompanied by two Indians Boytale did not know, but recognized as Cheyenne.

"So you have found the soldiers," Poor Buffalo said.

Lone Wolf nodded. "Yes, but you do not seem surprised."

Poor Buffalo shrugged and indicated the younger of the Cheyenne.

"We chased four white scouts after a big fight at Palo Duro Canyon," the Cheyenne said. "They escaped us, but we followed them here. Along the way, we saw unshod tracks mixed with theirs.

"I found the scouts this morning. They were with a wagons train guarded by soldiers. Among the soldiers was a white man with long red hair."

"What more proof do you need?" Mamanti demanded as he approached. "Our Cheyenne friends have seen my son. My nephew has found them for you. Attack, Lone Wolf! Bring my child home."

"All you men get ready for a fight!" Lone Wolf ordered.

As the warriors scattered, women began to sing praises and howl with delight.

"Shut up, women!" Poor Buffalo shouted. "This is a time to make medicine, to smoke a pipe and prepare for war. Be quiet before your screams cause someone's death."

Mamanti announced, "Those who bring gifts to the Owl will receive his blessing in this fight. A small gift will assure protection, a larger one, personal victory. Maybe a scalp; maybe a rifle. The choice is yours." He walked toward his lodge. "Don't be afraid to be generous, for the Owl will return in kind."

Boytale raced to his tipi. He ducked inside and grabbed his paints and the mirror he'd gotten from the settlers' store. He paused and looked around his home. What could he give the Owl Prophet to guarantee that he'd achieve greatness in the upcoming battle? Whatever it was, it had better be good—for his sake and Tehan's.

Marching beside the wagon, Rambling enjoyed the feel of his muscles stretching in the warm sun. Nights were getting cooler, and the days started cloudy. Walking helped with the chill.

Captain Lyman had decided to take no chances that Indians might be about, even though none had been seen since Moore's death. He arranged the train in two columns of eighteen wagons each, spaced about twenty yards apart.

The infantry was divided evenly and placed on the train's flanks. De Armond and his men walked along the right, accompanied by First Sergeant Mitchell. Half of the second squad was with them, including Sergeant Hay and Larsen. The rest of the second squad and Sergeant Koelpin's third squad guarded the left side.

Lieutenant West and his cavalrymen rode alongside or ahead of the wagons depending on the terrain. They would charge by in a flash of brass and blue, then fan out in front of the column. Each man would seek the highest point nearby and ride to the top. There they sat and peered in all directions, seeking the enemy. When the wagons approached, the cavalry regrouped and charged down the left flank to start the whole maneuver again.

Lyman rode at the head of the column with Callahan. He assigned Lieutenant Lewis and the assistant wagon master, Sandford, to the left rear.

Miles's Chief of Scouts, Baldwin, and two of his men had left at daybreak. The lieutenant had said little during the time he and his men had stayed at the camp. He told Lyman that he was leaving the Indian for Miles to question, and one of his scouts to tell the general what had happened to them.

The white boy Baldwin had captured was seated in one of the wagons guarded by two pony soldiers whose horses had given out. He wore a fresh set of clothes donated by various soldiers, and his bright red hair hung loose, blowing in the wind and flashing coppery in the sunlight.

"Injuns!" a teamster shouted. "There on the right."

Another called, "We got 'bout a half dozen to the left."

Rambling gazed to his right, trying to see the Indians. Then he caught some movement, and saw a group of riders on a hillside. Their mounts seemed to blend into the grass. The Indians stayed out of rifle range and looked content to sit and observe.

"Holy shit!" Greeny swore. "There's a heap of 'em in front of us."

Rambling grabbed the wagon's seat rail and stood on the step. A line of warriors crossed their path about a mile away.

"Captain Lyman," Mitchell yelled. "Take a look at yon bluff."

Rambling quickly looked to a tall ridge that towered over the plains. Along its rim Indians sat on their horses, clearly silhouetted against the blue sky. Even at a distance of eight hundred yards, Rambling saw their lances and feathered sticks.

Lyman abruptly called a halt. "Close up the wagons. Be prepared to corral on my order. Right flankers move to the head of the column. Left flankers to the rear." He signaled West. "Lieutenant, I want you on my right front flank, but be prepared for anything."

Long-range fire started from the hillside, the rounds falling short or pinging off in ricochet. The Indians didn't seem to be aiming at anything in particular. It was as though their intention was to intimidate the soldiers.

"Hold your fire!" Lyman ordered as he rode along the train's flanks. "The Indians on the sides pose no threat. The right skirmishers will concentrate their fire on the ridge crest. We will continue forward and to the left to achieve higher ground."

"You there," he said, pointing to the horse soldiers guarding their Indian captive. "If he tries to escape, shoot him." He looked at the prisoner. "Do you understand enough English to know 'shoot him?' "

The Indian nodded.

"Good. Then we shan't get into any mischief, shall we?" He addressed the others. "These men may be here to reclaim our prisoner. Since we know they will stop at nothing to recover their dead, I believe it is safe to assume that they will be no less vigorous in their pursuit of the living."

"Sweet Jesus," Hitchcock muttered. "We're in some kind of deep shit now."

Twenty-eight

Boytale waited with the majority of the warriors, ahead of the wagons. They'd planned to strike when the soldiers moved closer to the bluff.

"There, in one of the wagons—I can see him!" Mamanti exclaimed.

"What are they doing?" Lone Wolf asked quietly.

"They are leaving the trail!" Poor Buffalo said angrily. "Our plans were to attack from here."

Lone Wolf smiled. "Sometimes white people are so undependable."

"Joke all you wish," Poor Buffalo retorted. "But what do we do now?"

"Move with them. There are other places to attack from."

Boytale watched the wagons slowly roll across the prairie. He saw the occasional red flash of sunlight on Tehan's hair.

Soon, he thought. *Soon we will come to get you, cousin.*

"Would one of you fine gents have a shooting stick?" Mitchell yelled at the wagon train.

In response, a four-foot stick, forked on one end, sailed toward him.

He retrieved the prop and stabbed it into the

ground. Then he got down on one knee, laid his Springfield's barrel in the fork, and securely set the butt against his shoulder. He sighted carefully, took a deep breath, and squeezed the trigger. Before the smoke cleared from the first shot, he moved the rifle a bit, sighted, and fired again.

On the bluff, one Indian's horse dropped like a rock, spilling its rider. Before the rest of the warriors could react, a second horse fell to its knees, then over to one side.

Rambling stared in disbelief. Then he heard a bugle sound Charge. West and his men galloped across the open ground and up the hill. West's saber glinted brightly in the sun. The Indians, still shocked by the killing of the horses, broke under the onslaught and scattered, the unseated riders picked up along the way.

"That was one hell of a shot, First Sergeant," Rambling said.

Mitchell stood and pulled the stick free. "It's not so much the distance, boyo, as it is the wind. That's the real rub: How far do ye aim to the side to hit 'em dead on?" He handed the stick to Rambling. "Now, would ye be so kind as to return this to its owner? Then report back to yer squad."

Rambling trotted from wagon to wagon until he found who the shooting stick belonged to. No sooner had he rejoined his unit than Lyman called a halt.

"Gentlemen, there is water here, and as Wagon master Callahan has so rightly suggested, we are stopping to water the animals and fill our kegs. The delay should also allow Lieutenant West to recover his position, for I believe he is dangerously distant from us.

"Right skirmishers shall maintain their position. Left skirmishers will help with the wagons and mules.

Step lively, gentlemen. I don't think the Indians will wait all day on us."

"What are we waiting for?" Mamanti asked. "Look at them. They water their mules. We must attack now!"

"No," Lone Wolf countered. "The land is very flat. We have no cover, no advantage."

"But we are ten times their number," the Owl Prophet insisted.

"And they have rifles that shoot a very long way. Did you see the horses they killed? Do you want to ride down there and face that?" Lone Wolf paused. "I know you want Tehan back, but we cannot charge down there like the yellow Comanches did."

He gazed into the valley before him. "The time will come when their rifles offer them no advantage. Then we will strike."

When the wagons were ready to move again, Lyman ordered the skirmishers one hundred yards away from the train.

"Lieutenant West," he said.

"Yes, sir," the officer replied with a salute.

"How are your men faring?"

"I can put thirteen in the field, sir. The others have no mounts."

"Very well, divide those afoot among my men."

Before West could reply, shots sounded from the hillside on their right flank. A mule screamed in pain.

"Clear the hills, sir!" Lyman ordered.

"Yes, sir!"

West gathered his cavalrymen and charged into the hills. Carbine fire mixed with pistol shots, and the right flank fell silent. Then more firing sounded, this time from the left rear flank. West's men thundered across the wagon's trail and disappeared over the summit of a low rise. Again came firing, then silence.

Rambling noticed that the shooting was always aimed at the wagons. The Indians evidently intended to stop the train by disabling as many wagons as possible. When firing erupted in front of his unit, he aimed at the puffs of smoke he saw and shot back.

As the cavalry swept into view, Mitchell ordered a cease-fire.

"They've enough to do," he said, watching the horsemen vanish, "without havin' to dodge bullets from the likes of you."

A lone shot came from the left, and another mule cried out.

De Armond turned to Mitchell. "Y'know, if these savages kill the mules, we're done for."

"I know," Mitchell said, softly. "And they know it, too."

Big Bow galloped toward Lone Wolf, reining in at the last moment.

"We have found the spot," he announced.

"Where?"

"Near the Washita. The river is running deep, and the bank is very steep. Once we get them there, we can trap the whole wagon train."

"Good." Lone Wolf turned to Boytale. "Gather some of the young men. Ride to the different groups, and tell them to keep shooting the mules, but to ride away if the long knives attack. If we are lucky, some of the white men's horses will drop dead. Maybe we'll even capture one or two of them." He waved Boytale off. "Now, go."

Boytale called to Blue Shield and several of the other young warriors from his band. He quickly explained what Lone Wolf wanted done. Then the group rode off in all directions to deliver the news.

Boytale charged within three hundred yards of the walking soldiers, yet no one shot at him. He paused at the edge of the hills and looked back. He clearly saw the faces of the soldiers as they stared at him.

More importantly, he caught Tehan's eye.

Twenty-nine

Rambling watched the Indian cross in front of him, and marveled at the sheer effrontery of the man. With so many soldiers poised to shoot anything that moved, this warrior had not only ridden by in plain sight, but had stopped and looked back at them. It was either a very brave or very foolish gambit—or both.

Mitchell kept the right skirmishers about a hundred yards in front of the train. Rambling never thought three hundred feet could look so far away. It was only West's periodic charges past them that offered him any comfort.

To make matters worse, the Indians seemed content to hide among the hills and shoot at them, then vanish when the cavalry approached. Rambling thought of an old elk being chased and harried by a pack of wolves, the hunters constantly nipping at its heels until it grew careless with exhaustion. The fright and frustration gnawed at Rambling, and he grew eager to kill something.

A rifle popped in the distance, followed by the cry of yet another wounded mule. Mitchell signaled for a halt.

"Goddammit!" Rambling swore. "Why do they keep shooting the mules?"

Hitchcock snorted. "Why not? What surprises me is that they haven't killed a whole team of 'em. Then the wagon'd be easy pickin's."

"That it might," Mitchell said. "But if one wagon stops, the captain will circle the rest. Then we'll be harder to hit. As it is, the Indians can get a driver here, a soldier there, until they're ready for the kill."

"And if they gets no joy with the laddies," Sergeant Hay added, "a mule or horse is a mighty large and easy target. And I can guarantee these red bastards will take what they can. There's no sense of decency about them where whites are concerned."

"I can't imagine such wanton cruelty," Rambling said, shaking his head.

"You want cruel, hoss?" Hitchcock asked harshly. "You just let me get ahold of one of 'em. Buck, squaw, papoose, don't matter to me."

Boytale rode parallel to the train, keeping to the brush for cover. He had yet to fire his rifle, not because he was afraid he'd miss, but because he wanted each of his actions to be noticed. What good would it do him to shoot someone if no one saw?

He peered between the branches of a mesquite tree and watched Tehan ride by. He flirted with the idea of killing the driver and letting his cousin escape with the wagon. The sight of the two guards flanking Tehan squelched the idea.

After the last wagon passed, he waited for the walking soldiers. They were spread out behind the train. Part of them ran forward, then the rest followed. If only some warriors could get between these men and the wagon train.

Thundering hooves startled him, and he saw the long knives rush down the line of wagons toward him.

Afraid he'd be seen, Boytale wheeled his pony and dashed into the thickets that lay along the trail. Heart pounding, he hid among the brambles, scrub oak, and mesquite.

The soldiers rode past without looking in his direction. Then the formation wheeled like a flock of birds and raced back the way they'd come.

Anger quickly displaced fear. The long knives would have to be dealt with—and soon.

Hitchcock opened his canteen and took a quick drink before sagging to the ground. "Shit, man, is there no end to this? How long does he think we can keep going?"

Mitchell placed his fists on his hips. "Ye'll go as long as it takes, Hitchcock."

"C'mon, First Sergeant. I mean, goddamn, we're runnin' ourselves to death here. An' it ain't just us. Them poor bastards coverin' the rear—"

"Don't ya think the captain knows that?" Mitchell interrupted. "He's got to get these wagons back to Miles. I'll not let him down." He shook a finger at Hitchcock. "You won't either. Bitch as ya might, yer a born soldier. It's not the stinkin' uniform, the oath, or the pay for yer kind. It's the fight. Now get off yer great lazy arse, or yer fight will be with *me!*"

As Mitchell stalked off, Hitchcock got to his feet and grinned at Rambling. "Damn, Jim, I think he likes me."

The right skirmishers trotted up the trail, then stopped and waited for the wagons. A quick volley of shots sounded from the left, and dust kicked up near the men. The soldiers scattered, seeking what cover was available, and returned fire.

"Can ya see 'em?" Mitchell called. "If ya can't see

the enemy, save yer bullets." He motioned to Rambling. "You and Hitchcock run up about thirty yards, and see if you draw some fire." He looked at the rest of the skirmishers. "The rest of you lot, keep an eye peeled, and be ready to cover 'em. If we lose these two, two of you will take their place."

Rambling leapt to his feet and charged down the trail, Hitchcock at his heels. They'd no sooner started than Hitchcock yelled, "Down!"

Rambling dropped as though poleaxed and lay in the sand, gasping for breath. Recovering slightly, he blinked the sweat out of his eyes and looked back at Hitchcock. The other lay face-down. Slowly he raised his head, the red soil unable to hide his grin.

"You really enjoy this!" Rambling exclaimed.

"Ain't it grand?"

"You are crazy as a loon." Rambling looked past Hitchcock toward the skirmishers. "You and that big Mick back there."

The remaining skirmishers ran up, Mitchell in the lead. The first sergeant stopped and grinned broadly.

"Ya did well, boyos." He gazed across the trail at the brush on the other side. "They didn't shoot, though. This time try not to run so quick. Give the buggers a chance."

Rambling turned toward Hitchcock. "I am so glad he likes you now."

Keeping out of sight, Boytale raced ahead of the soldiers, then crossed their trail. He swung back to the southeast. Shortly, he crested a ridge and stared down a deep ravine at the creek below. It was running full to the banks, its red waters swirling and foamy.

On the other side, a small war party waited along the top, hidden among the scrub and rocks. Further away, the main body of Kiowa and Comanche warriors gathered for their attack on the train.

Here it will end, he thought. *The race, the fight, the lives of the white men, all will be decided.*

But where should he fight? Where would lie his best chances of counting coup?

He opted for the smaller war party. They would be the first to engage the enemy.

Boytale rode his pony back into the brush until he saw where the rest had crossed the creek. He forded the water, quickly found where the horses were being kept, and dismounted. Rifle in hand, he hurried to join his fellow warriors in their quest for glory.

West led his men down the hill, now cleared of hostiles, and rode straight to Lyman. He ordered a halt fifty yards from the train to allow his men and their mounts a chance to breathe. For the last four hours, they'd been constantly on the move. The horses were badly jaded, the men not much better.

He saluted Lyman as the latter approached. "Captain, we're almost to Gageby Creek."

"That's good, isn't it, Lieutenant?"

"Not really, sir. The creek is running full. Its banks are so steep, only one wagon will be able to ford at a time."

Lyman stroked his mustache and stared into the distance. "Hmm, I see, Lieutenant. Unfortunately, all too well." He glanced at West. "Indians? Any near the stream?"

"To be perfectly honest, sir, I didn't look too close. There are Indians all around us," he replied, indicating a small group of warriors four hundred yards to their right. "I would assume we can expect the worst."

"Indeed," Lyman said. "Would you please ride to

the rear and ask Lieutenant Lewis to bring his men in? Then circle the train, and ask the first sergeant to do the same." He gazed levelly at the cavalry officer. "I know your command is suffering, and I truly appreciate your efforts. However, I need you to assume the frontmost position in the column. Should the Indians attack before we ford, they will strike at you first. The few moments' warning that will provide may prove to be our salvation."

No matter the cost to my men, West thought bitterly. He saluted smartly. "Yes, sir."

The war party lay along a ridge's crest, peeking over its edge at the men below. The hill was not high, its slopes falling away gently. Scrub and broken rocks littered the sides of the hill, but near its base, all cover disappeared. The remaining area was empty and flat.

"See there?" Big Bow said quietly. "They can only drive one wagon through at a time. The long knives watch them. If we attack now, we can surprise them."

"But we'll have to run across open ground," Blue Shield said. "They will see us before we can reach them."

Big Bow shook his head. "It is of no consequence. Look at their horses; look at the soldiers. They are tired and unwary. Even if they see us, they will run away. No white man can bear to face an attack by the Kiowa."

Boytale gently rubbed the handle of his knife. If only he could get a scalp. He wasn't greedy. Others could count coup and gather honors, but he wanted the hair, a real trophy, a testament to his abilities as a warrior.

"How much longer must we wait?" he asked.

Big Bow grinned. "This little one is eager to fight. And he is right. Why wait?"

Boytale moved to one side, careful to remain concealed. He saw Big Bow's signal, jumped to his feet, and started down the hill. As he picked his way through the rock and plants, he kept one eye on the soldiers.

The warriors made no war cries to spoil their surprise. The scuffling noises of their moccasins were hidden by the rumblings of the wagons.

Then a soldier glanced in their direction. He shouted and pointed at the charging warriors. As other long knives looked his way, Boytale knew surprise had been lost.

He screamed his war cry, and he raced across the ground, envisioning himself as a wolf attacking its prey. They were all wolves, these Kiowa warriors, and the whites were sheep destined for slaughter.

Rambling stood on the edge of the ravine and watched the next wagon roll down the side. Fording Gageby had proved no great matter. No sooner did the rear wheels reach the water than the lead team of mules clambered onto the opposite bank. The real task was in climbing the other side of the ravine, where Lieutenant West and his pony soldiers waited. The drivers jumped to the ground and walked beside their wagons as they worked their mules.

Ten wagons had crossed before the first war cries sounded. Rambling looked across the ravine and saw a group of Indians charge Lieutenant West. The Indians were on foot, and had closed to within two hundred yards before the cavalrymen opened up with their carbines.

"First Sergeant Mitchell!" Lyman bellowed.

"Yes, sir!"

"Put as many men on each wagon as you can, and go assist the lieutenant."

"Yes, sir!" Mitchell turned to his skirmishers. "You heard the captain. Get aboard. It's time to earn that thirteen dollars!"

Rambling and four other soldiers grabbed the next wagon. They climbed under the white canvas cover and sat where they could, gripping the side boards. The wagon rattled and shook as it rolled down the riverbank. They heard splashing, and the vehicle lurched as it hit the water. The men held tighter to keep from being thrown out. As quickly as it started, the journey ended, and the driver was shouting for them to get out of his wagon.

The soldiers jumped from the vehicle and ran up the far side of the ravine, occasionally slipping on loose soil or rocks. Rambling arrived at the cavalry's side just as the attack was routed. Before he could fire a single shot, the Indians turned and fled, seeming to melt to into the earth.

Boytale ran for the brush and dropped behind a small stand of mesquite. He lay panting, eyes closed tightly, and listened to the soldiers' bullets scream past. Gone were thoughts of glory and coups, replaced by an urgent desire to live another day.

When he'd attacked the long knives, he'd thought they'd run from the onslaught. After all, they were greatly outnumbered by Kiowa warriors. Yet they'd stood their ground. Their faces had shown no fright, only grim determination. They'd fought as men with nothing to lose. It was then he'd felt afraid. The other warriors must have felt the same, for they'd quickly abandoned the fight and sought shelter in the brush and rocks.

The shooting slackened and finally stopped. Boytale slowly raised his head and peered at the soldiers from beneath the mesquite trees. Walking soldiers had crossed the creek and joined the long knives. They scanned the brush where the warriors had hidden, looking for a target.

Boytale ventured a slight movement of his arms. No one fired. Convinced he was hidden, he crawled away until he was back over the ridge. He lay there a moment, then grabbed his rifle and sprinted for his horse. Without waiting for the others, he kicked the animal into a lope and rode for the main war party.

One way or another, he intended to get that scalp.

Thirty

Lieutenant Lewis and the left skirmishers rode the last of the wagons through the ravine and up the far side, watching the train reform into two columns. Then Lewis requested that the skirmishers switch positions to allow his exhausted men some rest. Lyman agreed, and De Armond and Hay moved their squads to the train's left rear, while Koelpin and the unmounted cavalry started forward. Lieutenant West moved his mounted troops to the column's right front flank. Captain Lyman called the order, and the wagons moved out.

The skirmishers remained close to their charges, acutely aware of the hostile forces around them. Rambling stared at the Indians lining the ridges over him. Some had painted their faces in one color, while others had used slashes of paint diagonally from forehead to chin. Feathers, fluttering in the breeze, adorned the lances they held. Their horses were decorated with paint and bits of red cloth tied into their manes and tails.

The massed warriors remained in their positions on the ridges. They didn't brandish their weapons or scream like the wild savages depicted by Easterners. In fact, they seemed aloof, as though the column were nothing more than a line of ants crawling past them— to be watched, but not worth molesting.

Then Rambling had another thought. As he gazed at the Indians above him, he suddenly realized what the early Christians must have felt as they walked onto the Colosseum floor.

Movement caught his eye, and he watched a large war party crest a ridge to his left and pour down the other side. Lewis immediately called for his men to shift to the right and open fire.

Rambling darted across the back of the train and aimed his rifle into the mass of charging Indians. He pulled the trigger, felt the kick, and lost the scene in a pall of smoke. Other rifles fired, and he caught glimpses of Indians flying off their horses.

At one hundred yards the Indians shot back. Their bullets slammed into the wagons behind Rambling with flat thuds. Then the warriors swerved to the right, and Lewis ordered the men back to the other side of the train.

The wagons started to roll, Lyman shouting "Corral! Corral!" The Indians now swung past the left end of the train and made for the front. Distant rifle fire told Rambling that the right skirmishers had opened up.

Return fire from the surrounding ridges grew heavier. The aiming was less haphazard. Several rounds came past Rambling close enough for him to hear. He dropped to one knee, making himself as small a target as possible. The wagons had moved a short distance in their attempt to circle, and offered no protection at all.

Standing next to Rambling, De Armond calmly shot round after round. He selected his target, aimed, fired, then chose the next target while reloading. His demeanor was unruffled, as though he were duck hunting. De Armond grinned at Rambling while pulling another bullet from the Hagner pouch.

The smile was infectious, and Rambling found himself grinning like a fool in return. As he smiled, he felt himself grow calmer and was able to detach himself from the battle. He began to see the Indians for what they were—just men on horseback. Bloodthirsty, yes, but no less mortal than he was. With this insight, he also realized that to survive, he must make the enemy quit the field. That meant emptying saddles until the Indians lost their taste for battle.

Rambling slid another .45-70 cartridge into the Springfield's breech. He closed the rifle and brought it to his shoulder. Through the sights he saw a warrior resplendent in feathers and paint. His jewelry sparkled in the sunlight; his weapons flashed. Rambling set the sight on the man's breastbone. Then he took a deep breath and slowly let it out.

He took in another breath, led the Indian a short distance to allow for movement and windage, and squeezed the trigger. The rifle bucked. The Indian disappeared in a cloud of smoke. Moments later, the riderless horse raced by. Rambling nodded slowly and reached for another round.

De Armond reloaded and threw his rifle to his shoulder. In the next second, he crumpled, the Springfield falling from his hands.

Rambling scrambled to the sergeant's side and rolled him over, but the brown eyes were unblinking. They had started to dull, and a thin trickle of blood oozed slowly from the corner of his mouth. Rambling stared at De Armond's body, unable to move, unable to consider what he must do next.

A scream beside him snapped him out of his paralysis. The horses again raced by. Rifles boomed, pistols popped, and above it all he heard the scream.

He looked up and saw Lieutenant Lewis writhing on the ground, holding his left thigh. Bright red blood poured from a hole in the knee of his trousers.

"Goddammit!" Lewis shouted, his face contorted with pain. "My knee! My knee!"

Lyman appeared as if by magic, still astride his horse.

"The corral is complete!" he yelled. "Get inside!" He motioned to Lewis and De Armond. "Move those men! We'll leave no one to the Indians."

Rambling grabbed De Armond's left arm just as another hand grabbed the right. He looked up into Hitchcock's stricken eyes. For a moment, the two men stared at each other, both lost in grief. Then Hitchcock's face hardened.

"Move your ass, Rambling!" he growled.

The privates gathered their fallen leader, and dragged him to an opening in the corral. Inside, they dropped De Armond and fell beside him as the last wagon was rolled into place.

Boytale rode around the end of the train, one warrior among the many. He was excited beyond compare, and thrilled with the image of attacking the white man. He brought his rifle to his shoulder and fired with one hand. He knew he'd hit nothing except by luck. The jouncing of the galloping pony, plus his lack of practice with the weapon, made accuracy a joke. But he did not shoot with the idea of killing anyone. He wanted to announce his presence, to let the soldiers know that it was Boytale, the Mexican captive, who shot at them.

Riding down the side of the encircled wagons, warriors on either side of Boytale tumbled from their war horses. These soldiers didn't care who shot at them.

They weren't impressed with fancy riding or shots from the hip. They were intent on killing Indians.

Suddenly Boytale was angry. They were trying to kill *him*. He felt they had singled him out. Maybe it was his Mexican blood. Maybe they thought he was an easy target because he wasn't full-blood Kiowa. Whatever they thought, he'd show them.

Veering toward the train, he closed with the nearest wagon, ignoring the soldiers. A white man ran away as he neared, and he swung up the rifle and fired. The man's hat spun through the air, and he fell to the ground, covering his head with his hands. Boytale laughed, reared his pony, and raced away.

He rode back to the main war party and continued his charge past the wagons. Everyone had seen what he'd done, how he'd braved the soldiers' guns and rode in close. It might not have been a coup, but it would be sung about. He was pleased, but remained on the outside of the party, lest someone see the rifle shaking in his hands.

Lyman quickly ordered Sergeant Hay to take over the command of Lewis's men. West and his men abandoned their mounts and made for the top left area of the circle. Mitchell was moved to the right uppermost section and given the men there.

Lyman stayed in the saddle, riding from position to position, encouraging the men. Bullets zipped past him, but nothing hit him or his horse. He seemed charmed as he rode over the killing ground, ignoring the efforts of the hostiles.

Though the Indians aimed at the soldiers, the horses and mules took the brunt of the attack. Every stray round that went through the corral seemed to find a mark on one of the animals. Many had been hit, some mortally.

The warriors continued past the corral, disappearing into the hills. Then from four hundred yards away, unmounted Indians started firing from a ridge running parallel to the right side of the train. They occupied another ridge, higher than the first and a half mile distant, that partially encircled the stranded wagons. On the opposite side, Indians held the high ground at five hundred yards.

Lyman finally climbed off his horse and approached Mitchell. "What is your assessment of the situation, First Sergeant?" he shouted.

Mitchell shook his head. "They have all the high ground, sir. Lucky for us they can't shoot straight." He nodded toward the wagons. "As long as we have these boyos keep under cover, we should be all right, but come nightfall, I'd say dig in. Indians aren't known for their patience, Captain."

"I agree. We wait them out. Food's not a problem. How about water?"

"Some of the kegs are shot up. I can't say what the men are carrying." Mitchell paused.

"Something else, First Sergeant?"

"Well, sir, as you know, most of the drivers are unarmed, but we could use a hand with the ammunition."

Lyman nodded. "Very well. I shall suggest it to Mr. Callahan."

"*Kapitan* Lyman," Sergeant Koelpin called. "Look on de hill!"

A lone warrior dashed along the ridgeline. He wore an enormous feather bonnet and trailed a burning blanket behind him. He was quickly followed by another, who shouted at the soldiers, waving his spear so the light sparkled from its metal point. Then a third rode the ridge. He swung off his pony, let his feet bounce off the ground, and swung back into the saddle.

"Magnificent!" Lyman exclaimed. "It's almost like the circus."

"Aye, sir," Mitchell agreed. "Only, the fancy riders in the circus don't try to take your scalp."

The Indians continued their display of horsemanship one after the other, each trying to outdo those before him. Then Lyman noticed that all the warriors traveled the same direction.

"First Sergeant," he said, "have you noticed that the hostiles keep moving to our left?"

"No, sir, not really. I've been a bit busy, sir."

"Indeed." Lyman turned to Mitchell. "Give me some men. Make sure half are decent shots. I'm going to reinforce Lieutenant West's position. Unless I'm mistaken, the Indians intend to flank us there."

Mitchell saluted, then turned and began to shout names.

His troops gathered, Lyman ran along the edge of the corral until he reached West's area on the left side. No sooner had he arrived than fire from the Indians increased dramatically. The soldiers hid behind wagon wheels or each other, or lay on the ground. Lyman ordered the men to return fire whenever possible, but to maintain their cover. Then he moved to the rear of the corral, where Lieutenant Lewis and his men were posted.

De Armond, covered with a blanket, lay under one of the wagons. Lewis was beside that same wagon, where De Armond's body could serve as a shield if necessary. Lyman knelt next to his second in command.

"Granville, can you hear me?"

Lewis moaned, his eyelids fluttering.

"He's in no kind of shape to talk, sir."

Lyman looked up at Sergeant Hay and stood. "I gathered that."

"The hell of it is," Hay continued, "I canna do anything for him. We've no medical supplies to speak of, and certainly no surgeon. We've poured whiskey in him every chance we get, but he's so pale and shaky, sir. I'm afraid he's going into shock."

"Keep him covered, and continue the whiskey. Perhaps he'll live."

"That he might, sir, if the Indians don't kill him." Hay paused a moment. "You know he'll probably lose the leg."

"I hope not," Lyman said. "He so loves to dance." He cleared his throat. "And how are the rest of your men?"

"Fine, sir. Between the lieutenant and De Armond, they've suffered a blow, but they'll manage. After all, they are Fifth Infantry."

Lyman smiled at Hay's devotion to the unit. Like so many noncommissioned officers, he had come to regard his company as family. Officers came and went, but the old sergeants stayed.

"Then I shall leave matters in your capable hands. The Indians seem content to wait us out for the time being. I believe we shall return the favor."

Hay drew himself to attention and saluted.

Lyman returned the gesture and headed back to Mitchell's position.

Boytale looked over the ridge and down into the circle of wagons. He saw soldiers huddled beside and under the vehicles. He knew they'd shot at least two of them, because he'd seen them go down as he rode past.

Now the chiefs had again gathered to decide what to do. Boytale frowned. It seemed nothing was ever done anymore without every old man being asked his opinion. Even Lone Wolf spoke more than he fought.

With nothing exciting happening where he was, Boytale headed for the council meeting. Maybe some new attack was being planned.

He could feel the tension as he neared the group. Lone Wolf frowned deeply; Mamanti looked worried, while Big Bow just stared at the fire. The rest of the chiefs' faces mirrored their allegiances; they frowned, stared, or looked worried in turn.

"We must attack!" Lone Wolf said bitterly. "We have enough warriors to overwhelm the soldiers. Then we can take their food and bullets and leave this area."

"What of my son?" Mamanti asked.

"What of him?" Big Bow rejoined. "Does the magical bird not protect him? Can you not assure his safety?"

"Enough, Big Bow," Poor Buffalo said wearily. He faced the shaman. "Can the Owl predict the outcome of this fight? Are we to win?"

Mamanti glanced at the expectant faces around him. "The Owl has been strangely quiet on this point," he began, then glared at Big Bow when the latter snorted. "It does not tell me what to do, only what will happen based on the road we choose. When you have made your decision, I can tell you the outcome."

"Again no answers," Big Bow cried. "Maybe when the fight is over it will tell us who won."

"We will wait," Poor Buffalo announced, staring at the ground. "We have plenty of food and water, and we still have no news about the other soldiers." He gazed at the others. "Tell your warriors to shoot when they see a good target. We cannot afford to waste our bullets."

Boytale watched the council members walk away, each seeming lost in thoughts and plans. Mamanti approached him.

"We must think of a way to free Tehan. Sooner or later we will attack, and the soldiers will kill my son."

"But what can we do?"

"I don't know, nephew. I can make them wait one day, maybe two, but then Lone Wolf will get his way."

"Did the Owl tell you this?"

Mamanti gazed at Boytale a long moment. Finally, he said, "Yes, Boytale, the Owl told me that."

Boytale stared at his uncle's back as the medicine man walked away. He'd seen emotions play over the old man's face, and, for some reason, the answer he gave was not what Boytale expected to hear.

During a lull in the shooting, the unarmed drivers grabbed boxes of ammunition and carried them to the troops stationed within the corral. The process grew tedious, because they'd been instructed to remain close to the wagons.

Assistant Wagon Master Sandford grabbed a case of bullets and took off straight across the corral toward Rambling's position. A rifle shot rang out. Sandford dropped the box, clutched his belly, and sagged to the ground.

The men stared at the fallen teamster. Then Sandford moaned and stretched out an arm. Several of his drivers rushed forward to help him.

Gunfire erupted from the hillsides, bullets pelting the earth all around Sandford and his men. The rescuers quickly abandoned the field and retreated to the safety of their wagons.

Again, Sandford groaned and pleaded for help. Several troops darted to the man's side, but they had no sooner reached him than shooting started again. Angry soldiers returned fire, aiming at the Indians' gun smoke, but Sandford was abandoned a second time.

Hitchcock leaned toward Rambling. "You feelin' lucky?"

Rambling's mouth went dry. "Why?" he croaked.

"I've been studyin' the situation," Hitchcock replied with a smile. "You see the way the redskins pick up their dead and wounded? They just sorta scoop 'em up." He placed a hand under his upper arm. "Grab 'em just here. Now they can do that on horseback, but what's to say that a couple of white-eyes couldn't do the same afoot?"

"You think so?"

Hitchcock shrugged. "Aw, hell, there ain't nothin' else goin' on worth a damn anyway. Let's liven the place up."

Rambling leaned his rifle against a wagon wheel. "Why not? Going to get shot sooner or later. Might as well get it over with."

"All right," Hitchcock said, suddenly serious. "There's two things you got to keep in mind. First, we run at the feet, then the arm that's on our side. Second, we got to move together to get this done, so don't you run off and leave me. Understand?"

Rambling nodded.

"Okay. Get ready . . . go!"

Rambling and Hitchcock trotted rapidly to Sandford's side and slipped their hands under his armpits. Bullets kicked up dust around them, but neither soldier paused. They dragged the wounded teamster to the perimeter of the corral.

All the men cheered. Those near enough clapped them on the back and shook their hands.

While the men cheered, Hitchcock leaned close to Rambling. "Bet you a dollar I can beat you back."

Boytale stared at the circle of wagons and wondered what the noise was about. Then he saw two men race across the clearing in the center. They moved so fast that no warrior could get a shot off. He smiled.

These men were like the Kiowa. They openly faced their enemy unarmed and dared him to shoot. Boytale could respect that. It also made him realize that such men would not give up, and that could cost many warriors their lives. He almost wished he hadn't seen the men. It was much easier to attack a weak foe.

He sighed and headed to camp for a meal. Soon night would come. Then, maybe, the spirits would tell him how to save his cousin.

Hitchcock won his dollar, but the berating the two took from Sergeant Hay made the victory hollow. If nothing else, it certainly quelled any desire anyone else may have had about repeating the feat. Like a couple of whipped hounds, Rambling and Hitchcock slunk back to their posts.

Shooting continued throughout the day, but it was sporadic. The most troubling fire came from the highest ridges, where the Indians could shoot directly into the camp. No one was hit, but it wasn't for lack of trying on the enemy's part.

As night fell, the firing stopped.

Lyman ordered that rifle pits be dug close to the

wagons and fortified with sacks of grain. He also had four enclosed breastworks built down the left side of the corral, and one on the right. In these, he stationed small groups of men.

With the digging done, Lyman had the men check on their water supply. The consensus was there was not enough for another day. He called a meeting of his noncommissioned officers, Lieutenant West, and Wagon Master Callahan.

"Gentlemen," he said, "we are faced with a shortage of water. We could return to the river—"

"Begging your pardon, sir," Callahan interrupted, "but that water's so full of mud, it ain't worth drinkin'."

"Well, then, I am at a loss for what to do."

"It just so happens that one of the drivers can speak about as much Kiowa as that boy can English."

Lyman frowned. "I thought he was Comanche."

"Well, he ain't." Callahan laughed. "What's the matter, Captain, don't think Injuns can lie?" He waved his hand. "Don't matter what he is. Anyway, he's been parlaying with this driver about thus and such, when he says he's hankerin' for a drink of water that don't come from a canteen or bucket. Then he says there's a water hole close by where we can get clean, fresh water."

"And you believe him?" Lyman asked.

Callahan shrugged. "He keeps saying that he's glad we rescued him from the Injuns, and that he can't wait to get home. Sooner or later someone's got to trust him. Besides, we can always cut his throat if there ain't no water."

Lyman thought a moment, then nodded. "You're right, Mr. Callahan." He faced his men. "We'll need to put together a small squad, no more than six men. They can gather as many canteens as they can carry, then they will follow the Indian boy to this water hole." He paused. "Make sure they're well armed."

"Don't you worry, sir," Hay said with a small grin. "I've just the lads for this."

"They'll have to volunteer. I won't order a man to do this kind of duty."

"Ach, you can count on that, sir. Indeed you can."

Thirty minutes later, an angry Rambling stood near the corral's perimeter festooned with canteens. He looked at his companions and swore under his breath. Next to him stood Larsen, Hitchcock, two cavalry volunteers, a teamster who spoke Kiowa, and the captured Indian or freed white boy, depending on who was asked.

"Listen closely, boyos," Mitchell ordered. "Just because you volunteered for this mission, don't be thinkin' yer bloody heroes. Fetch the water, bring the water and the Indian back. If there's trouble, forget the water. If it's real trouble you have, forget the Indian."

The six men crawled under one of the wagons and slowly moved into the brush. The Indian led, the interpreter close behind him. They stopped behind bushes or boulders, or dropped to one knee, each time they heard a sound. The trip seemed to last forever, but eventually the interpreter announced they had arrived at the water hole.

As each man lowered his load of canteens into the water, the rest formed a circle around him, guns pointed out. Rambling was the last man to fill his canteens. As he dragged the vessels from the pool, he heard harsh whispering from the others.

"What do you mean, 'Where is he?' "

"Just what I said. You was supposed to watch him."

"I did," the first insisted. "While you was fillin' them jugs. Then I took my turn at the well."

"What in the hell are you two fightin' about?" Hitchcock hissed.

"That there Injun boy is gone!" the first voice replied.

"Shit!" Hitchcock said aloud. Then he whispered, "Let's git before he brings all them redskins down on us."

One by one, the soldiers ducked through the brush and vanished into the dark.

Thirty-one

Boytale heard a rustling noise and trained his rifle on the sound.

"Do you plan to shoot me, cousin?" a disembodied voice asked.

Boytale lowered the weapon. "Tehan?"

"Who else?"

Tehan emerged from the gloom, still wearing the clothes the soldiers had given him. His red hair seemed to glow in the moonlight.

"How is this to be?" Boytale cried. "They let you go?"

Tehan snorted. "No. I told them I would take them to water. Then I escaped while they filled their canteens. It was easy."

Boytale led his cousin to the campsite. Along the way, he announced Tehan's return. Tipi flaps flew open, and people rushed out to witness the event.

At Mamanti's lodge, Boytale stopped next to Big Bow and let Tehan continue on alone.

The Owl Prophet embraced his son, then turned to the crowd. "My son is home and safe. It is as the Owl foretold."

Boytale frowned. Earlier that night Mamanti had left him with the burden of rescuing Tehan. Now that

Tehan was back, Mamanti claimed the bird had told him all along this would happen. How could that be?

"I am amazed," Big Bow said quietly. "How it is that before something happens, the bird has no answers, yet afterward, it always has the right answers." He glanced at Boytale. "Remarkable, don't you think?"

Boytale was shaken. It was as though Big Bow had known his thoughts.

The other continued. "Now maybe you understand those of us who do not rely on the man with the dead bird. We believe the Great Spirit works through our medicine. We achieve greatness because we are meant to, not because Mamanti says so." He clapped Boytale on the shoulder. "Think about it."

Rambling awoke with a start. He quickly glanced around, disoriented until he remembered his whereabouts. The patrol had returned without incident. Before turning in, they'd distributed the water, saving a goodly amount for the wounded. Then he'd retired to the redoubt he occupied with Sergeant Hay and immediately fallen asleep.

He stretched and sat up. Immediately he noticed the smell of wood smoke and coffee. Then he saw Hay holding a cup.

"Is that what I think it is?" he asked.

Hay nodded. "Aye. We only get about half a cup, but it's better than no coffee at all."

"I don't recall any shooting last night."

"It was quiet indeed." Hay paused. "Sandford died."

Rambling sighed. "Too bad."

"I suppose. He was gut-shot, you know. Horrible way to die, but at least his sufferin's done."

Rambling stood and shaded his eyes from the sun while he located a cookfire.

The day passed slowly. No major action was started on either side. As the sun headed toward the horizon, Lyman once again called his commanders together.

"I don't believe the Indians have any intention of leaving. At least not any time soon. We must get word out if we're to be helped."

"Camp Supply is less than a day away, sir," offered Mitchell. "At least, by fast horse."

"Who's the smallest man in the outfit?" Lyman asked.

"It'd be that scout, Schmalsle, the one Baldwin left behind with the Indian boy."

"Very well. Will you send for him, First Sergeant? Meanwhile, I will prepare a message for him to deliver."

The men moved away, and Lyman took his writing materials from his saddlebags. He used a book as a desk and moved the lantern closer.

"Let's see," he mused, then wrote, *Commanding Officer, Camp Supply. Sir: I have the honor to report that I am corralled by Comanches. . . .*

William Schmalsle led the horse past the corral's perimeter and froze. He listened intently to anything that sounded out of place. Convinced he was undetected so far, he mounted, then carefully threaded his way through the tangle of mesquite, scrub oak, and prickly pear.

He'd agreed with Lyman that to proceed to Camp Supply offered the best chance of escape. Not only was the route shorter, but the men believed the Indians wouldn't expect an attempt back to the north.

Schmalsle swung to the east, intent on crossing the creek further away from the area. He walked the horse slowly, allowing it to pick the ground. After what seemed an eternity, he saw the plains open before him.

Then there was a shout, and a small party of Indians was hot on his trail. He quickly cocked his rifle, then kicked the horse into a gallop. He would fight if he had to, but relied on his mount's speed to effect his getaway.

He glanced back and saw he was leaving the Indians behind. His horse stumbled, and almost went down. Schmalsle cried out and clung for dear life as he was pitched sideways. He lost his grip on the rifle and it fell away, but that allowed him to hang onto the horse with both hands. Finally, he righted himself in the saddle. Clinging as close to the horse's neck as possible, he spurred the animal on.

Buffalo appeared from the darkness. He saw them alone and in pairs, then passed a small herd. Driven by fear and desperation, he steered the horse right into the buffalo, starting a stampede.

Careful to keep in the middle of the herd, he rode with his unknowing protectors until the Indians were out of sight.

Thirty-two

The third day of the battle brought nothing but bad news to Boytale and the Kiowa. The Kiowa and Comanche scouts had returned with news of soldiers arriving from the south. The chiefs gathered into what had become a daily council meeting and decided it was time to move on.

Poor Buffalo, Lone Wolf, Big Bow, and Satanta stood on a ridge and gazed at the trapped soldiers below. Mamanti, Tehan, and Boytale rode up, dismounted, and joined them on the ledge.

"So close," Lone Wolf said. "They are so close, and we can do nothing."

Boytale seethed with anger. These old men had robbed him of his chance to be a great warrior. What did they care? They all carried scalp–covered coup sticks, had many horses, and belonged to the best societies. Without a victory here, Boytale was left with nothing.

He sprinted to his horse and mounted. "I can do something!" he shouted.

Pulling an old pistol from his girdle, he kicked the horse into a gallop and charged down the hill. He rode straight at the soldiers' wagons, and jumped through a gap between two of them.

Charging through the middle of the camp, he fired

his pistol in all directions until he hit an empty chamber. Then, throwing the weapon, he charged back out of the camp and up the ridge.

The chiefs gathered around him, praising him for his bravery while chiding him for being so foolish. He wheeled the horse.

"Wait!" Poor Buffalo called. "They know you will be coming this time."

Boytale laughed and again charged down the hill. He raced back through the same gap as the first time, wheeled his mount, and sped out again.

Back on the top of the hill, the elders praised him until he once more wheeled the war horse.

"This is foolish," Lone Wolf said. "You have proven yourself a worthy warrior. Stop now before you are killed."

Boytale ignored them. He ran the horse down the hill a third time. This time the soldiers were not surprised. They fired at him before he was close to the wagons. He heard the bullets buzz past, and leaned to one side of the horse, hanging on with his legs.

Near the wagons, he straightened and leapt into the camp, tearing through campfires and chasing nearby soldiers. Then he ran for safety, but a few of the men were ready. He heard bullets hit his saddle and felt the tug of rounds as they passed through his war shirt.

When he returned to the men on the hill, they tried to grab his reins, but he eluded them, and started a fourth pass.

He felt the thudding hooves of the pony as it tore down the hill and across the land toward the soldiers. Almost immediately, gunfire came from the enemy, but Boytale ignored them as he had the old men on the ridge. He felt invincible, a force of nature that could no more be stopped than the wind or rain.

He and his horse were one. They breathed together; their hearts pounded in unison. He willed his strength into the animal until he felt as though *he* were running to the soldiers.

They flew over the wagons, bullets clipping the feathers in Boytale's hair. He saw soldiers spin and aim at him. He heard the boom of the rifles, saw the flashes. Yet no bullet touched him. He rode around the camp, then jumped the gap a last time, and bolted for freedom.

Riding to the top of the hill, he stopped and looked back. He'd made four successful passes against the enemy—three unarmed. He had bullets in his saddle, no feathers, and his shirt was torn, but his body remained untouched. It was something never before done by any Indian, much less a Mexican captive turned Kiowa.

Satanta rushed forward. "Did you see what he did?" he cried. "I could not have done it myself! No one ever came back from four charges."

Poor Buffalo stepped to Boytale. "We have seen what the Kiowa warrior is today. It is something that will be sung about for many years, and deserves special recognition." He looked at Boytale. "From this day forward you will be called Eadle-tau-hain. Let all men know him as He Would Not Listen to Them."

Boytale had finally achieved what he yearned for. A home. A place among the people he considered his own.

Rambling climbed out of his rifle pit and gazed at the hills around them. They were utterly deserted. After that Indian warrior had charged through their camp, the rest had just seemed to drift away.

"Can you believe what happened?" Hitchcock asked. "Man, I ain't never seen such a thing."

"You mean the Indian?"

"Hell, yes. Jesus, he come flying through here, and we all shoot and miss. Then he comes back. Not once or twice. Oh, no, three more times, and not one man here puts a bullet in him."

"To tell the truth, Seth, I hoped he'd make it."

Hitchcock chuckled. "I didn't even shoot at him on the last pass."

"Me neither," Rambling replied with a smile.

"My God, now I've heard it all!" bellowed Mitchell. "What is with you, Hitchcock? Didn't you get your fill in the Roman Colosseum or on the Crusades? Warriors! You're just like those coppery savages, living for the fight." He turned to Rambling. "And you! What a disappointment! Here I thought you was a good boy, a gentleman, as it were. Bah! You're no better than he is."

As Mitchell stormed off shouting orders at whoever crossed his path, Rambling glanced over at Hitchcock. The man Rambling had always pictured as a gladiator or Roman centurion held his thumb up and grinned back.

Epilogue

William Schmalsle made it to Camp Supply and returned on September 13, 1874, with Company K, Sixth Cavalry, under the command of Lieutenant Kingsbury. Lyman eventually linked up with Miles and transferred his supplies to Miles's depleted stores.

Afterword

Though the majority of the characters in this novel existed, Rambling, Hitchcock, Larsen, Bailey, and Ketzel are composites of the type of men typical to the Army.

Captain Wyllys Lyman was breveted to lieutenant colonel for his action at the battle for Lyman's wagon train, officially known as the Battle of the Upper Washita.

Lieutenant Granville Lewis was permanently disabled by his wound. He was breveted to captain for his actions in the battle and retired in 1879.

Congressional Medal of Honor winners are listed below:

Sixth Cavalry
Company H
   Sergeant Frank Singleton
   Sergeant George K. Kitchen
   Corporal William W. Morris
   Corporal Edward C. Sharpless
Company M
   Sergeant Josiah Pennsyl

Fifth Infantry
Company I

First Sergeant John Mitchell
Sergeant William De Armond—posthumously
Sergeant Fred S. Hay
Sergeant William Koelpin
Corporal John J.H. Kelly
Corporal John W. Knox
Corporal John James
Private Thomas Kelly

Among the Indians, all those mentioned actually lived.

Lone Wolf and Satanta were arrested at the end of the Red River War and died in prison.

Mamanti was also sent to prison, but died shortly after he claimed his magic was responsible for the unexplained death of Kiowa chieftain Striking Eagle, whom he considered a traitor.

No mention is made of the fates of Boytale, Tehan, or Blue Shield, but like so many of the other Indians who fought against the soldiers in 1874, they probably ended up on the reservation to die the slow death of warriors who have no war.

Western Adventures
From F.M. Parker

__Blood Debt

        0-7860-1093-2   **$5.99US/$7.99CAN**

They thundered across the Rio Grande as one of the most powerful fighting forces in the world. But disease, ambushes, and the relentless heat turned America's fighting forces into a wounded and desperate army. By the time General Winfield Scott reached Mexico City, some of his men had become heroes, others outlaws.

__Blood And Dust

        0-7860-1152-1   **$5.99US/$7.99CAN**

Grant had smashed Vicksburg and cut open the heart of the Confederate States. Still, the war raged on. But the fighting was over for Captain Evan Payson, a wounded Union Army surgeon, and John Davis, a Confederate prisoner of the Union Army. Now, two desperate soldiers have struck a deal: in exchange for his freedom, Davis will carry Payson home to die in Texas.